GH00480794

Before you read this book enjoy from Victoria Mosley

Free download

The Red Dragon Bed

& news of new releases.

Join me on my website

www.victoriamosley.com

Hurry to get it while you still can, the intelligent reader's

50 Shades of Grey!

[Please leave a review, thank you]

4

The House on Sydenham Hill

Victoria Mosley

Also available by Victoria Mosley

Fiction

Moonfisher

The Red Dragon Bed

Tallulah Thursday

Soul Snatcher @ Tobago Cays

The Nowhere Girl

The House on Sydenham Hill

The Angel Papers

Angel's Wharf

The Lion's Kiss

The Ship of Dreams

Ultramarine

The Medici series

For love of a Medici

The Medici Child

The Becoming

Poetry

The Dry Season

Crazy Love

Love bites

All @ Sea

Spoken Word　　God Bless America

Dedication

For Pete, to cheer you up!

Table of Contents

"The difference between past, present and future doesn't mean anything and has the value of an illusion, tenacious as it might be." Einstein.

Part One.

Chapter 1
Halloween Sydenham 1875

Nellie's twenty first birthday.

Her father calls her his "butterfly girl" because she is so bright and colourful and precious to him, like the jewelled pendant that he bought her for her birthday last year. She runs her fingers along the small seed pearls woven into the chain as she remembers his words to her as he clasped it around her neck, the sapphire glowing like a midnight summer sky and the rubies burning drops of precious blood against the white milky perfection of the pearls. He'd told her that he had bought the jewels individually and uncut from an Indian Prince and had them especially set for her. She sighs as she holds the burning core of the pendant up to the pale winter light; the stones are rough and feel heavy as she brushes them with her fingertips. She has worn it every day since then, sometimes hidden under her dress as it isn't really "done" to wear something as expensive as day jewellery. Not that she gives a fig for convention but her mother still does, and when Edith occasionally lifts herself out of her normal daily fog and actually *notices* Nellie, she will chide her for flouting the rules.

The country is still supposed to be in mourning for Prince Albert although he died so long ago now when she was only a little girl. She can still remember some of the hysterical outpouring of grief that rocked the nation that day in 1861 when the Queen's beloved had passed on to another realm. Tonight, however she must put her treasure back in its black velvet pouch and place it where only she will know where to find it.

The jewels have their own intrinsic meaning in the language of gifts, the pearls represent purity of course, and the rubies with their fiery core are for eternal love and the large blue sapphire anchoring the design together, what does the sapphire mean?

---She forgets----

Papa had mentioned once that a sapphire is a protection against envy, but to a large extent she isn't that interested in all the mumbo jumbo of Victorian sentimentality, with its secret language of stones and colours, flowers and scents. She is a modern girl and anyway she has her own mystery to bother about. never mind untangling the secret language of the stones Still it is the most divinely beautiful thing she has ever owned and she is loath to part with it if even for a little while: for she promises herself that that is all it will be.

Papa also thinks that she is such an impatient girl that she can never settle to anything much, all the normal preoccupations that young ladies are supposed to be interested in. She wonders if he thinks of her as a butterfly because he expects her to fly away at any second. She shivers as another thought crosses her mind, the vague knowledge that comes from a book she once read on the subject of these fragile creatures: where it is said that they only live for a brief moment in time, sometimes only a day at the most. That lifetime span can of course be shortened even further by being pinned on a piece of black velvet by some horrible collector. She pushes the thought out of her head and drops the pendant to swing brightly back against her dove grey dress, best not to follow her thoughts down dark alley ways especially today of all days.

She thinks back to this time last year; how little she knew then about what was possible in life and love. She falters in front of the large gilt mirror above the fire place noticing how pale she looks with bright feverish blotches on her cheeks her pupils black and dilated in anticipation. In the reflection, she sees the covered silhouette of her camera staunchly silent and disused on its tripod in the corner of the room.

Wistfully she remembers when she first discovered how to create photographs from pieces of glass and dangerous chemicals, that moment as a sixteen-year-old girl when she first saw the magic she could command from her fingertips and almost overnight she had become *avant garde* and really quite notorious with her work. Not as famous as her guide and mentor Julia Margaret Cameron though, but well sought after for the misty beauty of her portraits and her ultra-mysterious subjects that seem to appear out of the ether. The mirages of feminine longing that all the "in" set want to hang on their walls and gossip about over after dinner coffee, for the true identity of her subjects she keeps very secret.

The people in her portraits simply look nothing like the people one might see in normal society. That is partly due to her innovative composition, and partly to something that she has refused to talk about, until now. Brushing back her dark curls and twisting them deftly into a knot at the base of her nape she finally understands that her muses are only the manifestation of a projected image of her own longing, the nexus of her own mystery.

In the elite circles of the Sydenham artistic set she has surprisingly (for one so young,) found integrity and a sense of place; managing to deftly shoo away the unwanted advances of the lascivious young Arthur Sullivan, and other men of his ilk of which the neighbourhood seems to abound. She fingers a lock of silky hair that has escaped again from her chignon and smiles as she thinks to herself how she is indeed so fortunate in some ways and so very cursed in others. Nellie is fortunate enough to hold deep conversations with the elegant and intelligent Eleanor Marx when she isn't travelling with her father as his secretary. Eleanor has become quite a role model for the young girl and they have spent time together defining the intricacies of politics. She is welcomed as a frequent visitor to the drawing rooms of William Morris, though these happy visits have become less frequent since he put his foot down about the affair between his wife and his best friend Rossetti.

She has also shared the beauty of the muse of Rossetti the beautiful Jane Morris, wife of William, and has been asked to take her photographic portrait on numerous occasions. Rossetti is happy to use her images of Jane for studies for his paintings when the lady herself is unavailable and so she regularly swaps ideas with Rossetti and Burne Jones. She has a copy of Rossetti's volume of poetry by her bed and regularly delves into it when she can't sleep at night which is often recently. She's not that keen on the whole pre-Raphaelite idea of art though, she prefers her own images, and recently Rossetti himself has become increasingly taciturn and morbid, his depression reappearing and rendering him unfit for socialising, there are again whispers in the neighbourhood of his drug addiction and latent insanity.

However, it is the handsome William Morris who Nellie has a secret crush on. She sighs just thinking about it, dear William is so in love with his wife that he doesn't even notice poor Nellie. Yes, she has been lucky, she is sure her dear Papa would have built a house somewhere quite different if he had been at all aware of the kind of person she would be mixing with. This is quite apart from her innovative work which is formed around detailed portraits of the working sort of person, taken in natural light mostly around the coastal town of Whitstable where the family have a seaside house. This work is less popular with the fashionable London crowd, but she herself thinks that it is just as relevant as her society work, if not more so. Her darkroom in the cellar holds plate upon plate of negatives of fishermen at their work along the harbour wall in Whitstable mending nets and preparing the excess of their catch for smoking. She is prouder of these images than she is of the debutantes she occasionally poses and composes for their aristocratic parents.

That is only one side of her life though, the public part; yet the most important part, the part that she daily longs for; she has never told anyone about; not since she walked out into the woods and found "him" for the first time. On this day of her birthday this time last year. It seems like a lifetime away and the thing that she is about to do both appals her and fills her with a deep sense of the intrinsic rightness of it all. All of it is documented as logically as possible in her journal and one day someone will find her record of their fleeting times together. The mysterious and rather frightening moments that she could never foresee, that is until she discovered how she might be able to change it all. She isn't sure who indeed will believe it, mostly she doesn't believe it herself, but if disaster strikes and all is lost in the one deft decision she is about to make, then at least there will be some solid expression of the impossible left behind as an inheritance.

She sits in the pale blue silk window seat set into the bay window of the first floor sitting room overlooking the large garden and the park beyond. If she turns her neck and cranes a little she can see the glass and iron of the Crystal Palace, with its ornamental gardens and the spray of the 250ft water fountains catching the last of the autumn light. The pale sun glints off the glass and casts shadows in the park beyond, it's cold out there, cold and crispy just as she likes it. Today is a Sunday and the crowds from London will be visiting the pleasure park with its sculptured attractions and dinosaur park. They'll have bought a special priced train ticket with entrance to the park included and all the normal crowd, the richer crowd will stay away. Sunday is the only day that working families get to visit the theme park and the exhibitions in the Palace. The families might be riding the pneumatic railway through the tunnel that links one side of the vast two-hundred-acre site to the other. Somehow now it doesn't seem to be as shiny and new as it must have been the year they moved it from Hyde Park to the top of the Hill.

The Crystal Palace was Prince Albert's pride and joy: this rather large glass and iron monstrosity brought girder by girder from Hyde Park and rebuilt on Sydenham Hill is like a huge glistening greenhouse. One of the main architects in charge of its build, Paxton, was his name, had cut his teeth building greenhouses for the Duke of Devonshire.

Tonight, there will be a Brock's firework spectacular in the Park as there is every year on Halloween, and the Crystal Palace Parade will be full of snorting horses cavorting with their carriages, the local ladies bundled inside dressed warmly in their furs trying to get the best glimpse of the display. She smiles thinking about it, there will probably be one or two drunken coach drivers lurching about, always a potential hazard after a boozy Sunday spent in one of the many pubs and private cottages selling beer in the area. But that is later on in the day and now the sunlight blazes on the gold filigree of the paper-thin leaves of the oak trees and she thinks of how beautiful the woods would be to walk in.

Today she will escape the confines of her little life, and potentially step into something immense and miraculous, she will wrap up warmly in the mink that is her Papa's birthday present, to her; yes, today she will walk in the woods again for the last time before her journey begins. Another year of age has brought indeed its compensations although if she glances in the mirror the reflection shows her an image of a young girl, a beautiful girl, as if time has forgotten to mark her after her twentieth birthday, and as far as she understands it, it has.

Nellie sighs and turns over the pages of a scrapbook filled with postcards of the area before even she was born. Her father had collected them for his two children but now she sees them as a social documentary of the past, a past that is disappearing so quickly down the steam engine track of Queen Victoria's industrial Kingdom. A Kingdom that spreads its Imperialist might across the globe plundering and dictating its own brand of civilisation to fill the sugar bowls of the new middle classes and the drawing rooms of the rich with chintzes printed firstly in India and now in the Northern mill towns. She can't bear to think of all the injustices and tyranny of the Empire that has made them all fat and rich on the slavery and dominion over others. No, best just to concentrate on what she can do although there is a sneaking feeling inside her that she is rather running away from her responsibilities here, but it's not as if she is tied to anyone apart from Papa and he has his work and of course her mother to occupy him.

She turns back to the album shutting out the thoughts that disturb her, that well up within in her making her feel guilty, flicking through the gentle images soothes her and her heart stops beating so so wildly as she becomes calm again. The black and white snapshots show wide avenues of oaks with imposing houses set back behind high walls. Only a few houses are dotted through the photos before the Crystal Palace was built, bringing its legacy of trade and prosperity to the area, these pictures all looked tranquil and inviting and completely rural.

After the fields and common land were enclosed by order of Parliament then the houses had begun to appear. All these photos were taken by men of course, she really was the first woman to ever take up the profession in this area and with her connections she has done well in all the right artistic circles. Although compared to Nellie's youth and vigour the so called "artists" seem rather old and frumpy to her now. There are a few watercolours scattered here and there on the pages, even the famous Camille Pissarro paints here and she looks long and hard at his water colour of Longton Grove. She loves the misty tranquillity of the photos and smilingly remembers back to when they were one of her first passions as a child. She always found them much more fascinating than the illustrations in the children's books that lined the nursery walls.

Other older drawings depict the gently sloping fields of the common land, and the crowds clustering around the health-giving springs at Wells Park. There is the beginning of Sydenham high road with its rows of smart canvas awnings and the bustling shops on Sydenham Road on the year of her birth in 1854 when her father had first built them the house, on the site of the ruins of an old farmhouse. The shopkeepers are all lined up outside the doorways of their shops smartly attired in their aprons and boaters and it looks almost as splendid as any of the big shopping streets in the centre of London.

16

Her Papa had spent many fruitful evenings drinking punch with the locals at the Dulwich Wood Tavern, which he had frequented while looking for a plot to build on, and they had told him that the farmhouse he was interested in was supposedly haunted by the ghost of a highwayman. The man had apparently lived there and ridden the main London to Dover Coach Road in search of his bejewelled victims. But that hadn't put father off; on the contrary it had added an air of mystery and excitement to the whole thing. "The Old Coach House" it had been known as, when farmland was prevalent and the stagecoach used to pass on its way to Dover. He'd fallen in love with the large widely spaced oaks of the parkland and the view down across Kent, green and wooded and particularly luscious in the distance. No Papa was a pragmatist he'd not been put off by stories of ley lines linking the ground to Glastonbury Tor and Westminster Abbey, or of the local old wives' tales of elementals glimpsed in the woods on bright summer mornings. He'd not been frightened that his children would be spirited away, and he'd been right to be brave, until now of course but she Nellie can't save him from what is to come, she can only hope that somehow, he will forgive her.

Eventually he'd managed to buy the ruined house and lands for just the sum he wanted to spend; and while the glass and steel of the Crystal Palace was being winched into place on the hill nearby, he built his dream house nearby. This house that she would always know as home was soon rising stone by granite stone behind the gentle slope of the lawns and the high façade of the white wall, down a drive lined with imposing Cyprus trees. This was the year of her birth, the year that her dear Papa had thanked heaven for his insight in building here as cholera ravaged the rest of the English countryside to the north of the city. She thinks that the new house built on the foundations of the hold had kept some of the magic of the past in the stones that were recycled for its use. As a little girl she often felt whispers of something that she couldn't quite hear in the park, and glimpses of children running through the paddock down by the old stables. Back then she had thought it must be the spirits of the past but now she knows the real answer captured in the laughing in the leaves and the banging of doors down the long sunlit corridors just out of sight. Yes, now she understands only too well what it all means.

Theirs had been the first and smartest villa along the broad leafy lined street. Father was a German industrialist who'd made his millions by the age of thirty and needed to spend some of it in what was to be one of the most up and coming fashionable areas of South East London. He'd succumbed to the Victorian ideal of fresh air and exercise being necessary for bringing up a young family, and he had purchased the land with money made from steel and coal, grime and soot and hard graft that had got him where he needed to be. He'd placed his dream house high on the hill away from the smog and fog of the city that floated like a veritable cloud of Hades beneath them. Yes, he Henry Weinberg would take his new wife and build her a ''love castle' next to the German Ambassador's Residence high on the hill. Their other nearest neighbour was purportedly a Tea Baron returned from India a director of the East India Company but he kept himself to himself although the Memsahib his wife was often seen in native dress her carriage and his Indian liveried servants were the talk of the polite drawing room circles. The nearby railway station in Upper Sydenham would whisk him into the city for work in the offices that controlled his empire every day and only the best and brightest materials would he use to construct his mansion for his new life here in England. He was puffed up on success and Empire and proud to be one of those industrialists at the forefront of the great new age. If he continued the way he was going he could expect a knighthood at least and maybe later on a seat in the House of Lords.

Why the Prince Albert was also a German and he had married a Queen, and although he was only a Prince he was the veritable steam engine behind Victoria's reign everyone knew that. They had been introduced to the Royal consort at one of the most memorable concerts by Liszt in the glittering auditorium at the Crystal Palace. Victoria didn't much like classical music so Albert had come alone with his retinue and

Henry had managed to get the seats nearest to the Prince. The Saturday evening concerts conducted by Sir George Grove were absolutely the place to be seen and dignitaries came from all over Europe to attend. Nothing was too good for a "daughter of the realm," and Edith, Weinberg's newly acquired wife was just that, a titled Norman heiress that he had met at a social gathering at the great Exhibition in Hyde Park of 1851. She was no great oil painting and had that starry eyed haughty demeanour of girls brought up to be debutantes. That off time slightly startled look of the aristocracy that came from years of interbreeding. He just hoped that she didn't turn out to be as mad as she looked first thing in the morning. But she was a good match and marriage was all about money and contract and she moved effortlessly in the court circle no less; Edith was a former Lady in waiting to the Queen. Lady Edith Dartford became Edith Weinberg and he is determined that she shall have a greater title from her marriage, no matter how long it takes him to get it for her.

"Raven House", he called his pride and joy, his symbol of prosperity in the modern world and it is a huge Victorian Mansion at the top of tree lined Sydenham Hill in the leafy suburbs of South London; Henry had commissioned none other than Paxton to build it, the architect of the glowing glass Palace that is their nearest neighbour. The white fronted villa is set in three acres of its own parkland and filled with monumental oak trees that have been there since the seventeen hundreds. He'd hoped for many children in the Albert and Victoria ideal but only little Nellie and her brother Edmund were to run through the nearby woods, riding their ponies over fallen tree trunks and ducking out of sight of their nanny whenever possible.

Nellie thinks on this as she moves her hands in and out of the embroidery on her knee, the needle tracing a pattern of coloured silk through the bland starched fabric. She sighs and squints down at the detail of the tulip she is sewing into the design. It's a William Morris design of tulips and willow but it isn't turning out at all as it is supposed to look; the embroidery silks keep running away with her and turning up in quite the wrong places on the tapestry. It seems to be taking forever, but perhaps that is alright for she often feels now that time is on her side whereas before she was always running away from it. She turns again to the window and squints into the light, it's exactly the right moment to go now before the shadows start to lengthen in the wood and she might lose her way. She mustn't even think about seeing him again, if she does her heart starts to miss its usual beat and flips and flutters like a firefly on a summer's evening.

It's best not to think about it, but at this Halloween moment when the veils between the past and the future are stretched so paper thin that those with the gift can step through; when the ghosts of the past and future are rustling through the leaves, yes at this time of year she has her best chance.

She drops the embroidery and shuts the photo album and walks the short distance to her writing desk where the inkstand is full of the faintly purple ink that she likes best and the crisp sheets of high quality vellum are laid out ready for her in all their splendour. There is the small pile of precious photographs on their fragile albumen paper in a leather folder next to it. She carefully opens it and runs her fingers over the first shot. It's a misty outdoor shot of the summerhouse taken from the garden; she had used the usual three-minute exposure, framing the picture so that it would appear slightly out of focus, the way that she liked it. She smiles looking at it now remembering her wonder when she had first developed it in the cellar that stood in for her darkroom. She had expected to see a simple shot of the summer house and the large chestnut tree behind it, and this was definitely in the shot, but in the window of the summer house looking straight at her is the shadowy figure of a man.

---Tall, dark, indistinct except for his expression which is burning into the lens of the camera so that you can't miss him. --

She traces the faint lines of his mouth with her fingers and then with a sad sigh she shuts the folder. She has already started to pen the beginnings of her story but now she won't have the time to mould it into something worthwhile, something that might even be read by others one day. But she is too agitated to think on it long and slips the pages with the embroidery and the photographs into her small leather travelling case that is all she will take with her on her journey.

This view from the back of the house looks over the cornflower blue woodwork of the summerhouse in the distance, and she can watch the autumn sunlight turn the leaves to gold, she can watch the dog walkers throw balls for their charges. On days when she felt very alone and it all seemed like a pale dream with no conclusion she spent many hours here her pen idly in her hand, her body relaxed the house silent around her. What she likes doing best of all is to watch the children cross the park on their way home from school, the girls with their long plaits and crisp ruffled shirts from the high school for young ladies that she herself was taught in. Above the marble fireplace is a mirror spanning the width of the wall and when she gets too tired to sit in her chair she can rest on the day bed and watch it all go by reflected in the mirror, but not today: now she has to get ready.

The face that looks back at her from the mirror is oval with a high clear forehead, green eyes and masses of thick dark hair that just won't stay tidy in its place. The hairpins are always clattering out of their own accord and landing on the floor when least expected, her curls tumbling down and making her look rushed and untidy. It's a symmetrical face; some would say a beautiful face except at the corners of her mouth where there are fine lines which show certain sadness. Her figure is small and neat in its whalebone stays, but she refuses the large crinoline petticoats that are in fashion they stop her moving they stop her running; they prevent her from being Nellie. Her dress is dove pale grey silk with a high neckline and of course her beautiful pendant swinging over the crest of her small bosom and landing somewhere near her heart. Some say that her attire is bohemian but she doesn't care, she's of an artistic bent and from an early age she has learnt to stand up for herself and her way of life.

Moving across to the bed where her furs and hat are laid out, she feels lighter today than she has for a long time, her bones seem to ache less and the fog in her head has cleared just a little. She feels in her pocket of the black velvet pouch that will hold her necklace, just a few chores to complete the treasure of her negatives to store safely and then she will be ready. Maybe it really is time to finish her story, but does it really belong to her or does it belong more to the people that are passing through it with her? She closes her eyes for a moment and sees pinpricks of light jump across the red retina space, and she wonders what it will be like when everything is changed and she is no longer who she was.

. She wonders for only a second and then a dog barking in the distance brings her back to herself and she knows it is time to go, time to find out if he is waiting for her and if destiny will shine on them for this first and most brilliant of times.

*

Chapter 2
Sydenham Woods Halloween 1994.

John

John watches the children run through the leaves ahead of him, his two wonderful boys Oliver now a three-year-old ruffian and Toby five. The woods are golden and the spaniel puppy ruffles and barks in the leaves at his feet. Pieces of yellow leaf caught in his woolly ears, his wide paws a feast of mud, jumping and bounding around him in ever increasing circles of sheer joy. John smiles and lets him off the lead to follow the boys, relaxes and breathes in a huge lungful of the crisp air and realizes that he's happy. Today is his birthday and he's forty, although he doesn't feel it, he's what you would call ''a late developer'' he supposes, he didn't get married or have children until his mid-thirties. John has always done everything the right way around, it was his brother who was the black sheep of the family but he has always done exactly what was expected of him, if there is such a thing, and he has always believed that there is.

He'd had a reasonably successful career in the BBC and then it was time for marriage to one of his bright and pretty colleagues who was on exchange in London with *Paris Soir*. A feisty self-opinionated news reporter, she was more at home in the war-torn streets of Beirut than in London, and she wafted through the newspaper's open plan office smelling of Chanel No 5 and declaiming her unrest as she went. Five years ago, he had decided that it was time to settle for someone and as she was there and available, he grabbed her with both hands and she was now the mother of his two beautiful children.

Cecilia was small dark French and pretty with that mysterious twinge of the unknown that had always attracted him to foreign women. His relationships with English women had never seemed to work out; they were too clingy, too needy, too intensely in love with him; when he had started to become attracted to a French girl he had let himself go.

Cecilia for her part was charmed by the aloof manliness that he exuded, being a Parisian born and bred she was used to the over emphatic dramatics of the metrosexual French men she had always dated before John. She had thought that he would be a challenge, and he certainly was in that cool English public school way that made him emotionally inaccessible. It helped that he was tall and handsome, although the darkness of his hair had more than a few tinges of grey in it nowadays. She was bored with men falling for her so easily, completely fed up with the armloads of flowers and candlelit dinners that were the "de rigeur" rules of dating in polite Parisian circles. Then her parents were always trying desperately to marry her off to some faded aristocratic Parisian family that had managed to escape the guillotine by hiding out in the colonies somewhere. Those kinds of suitors always had the vaguely yellowing complexion of a malarial DNA, and her immune system had immediately decided that they just wouldn't do as the prospective fathers of her children. She'd read up all the relevant scientific articles in the French equivalent of *The Lancelet* about the best combination of genetic coding for the future of the human race. She was going to take procreation seriously even if most of the world bred indiscriminately like rabbits, as far as she was concerned people ought to be forced to have a license before they had babies. She understood that people might misunderstand and think it right wing of her to hold these views but actually she thought of it as a sensible option. Marriage for Cecilia was definitely about having children, why else would she give up her freedom, although two small children down the line and she isn't so sure that she made the right choice, but it's too late now isn't it?

John grins a little thinking to himself how ratty Cecilia has got of late, he feels a little guilty about that, it might be due to lack of sex. Every time he tries to get near her she shies away from him, his sex life has become virtually non-existent since the children were born. He has discovered the hard way that inter cultural marriages can be tricky; never mind a staunch Catholic settling for an atheist as he has always been. He doesn't really believe in anything much beyond what his five senses can tell him, especially not any form of "Godhead", although he might accept the existence of a Universe containing some kind of intelligent mind. What is one to believe in except perhaps love, and that's a tricky one. He loves his children and he's still very fond of Cecilia of course he is, but love? Has he ever really been in love, he doesn't think so?

These walks with the children at least give him time to stretch his mind in all sorts of directions although not all of them are comfortable. He shrugs to himself, thinking about the way his parents - in – law always insist on talking about him in rapid French when he is sitting at dinner with them, foolishly believing that he hasn't a clue what they are saying. Unbeknown to them his first ever girlfriend was an older French woman that he met in Paris on his gap year before Oxford, and not only did she divulge the intricacies of love making to him she also left him with a good grasp of the language, which he chooses to keep a secret from his wife. She knows he can speak French, just not how fluent he is. When they go and stay in the small but exclusive apartment in Paris that was their wedding present from her parents or the large Manoir in the Dordogne for family holidays, he takes pride in being able to conduct himself very successfully at the local markets with only a trace of an English accent to soil his bargaining skills. If he thinks about it he has been incredibly lucky up till now; his whole life has been one long symphony of middle class success.

He's a typical Englishman he supposes, boarding school, and then an English Literature degree at Oxford, followed by a research job at the BBC then he got lucky and bagged a job as editor of a prestigious financial magazine and now two wonderful children and a duty as a husband and father. Nowadays though he sometimes looks at young couples walking with their children or pushing babies in buggies and envies them their easy sense of togetherness as they croon at each other and the children as they cart home their weekly shop. He doesn't think he has ever seen Cecilia push a buggy, she is always too busy for that, and she definitely can't see the point of them going for walks together.

The leaves crunch comfortingly under his feet; he notices how thickly they are spread and how they are rising up above his ankles to the top of his timberland boots. Just these small details that seem to stand out more sharply today than usual as if he is seeing the woods for the first time through a very clear magnifying lens. He feels alert and very alive and a sudden sense of joy at the sheer wonder and intricacy of life itself almost overwhelms him. The two dark heads of the children are bent over something by the large oak tree at the corner of the descending slope, and he remembers vividly that as a child everything seemed to be imbued with exactly this sense of wonder that he is feeling. He watches them crouched where the leaf coloured path drops down to what must once have been the railway track in the distance at the bottom of the gully. He calls out to them, but they giggle and run around the corner out of his line of vision, whipping completely out of view for a moment. The puppy slides and scrambles happily after them, barking as he goes. John brings them down here every Sunday if the weather is good and today is one of those rare autumn days that feel like the end of summer, the suns heat burning through his shirt collar bringing him out in a slight sweat. He wipes the sheen of it from his brow and hurries down the slope to join the children. It's Halloween of course and tonight he will put fireworks out in the large garden and there will be a BBQ with the neighbours.

Life is good ever since he bought the house when he they were first married and Cecie was hugely pregnant with Toby. He'd decided a long time ago that when he had a family he would bring them to live on Sydenham Hill; it had a faded aristocracy about it that he couldn't find in North London. Its wide tree lined streets whispered of a heyday that lingered still just under the surface of things waiting to be rediscovered. He'd driven up and down the road many times imagining what it would be like to actually live here. It was something about the faded gentility of the place that drew him in, the large wide Crystal Palace Park at the end of the Hill, the row upon row of elegant houses that had now been turned into flats or care homes. Then Raven House had come up for public auction, due to a death in the family that owned it he supposed, though no explanation was given by the auction house. It was obvious at first viewing that it hadn't been lived in for decades, but the plus side of that was that it still retained all of its original features. Huge and neglected as it was he had fallen in love with its high-ceilinged rooms and intricate coving; with its dark wood panelling and carved oak staircase., the parquet floors and the dazzling music room with its floor to ceiling windows gazing out into the parkland of the garden beyond. As he walked through its empty rooms marvelling at the dusty chandeliers and the marble fireplaces he had felt a lightness and sense of rightness about being there. Almost as if he already knew the house and it in turn recognised him it almost felt as if it was welcoming him back.

With eight bedrooms, a music room and a beautiful wrought iron work conservatory it was far too big for them really. But Cecilia had been pregnant and for once in no mood to argue with him so he had gone ahead and bought it. He'd worried about the air of sadness and decadent decay that hit him like a cool rush of air as he opened the front door with his own key that first day. Almost as if the house itself was weeping for some long-forgotten love affair that had had an unhappy ending. But John was far too pragmatic for that to cloud his judgement of a bargain when he saw it. Renovation had been costly but he'd ended up with a large light airy home for the children to grow up in, with a garden big enough for several small ponies if they wanted them.

A slight cloud crosses his face as he thinks about his wife, she can be so aloof and let's face it so bloody infuriatingly French at times. Lately they haven't been getting on which meant no sex at all was on the horizon in the foreseeable future and the annoyance of her being called away to work in Paris more than usual was putting an even greater strain on the relationship.

----Or perhaps she's having an affair? -----

The thought fleetingly crosses his mind but then he dismisses it, with a quick flick of an on / off switch in his brain. It's not as if he cares all that much if she is, as long as she keeps the status quo and doesn't rock the boat of their lives she can do whatever she likes within reason. Reason is very important to John and he gets the feeling that women's minds work in a totally different way to men's. He realises that would probably sound chauvinistic but he doesn't care much.

He's almost giving himself a massive headache and he's supposed to be out here in the fresh air enjoying himself, so he lets the thoughts fade and he hurries around the corner and hears the sharp excited barking of the dog. His knee aches slightly as he catches his foot on the root of a tree, an old cricket injury and he stops to rub it looking into the light which is filtering down through the trees with its particular autumn gold. He squints a little shading his eyes with his hand trying to pick out the children who are a hundred yards or so away by the ruins of the Victorian folly. He can just make out their shapes and they seem to be looking up at something, he follows the line of their glance and sees a woman in a long skirt and furs rounding the corner of the folly.

Instantly, she is caught in the flare of the light, like the flash for an old camera, white phosphorus, blinding. He blinks and passes a hand over his eyes. He sees the laughter in her eyes; the gloss of the fur coat, the glitter of gold and pearls around her neck and the flash of a smile as she turns towards him. She's young and very pretty with acres of tumbling dark hair escaping from beneath her hat. She has an open innocent face with a radiant complexion and he thinks instantly that she looks like someone from a Victorian period drama. In fact he makes a swift survey of the surrounding area to see if they have walked onto a film set by accident, but no the woods are hanging, silent, shimmering the light tripping off the leaves and almost blinding him.

For a Nano second and it must be a trick of the light, the folly looks intact, with a painted blue doorway and glass in the window. She bends to take Oliver's hand and Toby is jumping up and down holding onto her skirts, she turns back to look at John and motions for the boys to wave at him which they do with wicked grins on their faces and then she laughingly leads them through the blue door and takes them inside and out of sight. He wavers in his stride and then speeds up but they seem to have completely vanished into the shadow of the folly.

It all happens far too quickly, and his heart begins to thud horribly against the wall of his chest as if it wants to leap right through his skin, as he hurtles down the slight incline and through the bare stringy remains of the brambles to arrive sweating at the folly. He stands there stupefied staring bleakly at it holding his hand to the stitch that is throbbing in his side at his swift descent. It is crumbling and falling to bits, ivy wound around what remains of the roof, flaking wood on the rotting surround of the doorway. There is no blue door, no glass, indeed no window and certainly no pretty woman with his sons. The little dog is whining and clawing at the ground around the empty doorway, his tail between his legs and the boys are gone. For a second he can't believe it, panic overwhelms him as never before and he begins to call them. His chest is tight and he can't breathe and he feels horribly sick as the ground beneath his feet seems to tremble and sway.

"Toby, Oliver,I know you are hiding from me come out now, Boys this isn't funny anymore, where are you?".

His last words end with a sob and he sinks to his knees on the crunchy leaves there is no reply and the woods have become strangely silent around him as if the branches are reaching out to clutch at him stop him from finding the boys. The light of the sun suddenly disappears behind the clouds and it is immediately very cold. He feels like he is in a glass bubble far removed from the present moment his senses torn apart from him. He begins to pick out insignificant details from the world around him, but he is no longer a part of it, as if he is being sucked into a vacuum with no air. He can hear the voices of the golfers on the golf course down below, a couple pass with their baby strapped to their back, the puppy winds itself around his legs whining miserably, his breath is coming in short sharp rasps, and he's having a panic attack. All he can think of is the impossibility of it, they were there a moment ago, and then there was a flash of light, a girl with laughing eyes and now they are gone.

Somewhere in his brain the neurons are still firing, his mobile rings harshly in his pocket and with a shaking hand he fishes it out and looks at it, it's his wife. Throat dry and with no idea what he is going to say to her he answers it, to the flare of her furious voice.

"John where the hell are you? I thought you were supposed to be taking the boys for a walk?"

He begins to stammer a reply, but she cuts him short with.

" You know damm well it's the au pairs day off but she's just found them playing in the summerhouse, they're on their own for goodness sake, how did that happen? They are both upset and yattering on about some woman or other, you'd better come home and sort this out, I simply can't cope with it all I have a deadline to keep for tomorrow and a train to catch remember?".

She hangs up on him and he sits on the low damp wall of the folly his knees shaking, his head held in his hands a flood of relief bringing tears to his eyes. He has no idea what has just happened, there is no rational explanation for it and perhaps he will never find one, but the boys are safe. That's all that matters, they are the pivot of his world and for a second there he had lost control and found his axis spinning, hanging wildly in the dark spaces of his own soul, without a clear way back.

He wipes his brow with a paper hanky from his pocket, there is sweat trickling down his back and suddenly he is very cold. The puppy whines and snuggles closer and he looks up hoping to see the flash of dark hair and rich furs disappearing up the pathway back towards the hill, but the path is empty. He can hear laughter in the leaves and smell the scent of something wonderful and unknown. The word "Ambergris" comes to mind although he has no idea where from or what it is, and he clips the lead on the dog and heads home to the recriminations that are his due it seems. He certainly can't tell Cecilia what has happened or she will think he has gone crazy or worse still that he is trying to cover up some kind of affair. He wasn't aware of the fierce jealousy of her nature when he married her, but he has to be very careful if he brings another woman up in conversation who she hasn't heard of before. He grimaces to himself, even if it might be a woman who can't possibly exist except as a tenant of his imagination, for surely there was nothing "real" about the vision that he has just seen?

He quickly runs an action replay sequence in his mind, now that he isn't worried about the children he can concentrate on the details of the girl. For he understands very clearly that she is a girl, a whole lot younger than him; maybe she is twenty years old certainly not a lot more although her clothes made her appear mature. He can only remember flashes of her: but they are so vivid as if they've been branded on the sea horse of memory in his brain. He can literally conjure up her smile the depth of colour in her brown eyes and the way that for a split second they had stared at each other as if in recognition. She reminds him so clearly of someone that he has met before, but if he had ever met her he is sure that he would have remembered her name and where she comes from.

Obviously he is having some kind of mid-life crisis, he has heard of some of his colleagues going off the rails, signing up for yoga retreats, running off with their PA's, but seeing beautiful young women in the woods who then vanish? He needs a drink and it had better be something strong like a slug of single malt whisky to bring him back to his senses.

Later there will be his BBQ and then a gruesome birthday dinner with a whole load of people invited that he doesn't really want to see. Cecilia in true French fashion thinks that the best way to cover up the possible failings of their marriage is by keeping their social schedule so busy that they never have any time alone together. No if they were alone they might have to talk about something other than the domestic workings of their life, and that might open a whole snake pit of worms. As he walks shakily up the steep incline he asks himself if he has too high expectations of his marriage. He'd stayed single for so long because he'd been searching for the perfect company his ideal woman for his "forever" marriage. He believes strongly in the vows that they both took on their wedding day, even though they were Catholic vows, her parents had insisted on that. Did it matter that he didn't really believe in any of the popery of Catholicism? No, he did all that to make Cecie happy, but it doesn't really seem that he has made either of them content. She spends her time travelling as much as possible and he spends his time working or looking after the boys. He supposes that most men in his situation would have an affair with the au pair, but luckily or unluckily depending on which way you look at it he doesn't fancy the Czech girl, Radna that they have hired. He sighs and lets the little dog sniff around a tree before continuing up the slippery steps towards the road. The shadows lengthen now, the sunlight has long gone and the woods are damp and uninviting, he shivers again.

His parents - in - law are in London tonight and he will have to do a lot of back slapping and effusive complimenting of Cecilia's hard faced mother. He ruefully hopes that it isn't true that women end up looking like their mothers, if so he is in real trouble. Before that though there is the rest of the afternoon with the boys, he'll try and get them to tell him what happened while setting up the evening's fireworks for them, He doesn't want to scare them but he is aware that something utterly magical happened today, he can feel it in his heart and the flicker in his body when he thinks of that brief glimpse of the girl.

Silly old fool he can't finally have fallen in love can he after all these years of not really knowing what people are talking about when they talk of the emotion. Not in the poetic sense of the word in any case, he's never really felt that strongly about anyone. Somewhere deep in his heart he is aware that although his marriage is shaky, the boys are still small and he has a job to do and a family to protect and that goes far beyond personal happiness, doesn't it?

The girl in the woods today looked so familiar to him again he wonders if he has seen her around, maybe in the local farmers' market on a Saturday in the grounds of Dulwich College? Quite a few of the girls in London have adopted Vintage fashion but there was something too authentic about her look, as if she had just stepped out of a costume drama. Perhaps they are really making a film nearby but then what would she be doing in the woods? She didn't look very ephemeral; she looked completely solid even though he was some distance away. He really is losing it now, she must be one of these young girls that spend their time dressing up in vintage outfits, she didn't look more than twenty, if that really. His thoughts are travelling in never ending circles and it's beginning to give him a headache, he's got to stop thinking about her and just concentrate on getting the puppy home.

As he walks along Sydenham Hill he pauses to stare in at some of the ornate looking houses set back from the road. He doesn't really know any of the neighbours and quite a few of the larger houses have been turned into flats but there are still one or two the same size as Raven House. The history of the area has become a source of fascination for him; and when he has time from work, (and when Cecie gives him the peace he needs or when she is away travelling); his favourite pastime is research. He's spent hours looking up old photographs and pouring over tithe maps, and he's got a fair amount of accurate research on his own house. He has the original deeds of the house showing that it was commissioned to be built by the architect Paxton by a wealthy German business man who had become anglicised as a lot of them did before the Great War. The public records showed that he was married with two children a girl and a boy Nellie and Edmund but that was as far as he had got in the research into the former occupants of Raven House. Thinking about it as he walks he speeds up now as he is nearing the gates of his house, if he gets time this week he really needs to go down to the archives at Lewisham Library and see if he can pull out any new information.

He is out of breath as he reaches his driveway and suddenly a flicker of feminine laughter echoes up from the woods on the other side of the road from him and he turns swiftly expecting to see her there. But no, it's only a pair of teenage lovers walking hand in hand on the path behind the iron railings and with a sigh he walks through the gates the cedar trees swaying gently as if in greeting and before him sees the house. The last of the sunset is gilding the windows turning them into the jewelled colours of stained glass. He is reminded of the rose windows of a great cathedral like Notre Dame or Chartres, he is almost blinded by the reflection and holds his hand up to shield his eyes. Then just as quickly the sun drops behind the tree level and the house is back to normal again. Where the light glittered before now the windows lour down at him like gaping eye sockets which he cannot hope to see behind, the dog pulls on its leash and a chill wind hurries around the corner catching him. He pulls his collar up and plunges his cold hands into the recesses of his pockets, these autumn afternoons quickly turn to evening and he has things to do: but first he must search out the boys and glean their side of this afternoon's drama.

*

Chapter 3
Sydenham Halloween 1874

Nellie

Nellie wraps herself in her new fur coat, the black Beaver fur that her father brought her from Marshal and Snellgrove in town yesterday as one of her twentieth birthday presents. Carefully she nestles her pendant under the furs where it can't catch upon anything or get lost. She can't believe how grown up she feels with all these expensive gifts but Papa again told her how proud he is of her with her business running along splendidly and the invitations for her latest viewing of photos laying ready to be addressed on the hall table.

Funny having a birthday on Halloween but she's always thought of it as lucky , as if all the fireworks and celebrations going on are specifically for her. .At least she doesn't have to go to the churchyard and polish bones as the French are purported to do on November the 1st although she thinks perhaps that's just a nasty story to make the English feel superior. .Today there is an expectant feeling in the air; she can sense it tingling in her skin as if new doorways into her mind have been opened up by what happened last night. It's not necessarily a comfortable feeling and she shivers turning to bend over and warm her long kid gloves in front of the roaring log fire before she rolls them onto her hands. She is standing in the music room looking out towards the summer house and she thinks she will take the tunnel into the woods today, so she doesn't have to meet anybody. Especially not the annoying gamekeeper who likes to keep her talking for hours about partridges and pheasants, as if she cares at all about such things especially the clutch of dead ones that he habitually has hanging from his gaming bag, neither does she want to soil her soft kid boots crossing the highway and she's definitely not in the mood for talking this afternoon.

Papa had the tunnel built from below the summerhouse down to the folly in the woods so that they never had to cross the road or go near the railway track to get out for their long walks. It meant that they could bypass the glimpses of the city beneath them which is all too often shrouded with its yellow fog of coal fire haze and the nasty smells that blow their way occasionally. No, here on the hill Henry had wanted there to be no sense of the pollution of industry to sully the lives of his small precious family, none of the sickness and consumption that comes with the labours of the workforce. His precious ones must have all that they desire, all that his very new money can buy and it isn't really necessary for them to know how he came by it. Her younger brother has been packed off to Oxford with all the trappings of a gentleman and so it is just his precious clever Nellie left at home now. This part of Sydenham is for the nouveau riche, the tone lifted by the artistic set, the music clique, and also the influx of diplomats, people like the German Ambassador in the next door mansion. It has become a playground for the rich with all the marvellous events and talks going on in the shiny Crystal Palace next door.

Last night was extraordinary if she thinks about it, which she does briefly before turning the key on the lock to the French windows and stepping out into the garden. Her mother had managed to inveigle the great Madame Blavatsky to hold a private séance in the drawing room. She had been giving an early evening lecture on Theosophy at "The Crystal Palace " and Mama had promised her plenty of money if she would honour them with her presence. She'd whispered to Nellie that she wanted to be able to talk to her little brother who had died of the consumption as a small boy and she still missed him. Madame Blavatsky has been causing a great stir in the press and polite "at homes", in the city with stories of her ability to talk with the spirits of dearly departed loved ones. It wasn't the first time that Edith had got all soppy eyed over something that had happened when she was four and her brother Richard only two. It was as if this early loss drove the melancholy tone in her life, as if her living children have never been enough for her. Nellie has become increasingly unsympathetic of the story over the years, but if a ghost child could actually be conjured up, for the evening's entertainment well that would be interesting. If the Madame could do that for her mother then she might truly become a believer.

Nellie loved her mother but was very aware that the once beautiful debutante was excruciatingly bored tucked away here in the quasi countryside far from the gossip and parties of Central London that she was brought up with. Was it any wonder that she provided herself with unusual entertainment to keep the melancholia at bay? That and the daily doses of laudanum for her headaches kept Edith from ending up semi hysterical, and bothering dear Papa with the dreaded hypochondria that brought the Dr and his formidable leather bag. Last week it had been wine tasting, lots of gurgling and spitting into silver buckets and talk of a hint of raspberry and overtones of oak in the red wine at table, and now it seemed that ectoplasm was on the menu for her entertainment.

All the important neighbours had to be invited, including the handsome but notorious Arthur Sullivan and his latest conquest no doubt, and the pretty Scott Russell girls Rachel and Louise with their lovely mother Harriet. All three of the Scott Russell women seemed to hanker after the young Sullivan although Nellie couldn't for the life of her understand why. Papa had declared that it was all tosh and nonsense and retired to his club in the city for the evening with Sir George Grove , but Nellie had been intrigued enough to attend.

Nellie walks across the leaves, her small kid boots crunching on the still visible traces of frost and she instinctively pulls the fur closer around her neck to keep at bay a sudden chill in the air. She looks around her, the day is bright and autumnal, later she will have to give that piano recital that she is dreading, why oh why do her parents insist that she take piano lessons? There is no doubt in her mind that she is totally untalented when it comes to music and it is a big embarrassment as so many of the young girls in the area obviously are. Why listen to Nellie when you can go to a marvellous Schubert or Liszt concert in the Crystal Palace instead? No she has definitely decided to put her foot down this time and refuse to do any more of these excruciating evenings, but now at least for an hour or so she is free to do what she likes.

Her chaperone Miss Tindley is resting and at twenty years old today Nellie is up for some measure of freedom and adventure, even if it's only an afternoon walk in the woods.. She has been educated for the last few years by Miss Tindley after a severe bout of pleurisy left her weak and susceptible to infection and so she has had to leave her beloved friends at the girl's school down Westwood Hill. She still sees them all sometimes in their uniform when she is on shopping trips on the high road with Mama, but if she if honest she doesn't really miss it all. She has her music lessons and the dance classes on a Friday at "The Palace" and lately she has become ever more fascinated with the art of photography, and it is no longer just a passing hobby but has become her main focus of attention. She has enrolled in classes with Mr Delamotte who took all the photographs of the palace being rebuilt here on the hill. He was a friend of father's and rather whiskery and disgusting but the magic of the darkroom is simply too engrossing to be denied and that is what she truly wants to become, a photographer in the genre of the wonderful Julia Margaret Cameron whose photographic exhibitions she has seen in the drawing rooms of private views in Holland Park along with the good and the great.

The whole process is fascinating in itself and Mr Delamotte has taught her all his techniques which she is pursuing in her make shift darkroom in the cellar. She has had to get the gardener to help her make all the platforms she uses for her trays of chemicals and the whole process is cumbersome and worryingly full of the use of dangerous chemicals; but the results she is starting to see make it all worthwhile .

First the sheet of glass is cleaned, she uses glass plates roughly 12 x 10 inch. A solution of collodion (gun cotton dissolved in ether and alcohol mixed with salts) is then poured evenly over the plate and made sensitive to light in the dark room with a coating of silver nitrate salts. The damp plate is then ready to be placed in the camera. Nellie uses a standard sliding-box camera and a French made Jamin lens with a fixed aperture of f3.6 and a focal length of roughly 12 inches. After removing the lens cap the exposure time required is between three and seven minutes. She then takes the glass plate back to the dark room still damp (thus 'wet plate' or 'wet collodion' negative) and a solution of developer is poured over it. The negative is washed and then bathed in cyanide to fix the image and remove unexposed silver salts. It's washed again and finally coated with varnish to enable multiple prints to be made from the plate without damaging it.

It has taken her quite a few months to hone the technique with many worrying mistakes but now she is perfect at it and she is ready to make her very own albumen prints. When she started taking photos at sixteen she had to get her negatives developed for her but now she is proud to be able to do it herself, and do it brilliantly. This is a very new process that only became widely used around four years ago. Thin plain paper is coated with a layer of egg white containing salt. The albumenised paper is then sensitised with silver nitrate solution and left to dry before use. Contact prints are made using a frame to sandwich together the negative and the paper in daylight, the image appearing or 'coming out' through the effect of light on the albumen paper. Thus the size of the negative generally determines the size of the print. The print is then toned to make it permanent and to add colour. On top of all this Nellie sometimes uses the process of water colours to tint the print , the whole thing is a huge learning curve for her and she is only just beginning to concentrate on the portrait side of it of which she is particularly interested.

Nellie sighs and sits in the warmth of the summerhouse, the sun making pools of rainbow coloured light on the floor as it soaks in through the stained glass windows. She gazes across the park and sees her old pony grazing in the paddock at the end of the trees. He must be twenty eight by now and she suddenly feels a stab of guilt at the fact that she hasn't been down to take him a carrot recently. She empties her mind and turns her face to the light feeling its pale warmth gently soothe her, she yawns with all the excitement last night it had been hard to get to sleep and her lack of rest is catching up on her.

She thinks back to the night before and smiles; if she is being honest with herself it really was rather terrifying! They had all filed into the dining room which was in total darkness lit only by the light of one oil lamp on a sideboard. Blavatsky herself looked extremely forbidding and rather stately, not a person to be argued with and so they had all immediately felt subdued, even the haughty Edith, yes instantly her mother had become as pliable as a child . It was almost as if from the moment that Blavatsky entered the house she had cast a spell on them, holding them hypnotised. Nellie would have loved to set up her tripod and camera in a corner of the room but had been forcibly refused permission and told that it was prohibited by one of the Madame's companions. Ectoplasm it seems is allergic to the science of photography.

They had been told to link hands and Madame Blavatsky asked for their forefingers to be placed on the wine glass in the centre of the table. Then the room had become really cold, even though there was a fire blazing in the grate and suddenly the glass had begun to whizz across the polished surface of the table spelling out answers to all the ladies questions. Mama had asked for the spirit of her small dead brother to come to the table but Blavatsky hadn't been able to conjure him up for her, in fact it was all going along fairly smoothly until it had come to Nellie's turn. She had asked first of all when she would meet the man she would fall in love with and all the ladies had been shocked. Was not she supposed to ask when she would meet the man she would marry?

Nellie doesn't really think that marriage is what it is cracked up to be, unless of course you desire cartloads of children. She herself would like one or two but she is not sure that marriage will suit her. If she becomes an artist or photographer then she can run away to Paris and have her own money and the crassness of Victoriana won't bother her. No, far better to search for love although she has fears that it isn't provident to go out looking for love , but better to let it find you . The glass had seemed to hesitate for a moment, hovering in the middle of the table and then began to whizz between them again spelling out the word "soon".

All well and good, but when she had asked how she would meet him that had seemed to cause total havoc. The wine glass had whizzed around in smaller and smaller circles and then simply flown off the table and smashed against the wall and at the same moment the oil lamp had blown out. All was confusion for a few moments and in the dark Nellie had felt a sort of intense warmth flow through her whole body as if she was being flooded with light. When it reached the top of her heads her brain exploded into a thousand fragments of blissful feeling like falling crystals, she can't remember any more than this but it was the most exquisite feeling that she has ever come across. Apparently she had fainted but she has no recollection of any of this, she just remembers gasping in disgust as Miss Tindley thrust smelling salts under her nostrils. She had woken in the music room ten minutes later, covered in a blanket and shivering wildly. Miss Tindley was looking disapprovingly down at her from above, her long aquiline nose pinched and red at the tip which seemed to make it stand out from her sallow face and she looked more bird like than ever. As she lay there trying to get a hold on what had just happened she could hear the hum of voices and the swish of heavy skirts passing the door, but the ceiling kept threatening to crash in on her and she was forced to lie back close her eyes and simply concentrate on breathing. The guests and Madame Blavatsky had all left in a flurry of

41

carriages and whispers and her Mama had taken to her bed with one of her migraines.

Nellie sighs and fiddles with her gloves buttoning the tiny pearl buttons and smoothing them into a straight line along her forearm. When she thinks about it, she does have this terrible habit of ruining things without really understanding how. Why, ever since she was a small child she could be counted on to say the wrong thing at the wrong time. After the séance an autumn storm had blown up outside in the garden as if in sympathy with the strange happenings in the house and all the gas lamps seemed to be sputtering and finally out of working order, even though they live near one of the biggest gasworks in London down at Bell Green in Lower Sydenham. She had lain in bed listening to the trees scraping against her bedroom window and had felt slightly scared wondering if they had unleashed anything seriously dangerous with their dabbling. She doesn't really believe in ghosts but there had definitely been a sense of the "other world" in the dining room that night.

The wallpaper in her room, a swirling design of ivy leaves around crumbled walls had become slightly sinister in the firelight and she was sure that she had the distinct impression that there was some person trying to escape from the clinging tendrils of the ivy. She'd had to shut her eyes tightly and bury her head in her pillow in order to shake the idea from her mind's eye. However this morning had dawned clear and bright, Mama and Papa taken the carriage to church and here she was escaping for a few hours, what could be a better birthday present that some precious hours of freedom?

She feels around beside the grate of the cast iron ornamental fireplace in the summerhouse and finds the small iron lever that is fashioned to look like part of the design on the grate. It pulls perfectly upwards on its oiled hinges and she steps back as the whole side of the wall moves silently away from her. The opening immediately divulges stone steps leading down into the semi darkness beneath, and she lights the lantern kept there specifically for this purpose. This tunnel had been one of her best ever birthday presents , her father had first showed it to her on her birthday when she was ten years old, and it was one of their many secrets, mother knew nothing about it thank goodness. Edith's imagination had a horrid habit of running away with itself as it is, they certainly don't need to provide compost for it by letting her into all the mysteries built into the fabric of the house. This isn't the only tunnel that the architect incorporated into the designs but it's the one that Nellie loves to use the most.

The opening to the tunnel recedes to a round globule of daylight behind her as she descends further into the gloom, she turns a corner and there at her feet is what appears to be a pathway of coloured light. The roof of the tunnel is covered in mosaics depicting the judgement of Paris. Floating Goddesses flit above her head and Aphrodite holds out the golden apple of discord to the handsome dark haired boy promising him the love of the world's most beautiful woman Helen of Troy if he will only choose her.as the most glorious of the Goddesses on Mount Olympus. The light is funnelling through the ventilation shafts cut into the roof, small slits where the daylight seeps in, carefully disguised from above and perfectly aligned to the gradient of the hill so that no rain water can infiltrate. Nellie loves it down here; she feels like she has stepped into a fairy tale, there really isn't enough magic in her daily life but living in a magical house helps towards soothing the bonds of being a young single woman in a man's society. Why she'd be more useful joining the women's suffrage movement than learning embroidery with Miss Tindlay but there is no telling her mother that.

It's silent in the tunnel as if she the butterfly is in a cocoon, or even in nature's womb, in hibernation waiting to burst forth in the spring like Persephone. She blushes slightly as she thinks of the rape of Persephone , she's been reading an awful lot of Greek legends and tragedies recently;, she had discovered reams of them at the British Library on her trips into town when she was supposed to be dress shopping. Often she wishes that she didn't have a brain at all because that is what seems to cause the trouble, too much thinking which leads to yearning after things that she can't have. The air shifts in texture and lightens as she reaches the end of the tunnel, a twitch of a small lever on her left at shoulder level and she is in the folly in the woods, the golden light of the sun blinding her for a second before she steps out into the demure light in the folly. Papa built it here for picnics on summer days and also roasting marshmallows and making hot chocolate on the small stove in the crisp autumn days when they go for one of their long walks.

It's hot and musty in here and she flings open the blue door and steps out into the strong sunlight in the woods. It's still warm outside her fur feels almost cumbersome to her and she unbuttons her coat, her pendant swings out from her dress catching the light and she hurriedly scoops it back to rest once more against the dove grey silk.. She takes the downward slope towards the small stream, her boots sinking into the soft bed of leaves and not making a sound. She walks for a full ten minutes in a large circular path thinking about nothing in particular only the sound of squirrels rustling through the leaves as they scamper up the trees with their winter hoard. The small stream is trickling its watery music somewhere to her left and the holly bushes are bright with berries, making her think of blood and Christmas. Soon too soon there will be the long winter months to come when it will be too snowy to do much walking. There will be long boring "at homes" where mother will trot out the local hideous candidates for her perusal,

------Does she seriously think that Nellie is going to marry one of these bores? ---

Even the lascivious Arthur Sullivan has been invited to try his luck and it's fairly common knowledge that he has bedded more than one of the young ladies of the neighbourhood. He might be a musical genius but his darting eyes and bushy whiskers do nothing for Nellie, she can't imagine why women should fall for him, nor does she intend to find out as he would so obviously like her too. Her clear brow creases into a furrow when she thinks of the last time he came for dinner and insisted on trying to put his hand on her leg under the table. It's time she told Papa to send him packing

The woods are empty of other walkers and for this she is grateful, but then in the distance she hears the laughter of children and suddenly realising that she has left the folly unlocked and that it might be a dangerous place for small children she hurries back. Rounding a corner she sees two small boys dressed in unusual garments their dark heads bent together over something in the ground by the folly. They look up and see her and hesitate for a second , but she is good with small children they seem to immediately trust her and she gives them one of her huge smiles and a wink and holds out a small gloved hand in greeting.

"Good afternoon, I'm Nellie, who are you two handsome boys?"

The smaller one is shy and looks down scraping the leaves at his feet into a muddy pile but the elder pipes up with.

"We're Toby and Ollie, and we live in a big house on the hill, and our Dad is just behind us and he's John".

Nellie looks behind them for a second and sees a tall handsome man descending the hill towards them, for some reason just the sight of him in the distance makes her chest a little bit tighter and her heart skip a beat. Then she remembers the children and looks to where Oliver is holding onto her hand tightly and looking up at her in a bemused fashion.

" Why are you wearing these kind of clothes"

Toby asks stroking her fur in a kind of wonderment.

"'Are you in a play in the theatre about the old days, some sort of history thing, because normal ladies don't look like you. You look like you come from a book or a fairy tale. Look Ollie she's got kind of stardust in her hair".

The boys look up to where the sunlight is indeed surrounding her in a sparkling gold halo of light, Toby looks down at his hand, it's very cold and where it is grasping the girls hand his fingers seem to be touching ice, he tries to take his hand away but its stuck and for a second he feels frightened. But then no, there's his dad not far away and Ollie is looking at Nellie adoringly, playing with a very sparkly necklace that she has around her neck and she has such pretty smiley eyes, surely nothing can be wrong with them talking to her can it?

Nellie is delighted with her find and even more so with the handsome father in hot pursuit who has nearly reached within calling distance to them. On a complete whim she bends and whispers to them.

'' Would you like to play a little hide and seek with your father? If you come inside with me I have something to show you that I think you'll find interesting. ''

Her face is so open and trustworthy that Toby doesn't hesitate, only Ollie holds back a little and tells her.

''Mum says never to go with strangers, and Dad might be cross''

Nellie pushes the curls back from his small worried face and tells him reassuringly.

''Well it seems we are practically neighbours, I live in a big house on the hill too, and it's only for a second, your father will easily find you, this I promise.''

She has no specific plan in mind, she simply thinks that the boys might like the adventure of the tunnel and if she leaves all the doorways open then their father will follow them inside and that will be a meeting that she simply can't wait for. Niggling at the back of her brain is a feeling that something is slightly out of kilter, that the boys don't really look like any of her older cousins children, that the air around them is too bright, that she has a ringing in her ears which she has never come across before, but she ignores all the hints at differentness. She's simply a little oversensitive after last night's séance that's all.

She turns and moves through the blue door of the folly, the boys giggle and turn to wave briefly to their father, once inside they gasp in surprise as the stare into the tunnel. The tunnel door is open and almost instantly they are all three of them skipping down into the cool mosaic archway with its smell of deep moss and the sunlight through the slits in the roof playing over the Grecian Goddesses at the feast of Zeus. For a few minutes they move in unison down the passageway together, she looks behind her for the handsome father but behind them there is only the empty passageway and the echo of her footsteps. The boys are running ahead shouting and jumping in the air, and they turn the corner just before the entrance to the summerhouse and in so doing move out of her line of sight for a moment. The door up into the summerhouse is now open in front of them although she was sure that it had closed behind her.

Suddenly she realises instinctually that something is going very wrong; the air is thick and dank and the sun has disappeared. There are puddles of water at her feet while the mosaic on the ceiling is overgrown with creepers, the light almost non-existent. She calls out to her two companions but they are gone, vanished as if they had never been and she is alone and dishevelled, slightly out of breath and unsure of what is happening. From somewhere behind her she hears the sound of a man calling frantically, his voice echoing and bouncing down the now empty tunnel.

Without looking back she picks up her skirts and runs and she doesn't stop until she stumbles up into the light of her own summerhouse and collapses on the cushions breathing heavily. Her gloves are gone, her hair is all over her shoulders and her new fur coat has a tear, but apart from that everything is the same as it was. The little boys are nowhere to be seen, this troubles her for a moment but then she imagines that in the

47

confusion of the past few minutes they may have doubled back and joined their father. Yes that must be it what other explanation could there be?

Catching her breath she hears the bell for tea and pulls herself together. Maybe it was all just one of her own fantasies, but where did the little boys go and who was that man? Patting down her hair in the glass of the windows and rubbing at a grass stain on her skirt she walks briskly back into the house. She is just in time to take tea and a long hot bath before getting ready for dinner and her piano recital. No doubt Mama will have invited the usual pasty faced youths or a few dowager old men whose wives have died some gruesome death in childbirth in order to pursue her out of her singleton life, but this time she is very sure that she isn't interested in any of them, it doesn't matter how handsome they are.

Now she is determined to meet the man in the woods and if he lives in one of the houses along the Hill then it shouldn't be difficult to find him. As for his wife, well, wives can be dealt with, she has seen it done before and in the very worst case scenario they can always elope to the Italian Riviera with the two little boys and she can become a monumental scandal. She can make her livelihood taking photographs of rich Italian weddings and he can grow an olive grove or whatever it is that you do on a hill in Italy

She smiles to herself, yes if nothing else she is determined that her life will be interesting in a way that her mother's never was nor can ever hope to be. Only a tiny part of her brain tells her that she is behaving like something out of a 2d novel and not at all as she would wish, but something in the light today has turned her from the 'rational' to the 'extraordinary' and she can't wait to find out what it is.

*

Chapter 4
November 1st 1994.

John.

He hadn't slept much last night and this morning as he looks in the mirror he sees his face is as grey and misty as the fog outside the window. All his bones ache, and he feels suddenly old and slightly shaky, all his points of reference have been shifted and returned to him misaligned. It's as if the end of the world is coming and there is nothing he can do about it, but stand and wait: he feels an imminent sense of impending doom which he can neither explain nor shake off. The fog is billowing around the garden in great swirls of obscurity as if the leaves are smouldering in some long forgotten ice fire that has burnt since the beginning of time. For a moment he feels the lingering outlines of the ghosts of the past rustling through the house and this time they don't feel particularly friendly.

He shakes the shaving foam from his chin shivering slightly in his T shirt and baggy boxers and he looks out over the lawn to the summer house. Somewhere down in the kitchen he can hear the boys arguing with the au pair about whether they want boiled eggs or pancakes for breakfast. At least they sound fairly normal after yesterday's bizarre occurrence , even if he feels shaken up by it, but he's just tired, he's beginning to sound like a superstitious idiot, and he's always been the pragmatist around here. He sighs and washes the razor in the murky water of the sink. Thank God they were both unharmed after yesterday's little shenanigans. In the end he hadn't bothered to explain anything at all to Cecilia. Life is becoming a bit like that; they simply didn't really talk any more, not as they should do. His marriage is falling apart and he has no tools at his disposal to save it. It's as if they are living on parallel tracks and only turn to glance and wave at each other in passing, it shouldn't be like this, he knows it deep down in his bones but feels powerless to do anything about it.

By the time he'd got back puffing and shaking from the woods Cecilia had been all packed up and ready to be off to Paris for some urgent meeting or other with her boss. She doesn't even take the time to explain to him why or how anymore. As he watched her long slim legs slide elegantly into the back of the car as the uniformed driver carefully closed the door behind her he had a eureka moment.

---She doesn't even notice me anymore----

It's as if he has become part of the interior furnishings of her life, as unimportant as a chest of drawers or sideboard, certainly less important than her personal trainer, her Pilate's group or her weekly pedicure.

--- His presence in her life is as automatic as putting on her eyeliner and a good deal less interesting. ----

She had scurried into her sleek company car with barely a wave, leaving him to sort out his own birthday dinner, marinate the meat for a BBQ for the neighbours, pitch the fireworks in the orchard and of course entertain her bloody parents. He'd got through it all though with the help of several pints of mulled wine, and a jovial expression pasted to his face. After a while his cheek muscles had started to ache with the strain of his fake smile and now he had the mother of all crashing headaches to prove it. He'd been more than worried about the boys, and in between his hospitable front he had tried to see that they were alright and not traumatised in any way, while trying to gently glean some information from them about exactly what had gone on. Toby had looked up at him with wonder in his eyes and told him.

"Lady has stardust in her hair Daddy, and she is called Nellie, when can we see her again?".

Ollie's face had just clouded over slightly and all he'd said was.

''Nasty dream daddy, all these old smelly leaves and we boys got lost in a tunnel, one of our fairy tale stories, but real. Ollie didn't like it''.

The tunnel bit seemed to make some sense, John had heard that when the house had been built various tunnels linking it to Crystal Palace had been installed so that the ladies didn't have to get cold when venturing forth to the Saturday night music extravaganza's that were so popular.

---But a tunnel into the woods? ---

Did it really exist and if so how the heck was he going to find it without the original blueprints for the house?

In the end he had left it at that, tried to dull the swirling questions in his brain and concentrated on the evening, and it had proved to be quite interesting as evenings in suburbia go. According to the woman next door, he can't for the life of him remember her name now only the hybrid red dye of her hair; there is an exhibition at the Dulwich Gallery of photos of exactly the same era as the house. Various portraits of local celebrities of the time taken by a woman photographer who might herself have lived in Raven House. His pulse quickens and he realises guiltily that he has to find out more about the girl he saw yesterday, already he knows with a fateful sinking of the heart that he isn't going to find her living in one of the houses along the road as the boys think he might. For a brief instant he had wondered if she was a local girl, but the whole vanishing act scenario was too bizarre for any of it to be a hoax. He knows for the first time ever in his life that he has come across something and someone who he can't rationally explain away in one of his theories. Life has thrown him a beautifully obscure curved ball; something extraordinary to deal with and even he has to be bound by the sacred feel of it all. Thank goodness he doesn't believe in god or the devil otherwise he might be beginning to feel very frightened.

He scratches the top of his greying hair, cropped short for convenience but still thick and abundant, yes today he will work from home, make sure that he has a long chat with the boys and see if he can find any evidence of this tunnel that they keep telling him about. Logically the only explanation for them turning up back in the summer house after leaving him in the woods is the existence of some kind of tunnel leading from here down to the woods. Seriously though there is no logic about the whole situation. Then later either today or soon when he has the time or when they are busy with tea and homework, he will make a foray down to Dulwich Village and see if any of the faces in the portraits are familiar.

----If not he can always go and scan the archives at Lewisham for information as to who lived here, and when. -----

He isn't a journalist for nothing, if he can discover financial double dealings and forecast the markets he can easily sort out this little mystery on the home front.

The one thing that is beginning to bother him is the throbbing in the lower half of his body that he's had constantly since he caught a glimpse of the girl in the woods yesterday. For a while he'd wondered what it was and then he'd understood that it was desire, something that he can't remember feeling for a long time. The thought that one glimpse of a girl in the woods had made him feel like this makes him also feel incredibly guilty, he's never felt this way for Ceci, or anyone really since his first proper girlfriend when he was just twenty one. Funnily enough her name was Ophelia and she had been very beautiful but a total loose cannon. For some reason his reasonably conservative parents had loved her verve and charisma, maybe he should never have dumped her, but she just wasn't solid enough for him, not perfect enough. He'd heard in the grapevine that she'd gone on to make a good marriage but it had gone wrong and she had divorced.

Maybe instead of thinking about some elusive woman in the woods who might not even exist he should ring up

Ophelia? His elder brother sees her regularly so he still has her number. He grimaces at himself in the mirror, silly old fool, now he's trying to undo the choices he made years and years ago. No far better to chase after a phantom than try and stitch together something that he ripped apart and threw away without a second thought. Ophelia probably wouldn't even want to speak to him, but then again she did have a big soft spot for him and she might be there as a friend or sounding board if he needs one. It's strange how because he has been so busy with his life and career that all his old friends have just drifted away from him. There is no one he can trust to talk this over with, no one he can ring up and go for a drink with, he has managed to completely isolate himself without really meaning to. All those shiny successful people that he does business with wouldn't be at the end of a telephone for him if he needed them, they would simply vanish, like the wind.

He pulls out the plug on the soapy water in the sink and watches it gurgle down the plughole before studying his face dispassionately in the mirror. Not a bad face, looking a little grey and peaky now but he was still what you would call handsome. A plethora of useless arbitrary thoughts flit annoyingly across his mind. It occurs to him that in Australia the water goes down the plughole in the polar opposite direction, it crosses his mind that his marriage is a mess but he has the children doesn't he? What more should he want or expect? An inner voice challenges that supposition, he should want to be happy and he certainly isn't that. He wonders what it would be like if Cecilia just disappeared, if she never came back from Paris and he suddenly found himself single again. He brushes the thought away as he splashes his face with some kind of potent aftershave that the in laws gave him as a present last night and winces at the sting of it on his raw skin.

He's forty for god sake, time to try and grow up a little at least, but he still feels twenty two although the face in the mirror tells him something different it's not a craggy face but it definitely has a "lived in" look about it. Cecilia constantly reminds him that he is a cold uncaring English man, with that lilting French accent of hers that he used to find so fascinating but nowadays he simply finds it irritating. He doesn't agree with her, he never used to be cold with his girlfriends he remembers being quite affectionate back then. He did all the usual things like hold hands but recently he's just shut down. He doesn't even feel like sex with her any more, she is too angry with him, angry with a cold dark unnameable fury that lurks beneath the surface of their daily interactions like the iceberg that sunk the Titanic. More than this he just doesn't find the lean toned blankness of her body all that interesting.

It happened sometime after the birth of Ollie, she had turned, inside his head anyway, from a lover to a mother overnight. Just like that he had suddenly shied away from seeing her in anyway as a sexual being, he knows that it's a cliché but you can't fuck your mother now can you, and so his wife had in some strange way become taboo sexually. He examines the harshness of the word "fuck", not one that he would normally use but quite honestly if he had the choice that's what he would do now. Go to his club in Soho get drunk and pick up someone who meant absolutely nothing to him, take her to a hotel and fuck her brains out. It would clear his head, it would stop all this confusion, and it would be just what it was and what he hasn't had for months now, just sex.

The door is flung open and the boys whoop in and suddenly his mood lifts, they have this capacity to lighten the mood of any situation with their innocent exuberance, which he supposes is the blessing of having children. They tussle with him on the unmade bed and he smells their clean child smell before Radna comes to shoo them away to get ready for school. Crossing to the window he catches a glimpse of movement out by the summerhouse and his body instantly tenses expectantly, but then he thinks that it is probably only the gardener. When he had first bought the house he had had grandiose ideas of doing his own gardening but that hadn't worked out so now a local landscape design company just sends in a man once a week to keep everything in trim.

The morning has taken on a staccato feel with its series of unconnected events and he feels like he is watching himself watching everything. As if to emphasis this, the house phone begins to jump across the bedside table, as if through its own volition. But he ignores it studiously; he pulls on some jeans and an old cashmere sweater over his T shirt as he hurries downstairs. The spaniel gambles around his socked toes trying to chew them but he shoves him gently away and shrugs on his waxed jacket and his boots heading out into the calming cool of the morning. The trees are just getting to the stage where they look slightly forlorn, the last leaf hanging from bare hand like branches, and the gardener is trying to rake them into piles that keep on scattering away in the morning breeze.

He stops and listens, only the usual Monday morning noises out on Sydenham Hill, the stoic parents of South East London battering their way through morning traffic to take their children to the super rich schools in the area, schools, to which of course his own children belong. He waves as Radna propels her little Kia down the drive on her way to deposit the boys at Dulwich Prep, and decides to take a tour of the orchard to clear his head and while he is at it remove the burnt out husks of last night's fireworks. He pops them into a recycling bin bag placing it down by the compost heap for the gardener to pick up later and smiles as he remembers the children's' expressions of joy as they watched the power rockets fling themselves into the sky.

The sun is hotter than ever now and he unzips his jacket and pushes open the door of the summerhouse, it's empty of course, what exactly was he expecting? He gazes blankly at the slightly dilapidated interior, the floorboards warped from the damp, the window frames and door in need of a coat of paint. That will be one of his summer jobs to restore it to some semblance of its former glory; there is no point in just letting it fall to bits. He takes his jacket off and places it on the bench under the window and then diligently makes a tour of the walls being careful not to get splinters in his fingers. When he gets to the small iron grate of the fireplace he stops and bends down, feeling all the way around the ornamental wrought ironworks for

55

something, He's not sure what, but images of Harrison Ford n the lost city of the Aztecs comes to mind. He pulls and prods and is just beginning to get stiff when something of a sixth sense , the one that tells you if someone is looking at you from across the street, that sixth sense, starts buzzing in his ears and he realises that he's not alone.

The hair on the back of his neck stands up and it's got very very cold in here almost icy. The light is too bright and he's suddenly afraid when he hears a voice, thin and clear like the ting of a Tibetan bell talking to him.

" Hello, are you lost and looking for something?"

It's a woman's voice and it's very faint almost as if it's coming from inside his own head, but he knows immediately without question that it's her. He twists slowly on his heel and looks up into the light and the softest most beautiful pair of wide brown laughing eyes that he's ever seen. She leans over him and he can smell that smell again, musky potent unknown. Something cold and paper thin brushes his hand and almost pushes it to a knob he hasn't noticed at the side of the fireplace. He opens his mouth to reply to her but he can't speak, and his mouth opens and shuts like a fish. She leans in towards him again and the softest of leather gloves brushes the corner of his cheek, or does it? It feels like ice, it feels like winter, it feels like death and an icy band clutches at his heart, as he gasps for breath.

" I'm Nellie and you're in my Summerhouse, we almost met in the woods yesterday don't you remember? I think you are looking for this".

She leans in past him, towards the wall and it's her perfume all around him that's making his head spin. He looks at her skin, pale translucent, the hint of pink in her cheek the fullness of her breasts under her buttoned up coat. She leans in past him and pulls a small hidden lever down by the grate of the fireplace. He just has time to whisper.

"I'm John, who are you really? ".

There is a grinding noise and the wall begins to disappear backwards away from him into the darkness which drops downwards. It's the tunnel the boys have told him about. The whole wall has swung away into the tunnel, but the girl is gone and he is crumpled up in pain, the tingling in his arm and the tightness of his chest tell him that he may have suffered some kind of heart attack.

Later, much later he can't tell how long he's been laying there he wakes up in the same spot, but the fireplace is back where it was, the summerhouse intact and normal around him. Painfully he bends his head and looks to the window, it's getting dark outside he must have lain here for hours and he's cold, mortally cold and he needs a brandy quickly. Shuffling to his feet the room spins around him and he fumbles for the wall, the pain is still there in his chest but now it feels like the pain you get after crying too many tears. Somewhere back in his memory of being a child he can remember this feeling from crying himself to sleep the first few months he was at boarding school. Yes he feels an incredible loss as if he has just heard of the death of someone whom he loves very much, and he begins to take deep breaths as if he is in need of oxygen. The survival mechanism in his brain is telling him that he needs to get back inside the house, he needs to be warm and everything else will be sorted out later, everything else will drop into place as soon as he can find some way through to the girl.

For it is obvious to him now that life will never be the same again and his life will only be worth something if he is able to love her. By the time he slams the front door behind him he is shaking violently his teeth chattering away. There are the normal sounds of the boys having their tea coming from the kitchen and he staggers into the drawing room to pour himself that drink. The alcohol puts the fire back in his blood and he thankfully collapses in one of the big comfy chairs next to the radiator that is pumping out heat. He's very tired and falls into a light dose probably from the shock of it all more than anything.

As he drifts away to a dream of the orchard warmed by the summer sun a voice in his head soothing tells him that tomorrow he will discover who she is and tomorrow he can decide what to do about all this , but for now he must sleep and heal and let the Angels guide him

*

Chapter 5
Cecilia Halloween 1994.

Daylight is a distant whisper as she stares out of the train window at the flat Kent countryside with its pylons and its container yards. She's been given a complimentary ticket on the Eurostar before its official opening in a couple of weeks and she leans back and wriggles into the comfy first class seat sighing contentedly A small part of her feels a tiny bit guilty at upping sticks and leaving John with the kids on his birthday, all the neighbours and their children coming over and the BBQ laid out outside the conservatory so they can watch the fireworks. Of course it was definitely slightly sadistic of her to leave him to entertain her parents but at the thought of it a wicked smile crosses her face and she chuckles. Well she Cecilia had put up with his boring parents often enough it's time for him to return the favour. So only a tiny piece of her feels guilty, not enough to bother about and she metaphorically expands into the contours of her being giving a little jump for joy at getting back her own sense of freedom and purpose.

There is a tall salt and pepper haired French man in the seat opposite her, the English would call him a "silver fox" and he is blatantly giving her the eye. She studiously ignores him, but she's really pleased that she's still attractive enough for men to bother with. She is scared of getting to that point which women do at one stage or another where they become invisible to men, but luckily it doesn't seem to be happening yet. She supposes that it is hugely vain of her to care, but she is vain so why not admit it? At thirty seven she's a few years younger than John who seems to have settled into a morose kind of middle age since he bought that bloody house. All he wants to do is play golf and go to the Opera neither of which do anything at all for Cecilia. Golf is for old men and Opera is totally incomprehensible, all those overweight women bellowing in a language she doesn't understand. The train bounces and changes tracks and a waiter pop's his head in the carriage asking for her dinner order. The man opposite her seizes his chance and presses a cool hand on her knee and with wide enquiring eyes asks her in heavily accented English

"If Madame is dining alone perhaps you would care to join me?"

She looks piercingly at him for a moment and blatantly shifts sideways to dislodge his presumptuous hand, a small swell of irritation flickers over her aquiline face and she replies in perfect Parisian French.

"That's so kind, but unfortunately I have an article to write before we reach Gare du Nord so I'm on a bit of a tight schedule".

She quickly orders the Cassoulet of Lamb and a good red wine to go with it, as its cold outside and she's tired; she needs something to keep her going. They won't reach Paris before midnight and her meeting at the office is first thing in the morning. It's been hard to do the commute while the boys are small but John had point blank refused the idea of living in France, so what else was she supposed to do? He would have liked it of course if she had become a carbon copy of his mother who was vaguely reminiscent of the Queen and seemed to spend her time doing very little for various nefarious charities, or playing bridge and going to the Opera. Cecilia can't see the point of the Opera; give her a good film any day, anything rather than all that emotion and drama usually in German which she detests. All she can ever think about when he takes her to the opera is that the women onstage need to go on a diet and how she's going to escape with the least possibility of an argument. John's eyes become glassy and he is so engrossed that he doesn't notice her sighs and fidgeting and her usual exit to the bar where she drinks her way through a solitary bottle of champagne and ends up slightly drunk saying regrettable things to him when he eventually appears in the interval.

She notices that her companion is just waiting to make another foray into desperate conversation with her and very firmly plonks her large Chanel spectacles on her nose and takes her notepad out of her briefcase. She is dressed top to toe in Agnes B, elegant sleek chic and totally work woman like with just a hint of sexiness in the hue of her stockings and her Jimmy Choo shoes that delicately frame her small ankles and perfect legs. She crosses her knees provocatively letting her skirt ride up her thighs, let him sweat a bit, it'll do him good. Wasn't it Lacan that said that every time you have this kind of direct eye contact with a member of the opposite sex you are opening the door on a relationship? Well he must have been wrong because nothing would induce her to consider even kissing her travelling companion, let alone anything else. She flicks her eyes rapidly over her neat writing and absentmindedly twirls her wedding ring around her finger, carefully checking herself to see if any part of her is missing the boys.

No, she's fine, no mother's angst in sight, yet after that debacle this afternoon she'd been slightly averse to leaving them all. Little Oliver had looked very red cheeked and slightly feverish and confused when the au pair had brought them both into the house after finding them cold and shaking and crying in the Summerhouse. They had seemed to be locked in and through the tears came a story of leaving Daddy in the woods and going down a tunnel with a lady. None of it made any sense at all and she had been quite sharp with Radna who had obviously been reading them spooky stories again. That's the trouble with au pairs, you really have to keep a tight rein on them or else this kind of thing happens. For a split second she'd wondered if John was having an affair and the twins had stumbled on him in flagrante so to speak, but then she'd immediately thought better of it. He certainly didn't look like someone who was flushed from the rigours of sex, she'd suddenly seen him as the middle aged man that he is, going grey with a slight paunch and more likely to have a heart attack than a *"Liaison Dangereuse !! "*

She'd just had time to bark a swift rebuke at her husband before the company car came for her. At least the drama had given her a let out clause from her sudden departure and she smiles suddenly thinking of him having to cope with this evening's entertainment issues and her own parents who were turning up expecting to see her. She quite likes the idea of creating a birthday party scenario which she will be absent from, sometimes she's just a complete bitch, she utterly realises that and she also understands deep down that she sort of loves him really. But she is punishing him for treating his career as more important than hers yes all this is her reaction to him not doing what she wants. For not letting them live at least half the time in Paris. Cecilia so wants the boys to be bi - lingual, to grow up with at least some of the panache that living in her home city would anoint them with, but he won't budge an inch on this one.

She shudders inwardly thinking of the big draughty house in Sydenham echoing with children's laughter and footfalls on the polished wooden floors. She hates the house, there's no getting around that, ever since she laid eyes on the complicated red brickwork and stared in through the stain glass windows adorning the porch. She is very aware that the house doesn't like her much either. The taps clang too often in the echoing bathrooms, the doors get stuck locking her in places she doesn't want to be locked in, and on the rare occasions when she is there by herself with the boys she can't stop listening to its voices. The voices follow her into rooms slamming doors and swishing curtains, she can't distinguish the words but she knows that their intent towards her is ominous. Someone or something in the house hates her and wants rid of her. She occasionally sees the figure of a woman in furs walking away from her in the park, and although she certainly doesn't believe in this stuff she is beginning to think that Raven House is haunted. She hasn't dared mention it to John, he would just laugh at her and call her menopausal, and indeed she is having night sweats and hot flushes these days but she is dam sure that it's the house not the battering of hormones that is effecting her like this. When she's not there she feels perfectly fine and so she spends less and less time at home now and *tant pis,* what else is she to do if he won't let them move. A few years ago she would of course have stayed this evening and played the dutiful and ecstatic lady of the house , but too much has passed between husband and wife and she's just not sure if she still loves him enough anymore, at least not in the way she should.

When they were first married she was mesmerised by John's soft concern and love for her and the children especially when they were tiny. He was the perfect man to have around small children always there to soothe a fretful child in the middle of the night when Cecilia needed her beauty sleep All was loving concern until the boys became toddlers and she supposed that he thought it was time for her to "get on with it" in the time honoured fashion of upper middle class families. She soon found another cold calculating side to him cobra like rearing its head. He was ruthlessly career orientated and that didn't include being the least bit bothered about supporting her in her career.

He had this antiquated English notion that she was the mother so she should get on with all the mind numbing and painful tedium of tiny child rearing. She should have guessed really, his army background and his own mother never doing much but hold tea parties for the Women's institute should have told her something, but she had been too glazy eyed with obsession to see through his charming exterior. For a while she had gone along with "the little wifely bit" literarily strapping babies around her shoulders and pushing buggies around the South London Streets, and joining desperately tedious coffee mornings with other mothers.

That was when she found out that she definitely had a "fluffy mother gene" missing. She simply couldn't have cared less about breast milk and potty training, first words, or documenting smiles, or rushing home from the office to tell bedtime stories. She'd far rather go to the pub and have a good bottle of red with her colleagues No she'd soldiered on for a few years but then one morning she simply hadn't been able to get

63

out of bed, or do anything other than burst into tears. The Doctor was called and the household wandered around talking in hushed voices about "depression" It wasn't bloody surprising she'd become depressed , who wouldn't have in that draughty windy old house with its creaking windows and a certain sense of malevolence she'd always felt it held towards her.

From the first day that she'd walked into it she had this irrational feeling that the house hated her. John simply wouldn't listen to her pleas to sell up and move to Chelsea or Islington, the houses were just as big there for God's sake, and no creepy woods at the bottom of the garden to freak her out on storm filled nights when she was alone with the children and he was at "a meeting" or at his bloody club talking to really interesting people that he never introduced her to.

That was when the rot had begun to set in. She took the pills the florid Doctor prescribed, pulled herself together, got an au pair and got her life back, and begun to hate her husband. It was precisely because everyone thought he was so charming that she had married him in the first place, no English girl had been able to tie him down and he was the best "journalistic" catch in town, with his connections to government and a huge future ahead of him. But since her "melt down" she had begun to understand just why he had never married before her. He was totally emotionally unavailable. His boarding school upbringing had cut him off from his feeling self. Yes like any man in the bedroom he could get slightly misty eyed after a particularly satisfying orgasm that she had given him, but he couldn't translate that into real intimacy and affection, he couldn't understand what it was that she needed from him and why she had become so bitter.

----Did it really matter? Now she was letting her mind wander when she absolutely needed to concentrate   ----

The train flew on into the darkness and she pressed her hot brow against the cool glass wishing that she could go to sleep for a week and wake up single again, but that was a terrible thought, she shook herself out of it and wondered when dinner was going to be served she was getting hungry. There were ways to cope with an ailing marriage, it is time she got a little more "French" about it all. She needed to keep it going until the boys were older but she would no longer cow tow to John professionally. No she needed to work more in Paris now and he'd just have to sort out the everyday stuff with the children. It's not that she doesn't love her children, she does, but she needs more, and her job and an adoringly beautiful toy boy in Paris is beginning to make her feel a whole load better about herself.

Louis had been given to her she felt almost as a present from the Gods, to be her intern a month ago by her boss, who had an uncanny understanding of these things. Cecilia was his best woman reporter and the way things were going in France and abroad she needed to be kept sweet, and why not with a lover. That dolt of a husband of hers didn't know what she was worth, but the Berenson newspaper empire needed her, and money was no object. She had an affinity with the underdog; and she could make men talk as if they were talking to their girlfriends and women gave her their stories because they trusted her to speak out for them. She had an incredible icy calm under pressure and now that the children were older he wanted to send her back to report in the war zones, next stop for her was Bosnia if he had his way, but she had to be softened up first . Yes she is one in a million and he can't have her tied up in London with childcare.

Cecilia sighs and looks out the window again but can only see her own reflection, her small pale face with its adequate aquiline features and her hair, dark and straight slicked tightly back into a bun. She looks her age there is no doubt about it, her lips have a thin "no messing" steeliness about them and the fine lines around her eyes aren't going to disappear any time soon. She wonders if she should pop into one of the dermatologists in town while she is there, but Louis likes her the way she is, and the adoration of a twenty five year old is keeping her young in ways that she never would have imagined.

The train stops with a jolt and she gazes out onto the slick wet platform of Calais, the gendarmes are passing through the carriages and she gets out her passport avoiding looking at the man in the carriage who is smiling in what he deems to be a beguiling fashion at her. Then the carriage door burst open and there is Louis, all dark wet curls and smooth cheeked cold from the rain and shrugging off his anorak to sweep her up in his arms.

''Surprise surprise Cherie ! Un bon j'espère, oh je t'adore, c'était trop long !''

With that he lifts her from her seat and engulfs her in a flurry of kisses, her feet are completely suspended from the floor and she doesn't know whether to laugh or be angry, but the look of sheer horror on the face of the sleazy man in the corner is enough to make her laugh out loud.

'' A good surprise of course silly......it's lovely to see you but can you put away that dripping anorak you are making me feel like a wet dog, and it's not a good look.''

He holds her face in his hands and looks at her intently, and then taking her by the hand pulls her into the corridor and presses her up against the wall where no one can see them. His voice becomes husky and he runs a hand over her hair down her neck and lightly, so lightly, just the faint impression of his fingertips over her small perfect breasts. The nipples rise like evening primrose flowers after the rain to greet him and his voice drops to a husky growl.

'' It's been too long, how long? A week, ten days? Why do we have to be apart, leave your boring husband and come we will live together in Paris''.

Her pulse has quickened and a liquid feeling is permeating her body, she knows that she has to get herself under control or she will regret it. Gently and with a sigh she pushes him away slightly and cups his face in her hands giving him a slow sensual smile and running her tongue lightly over her lips.

" The boys, I have the children to think of , let's go and have supper and we can talk about this, we are on a train Lou Lou , there will be time , plenty of time for love later, be sensible Cherie , let's go talk"

He grabs her hand and a slight pout appears on his oh so pretty face, she watches him from under her eyelashes and thinks how lucky she is. He's exquisite, like something out of an underwear ad, all lean muscle and long symmetric lines, the eyes that he turns on her are so dark as to be almost black and she can't stop looking at him. The waiter shows them to a table at the corner of the carriage and they settle into the seats opposite each other. He still holds onto her hand tightly over the white starched table cloth and underneath the table he has shrugged his converse off and twined his toes around her legs. She smiles, he couldn't be more different from John; Louis is intent dark Jewish French passion, all coiled spring ready to unfurl around her. Just thinking about what will happen later with him makes her cheeks heighten in colour and her mouth salivate slightly with anticipation. Now she is floating so far away from hunger that it's ridiculous but they go through the motions of eating. All the while he whispers intimate promises to her under his breath in his throaty English accent.

Looking at him over the table top with the blur of the other passengers in the background she eats him up with her eyes. As she plays with the beans from her Cassoulet she thinks that she would be happy simply to sit looking at him forever, he is so beautiful he simply takes her breath away she doesn't even feel the need to touch him. It occurs to her with a flash of utmost clarity that she is in love for the first time ever and that she is in a really dangerous place. To be in love with a wild cannon of a boy who at twenty five is twelve years her junior is foolhardy to say the least. At this moment in time with him sitting directly opposite her murmuring filthy suggestions at her over the dull red glow of the wine all she really wants is to be naked next to him, skin on skin in that place that is solely theirs and for the rest of the world to disappear and leave them in this magic circle of desire.

Louis is impatient, but then that is his nature. He had first met Ceci at a press conference when she was covering a story on the province of Ethiopia from where he imports his coffee. He runs a very successful pop up internet coffee company from his apartment on the left bank, his verve and charm having made a success of a business that his parents had muttered about. He is ambitious, he was bored with the young girls he usually dated and then there was the fabled Cecilia de la Croix right in front of him and he found her quite stunningly beautiful.

At first the lure of her famous family had been part of the string that drew him to her, until they got into bed together and then he too was lost in the intensity of their chemistry. So he had persuaded his father that he needed a sabbatical from the firm in order to gain more experience in international politics and taken up the position as her intern. The head of the newspaper empire is a family friend, that is the way all things work in business in Paris, and so it hadn't been a problem. A bit of research a few phone calls and "voila":

He tells himself that it's just for a few months, just to be near her, just until he can persuade her to leave her husband. He spoons sugar into his espresso and frowns, leaning forward slightly to cup her chin in his hands and gently kiss her. As soon as their lips touch it is like some kind of a drug that he can't get enough off, he feels his body lurch towards her and she draws away from him her hand shaking slightly with the buzz that wires them together and with a sharp intake of breath.

"How long do we have this time ma biche?"

The long clean toned lines of her body often make him think of the gazelle that roam the plains of Africa, if he could

68

he would scoop her up in a net and carry her off to a mountain cave and never let her leave. The fact that she is older than him, married and a mother , is simply not of consequence to him, all he wants to do is help her escape , help them be together .

Cecilia is feeling tired now, all the adrenaline at seeing him seems to have seeped into her bones and she is weary of the black and white way he sees the world, all from a young man's perspective, all from a young man's ego. It crosses her mind that it is an enigma, the things she loves about him are also the things she hates about him, but really she doesn't intend to change her life for him. This is the battle of wills that they play out when they are together. She wants him in the bedroom only, he wants her forever, or thinks he does. If they were together all the time it would begin to fray at the edges and fall apart, she knows this, she's the grown up here, and he is very obviously a boy. Gracefully she gets to her feet, the train is slowing down passing through the Ban lieu of Paris, the lights of the high rise apartment buildings throw blocks of light and dark through the windows, she looks down at him and strokes the shiny dark curls, rather like she would stroke a favourite dog.

"Vazi, on y va ! We should go, I've work to do before we sleep, and we have love to make before that "

She laughs as she dances away from him down the narrow corridor.

"First one to the taxi rank wins, and the loser has a forfeit. "

He lets her go with a grin as he pays the bill and gets up to follow, sometimes he isn't sure who is the grown up, but he will play her games until he decides he's had enough and then he will take her away from all of this, whether she likes it or not Cecilia de la Croix will be his and his entirely one day, whatever he has to do to get her.

*

69
© Victoria Mosley 2016

Chapter 6
Nellie Christmas 1874

The snowflakes drop outside the window, huge crystalline stars, mesmerising, perfect, each one unique in size and form, she watches transfixed: her small cold fingers following the line of them sliding down the window pane. The park beneath the window is silent covered in a shroud of white, no noise apart from the gardener clearing the pathway with a shovel from the front door down the drive to the vast black gates, the sound muffled by the coating of powder. It's a pointless task; the snow fills in the spaces that he is doggedly clearing with effortless silent relentlessness. The cedar trees point their bare branches to the sky like huge black threatening fingers and it is utterly silent, the sounds of nature truly muffled as only snow can make it. As fast as the gardener shovels the snow banks up behind him and she is watching how every now and then he stops to wipe his brow and cough; his cheeks bright achingly red, his nose sore from the influenza. He should be inside wrapped up and warm, but the winter is cruel and the work has to be done. She shivers thinking how unyielding this yielding mass of frozen water is, how intransigent the revolving of the planet and the march of the seasons. Just last week she had finished reading Darwin's "The Descent of Man ", and found his theories to be utterly fascinating but illogical in the light of her own personal experience .

It's been a month since she last saw" the man", and almost touched him, well she did in fact touch him but he seemed to slip through her fingers like ice. One minute she had been bending over him, so close she could have kissed him, she heard his voice, she heard him tell her his name "John" and then some switch clicked in the universe and that blinding light flashed again and when it was over he wasn't there anymore. She'd felt dizzy , she felt almost as if she was having one of those seizures that she's read about, the hysteria thing that happens to some women apparently where they manifest all sorts of unusual phenomena. More than that though she had felt bereft, as if for the first time ever she had found the missing piece of something that she had been unaware that she was even searching for. Yes she had found it all for a moment only to have it wrenched away from her. There had been a pain for days afterwards in her solar plexus region as if she had been punched or as if she was bodily connected to something and it was pulling away from her fast, wrenching her very insides with it.

The next day she had tried to make an appointment with Madame Blavatsky only to find that the dratted woman was off on her travels again, but she had managed to book an appointment with her in Paris in four days' time. She has presented herself as a photographer who wishes to document some of the meetings and séances of the small bird like woman and has been granted an audience. In the meantime she has been to the library to try and ascertain whether the woman is indeed a mystic or simply one of those music hall charlatans that the theatres are full of at this time of year. Nothing much was forthcoming and reports of Helena Blavatsky's life seemed to contradict themselves at every turn, but there was no trickery the night of her birthday when the glass had smashed in her own dining room, when a door had opened into another world, though whether it actually exists somewhere in time and space she has no idea.

Nellie is not sure how time had shifted that night , how it came about that she met a man and fell in love with someone who quite obviously doesn't exist in her present, but she's hoping that Blavatsky's eminent studies in Tibetan monasteries and secret trysts with High Llama's on Himalayan mountain tops will provide some sort of solution. She's been reading up on all the material she can find about her, both complimentary and otherwise, and Helena Blavatsky is certainly a courageous and extraordinary woman. For all the table rapping and spook manifestations it seems that she has really travelled to lamaseries in Tibet and studied with Buddhist monks. That Halloween night Nellie had certainly noticed a

71

presence and authority about her that she had never come across in anyone else before.

She has found that if she thinks hard enough about John just before dropping off to sleep at night, he will come to her in dreams. More often than not he is walking away from her down a long descending pathway towards a storm tossed beach. But some nights there are moments of sheer delight when suddenly he seems to be there at her bedside, holding her hand kissing her brow, talking to her softly , telling her over and over again how beautiful she is, how he loves her .

Yet in the morning she wakes to grey winter light and he is gone. As she sits there staring at nothing in particular on the snow laden lawn she notices the path of a robin hoping towards a line of holly bushes red with berries. As she concentrates her eyes on the small bird she begins to see something else in the snow that makes her heart beat wildly and her breath come in gasps. Appearing from nowhere and coming towards her window are footprints, she watches in awe as one perfectly formed foot print after another with no visible creator comes towards her. With a cry she rushes out of the room down the stairs and flings open the front door only to be met with a blast of icy air. Without thinking she whirls around the side of the house lifting her skirts above the snow trembling with heat and anticipation. Five crows fly up in consternation, the gardener drops his shovel in surprise, she arrives out of breath under the window and there just beginning to be covered by fresh snow is the last of the footprints as it disappears from view.

"Are you alright Miss, can I get you anything?".

Clarkson the gardener stands there in front of her twisting his cap awkwardly in his hands, shuffling his feet and sniffing. The snow is gathering in her hair, a powdered puff of coldness stinging her cheeks and blurring her vision and a supreme weariness suddenly comes over her. She wants to lie down in the snow and sleep but she can't: the carriage is being made ready; she has a train to catch to Folkestone and then the steamship to Boulogne before the snow becomes too deep and the lines are blocked. She looks up at him and smiles gathering her shawl around her shoulders and focusing on the kindness in his eyes.

"No thank you Clarkson, silly of me, I thought I saw something from the window but it must have been a snow mirage, you can tell the stables to bring the carriage around in half an hour I will be ready to go to the Station then.. Why don't you go into the kitchen and ask cook to give you something warm and comforting for your cold, you shouldn't be out here in the snow.".

With that she realises that she is freezing and her feet are soaked through in her small velvet slippers. Miss Tindley is banging crossly on the window above her and shaking her head at her, it is time to change and get ready to travel. She had managed to persuade Mama and Papa that she needed to go to Paris to get some new hats for the spring and do some Christmas shopping. The governess would of course be accompanying her but she will have to come up with some kind of story to pacify her and if the worst comes to the worst she can always bribe her .Then if things go according to plan she could take up her new post as photographer to the great Theosophist and send for some of her things while she travels with the woman. She wouldn't need much and she's already packed a small travelling trunk which she's placed at the end of her bed. She looks around her at the still garden under its burden of frozen white slumber that the snow brings. One solitary leaf falls from the bare branches of the oak tree and a squirrel scurries by its fur standing out against the cold. She doesn't want to go, leave the house which connects her to him; it's as if an invisible force is holding her here, she feels that if she leaves she is leaving any chance of seeing John again behind in the dust and dreams of the house.

Ridiculous really, if they are not bound by time why on earth should they be bound by place? She talks crossly to herself , if he has children it stands to reason that there must be

73

a wife lurking somewhere so all this "love" they seem to have instantly fallen into may very well be doomed before it has even started. Yet if she "feels' with her body the whole of it is telling her that even though she can't see him or touch him they are connected by a tie as strong as the iron pylons of the railway bridges crossing the Thames. Wherever she goes he will be with her, there is no doubt in her mind about that, and if both of them are straining towards each other surely the meeting will be inevitable?

All this churns in her head as the carriage makes its slithery journey down Sydenham Hill and towards London. The driver is crooning at the horses and the boy at the back of the coach is ready with the extra weighted chocks to slow them down. It's dangerous going out in this weather especially on such a long journey and the white pinched flapping face of a nervy Miss Tindley chatters incessantly at her from across the seat. Nellie blocks it out, as surely as her Mama's tearful goodbye. Sydenham Hill station and the Crystal Palace station had closed due to the mounting banks of snow and she just hopes that they have managed to keep the line open from Victoria to the coast.

Luckily Papa had given her her own bank account when she was eighteen so she has more freedom than most women, let alone young women. She doesn't have to ask her parents' permission to do things anymore, it has made her quite independent and Papa seems to think that she has more responsibility in her little finger than her brother Edmund. That wouldn't be difficult Edmund is proving quite a trial with his drinking and carousing now he has left Dulwich College. Thank goodness Oxford has claimed his illustrious presence; at least she won't have to put up with his odiously gauche friends making eyes at her anymore.

Nellie has never really been attracted to young men she finds the older handsome sort much more acceptable, which is lucky really seeing as John must be around forty. The thought of him in that way makes her flush and she stares fixedly out of the window to divert her attention from her own beating heart which is suddenly thumping so hard against her ribcage that she thinks that Miss Tindlay must be able to hear it. She concentrates her mind on the mesmeric falling snow and more mundane matters, like money. It's fairly obvious to her that money is freedom and she intends to use her own to live her life as she sees fit and not how convention expects her to be.

She has been filling the coffers of her bank account over the past few years with the money she earns from her photographic commissions, and they have been plentiful with the summer wedding season and even more so from the men of the village wanting her to make their portrait as a way of flirting with her.

---The most recent being the rather touchy feely revolting Arthur Sullivan. ---

He might be a great musical libretto but he isn't someone she readily relished being in a room alone with.

Everyone knows of his seduction of the two Scott Russell sisters Rachael and Louise. Yes Rachael had been publicly shamed when a notice in the newspaper had been given of the tale of Sullivan taking complete advantage of the girl in a dark part of the woods out by Sydenham Hill station. It gave her an insight into the skulduggery of the male sex drive which popular female fiction always seemed to glorify in one way of another. The last fiction book that she had read had pages and pages about a man's bursting tulip swimming in the channel of some poor woman's "secret river " It would be laughable if it wasn't insulting in an age when women like Helena Blavatsky donned men's cloths and travelled around the world often unaccompanied. Sullivan's behaviour had been atrocious but because he was a man and quasi famous, he had been allowed to get away with it over and over again. Nellie had been expecting someone debonair and exciting to turn up in her makeshift studio above the stables for his appointment for his portrait, but instead Sullivan turned out to be rather pale and insipid with huge whiskers and with the promise of a paunch as he grew older.

She smiles now out into the whiteness of the descending snow, yes Arthur's silky seduction technique had fallen on deaf ears where she was concerned, she'd produced the adequate portrait that he had asked for, given him his bill and sent the finished piece around by carriage the week later. Then she had proudly placed the hundred guineas in the bank account and forgotten all about him until her father called her into his study the following week and told her that Sullivan was so impressed with her that he had asked permission to call on her.

She had met the proposal with an unbelieving laugh.

'' Not if he was the last man on the planet would I ever contemplate the idea, it is totally laughable Papa''.

She had ended the interview by ruffling her father's hair affectionately and swishing out of the room in her long silk skirts that she had taken to wearing. They fell softly around her hour glass figure and she looked a little like the Greek goddesses of old. She had decided to adapt all the dresses in her wardrobe to her own style and inclination enabling her to move with ease and flexibility in her work. She wears them with the soft leather Chameleon shoes that are all the rage at the moment, Italian leather with a cut out mosaic of silk at the front, very William Morris; but today she has a pair of fur lined kid boots tucked neatly under the seat keeping her frozen toes warm. There is no possibility that she could be capable of bending and stretching in all the ways that photography demands in the present bustled nightmare dresses and crinolines which fashion dictates that young women of a certain class are supposed to wear. No leg o' muffin sleeves and the sharp velvet and taffeta creations that Mama would like her to wear for Nellie anymore; these have taken their place at the back of her cupboard. It was when she threatened to dress like a man if Edith forbade her to wear her own designs that her mother had given up and sulked for a complete week, she smiles now remembering all the door slamming that went with her new found freedom of costume

She puts a hand on the leather trunk stowed under her knees, in it is her camera and carefully prepared glass plates , just in case she receives the commission she so desires. The carriage is passing the Orphanage now on Lordship Lane, always a curious building it had given her nightmares as a child. The thought of being locked inside its long dark corridors and dormitories with the rag tag and bobtail children, her parents mysteriously absent had night after night woken her. Now she glances in briefly at its carved and curved windows replicating the windows of a church. The stark parsonage sits snug and slightly smugly behind it, smoke coiling out of the chimney and upwards into the icy air

At least she is lucky enough to have everything she wants in life and the freedom and talent to make something of it. Living up there on the hill she is protected from the harshness of London's reality with its workhouses and sickness. Papa always says that industry must have its workers and those workers are well treated, but lately listening to the talks of Eleanor Marx the great Karl Marx's daughter she isn't so sure that he is right. There is perhaps a need for some kind of socialism in this country that emphasises its democracy, and not the superiority of Imperialism that seems to be rife in the factories, but who is she to have an opinion about this? This is the first time she has been out of England since a trip to the Italian Riviera with her parents when she was fifteen. She blushes at the memory, all those beautiful boys staring at her in the street; she might have died and gone to heaven. The buildings were so elegant, the smells so enticing and the sun burning above them every day as they made the trip to Roma and Venice and of course a pilgrimage to Verona to see Romeo and Juliet's house. Sometimes her mother has good ideas and that had been one of them, the art and culture of the country had inspired the small pretty teenager to want to create something great of her own.

77

She looks out at the billowing snow, falling in blankets now, the only good thing about it is that it has kept traffic to the minimum and they are across the bridge and pulling into Victoria Station before she knows it. She peels on her long kid gloves and picks up her fox muffler hooking her hand into the handle of the heavy case that carries her camera. She's not sure that she would call her photography great, but it has a certain something about it that people seem to like. She herself loves the magic of the developing process even though the chemicals that she uses are potentially deadly, but now isn't the time to ponder on such things. She has a train to catch and as she sweeps through the forecourt and onto the platform a huffing puffing muttering Miss Tindley is left far behind with the porter as a bevy of butterflies hit her stomach and she almost feels sick with anticipation. She's about to make her first voyage abroad on her own and she's going to visit one of the most fascinating women alive. More importantly she hopes beyond hope that she can find some of the answers to her questions, and find a pathway through to the man who has nightly come to her in dreams calling her to him, calling her to love. Calling her beyond the boundaries of the here and now to something that bears the sparks of the divine.

*

Chapter 7
Place Vendome Paris 1874

Helena Blavatsky

She sits by the fireplace staring into the red-hot coals, but if you look closely you would wonder at the expression in her eyes for she seems to look beyond the flames, the black pupils huge in the dark brown eyes. She seems to be looking out into eternity; the eyes eerily empty, the breathing deep and slow and at times hardly perceptible. The room is high ceilinged and majestic in typical Louis xvi style with heavy brocade curtains that mask the view of the circular square, one of the most beautiful squares in Paris. She is large, eminently large she herself readily adopts the nickname hippopotamus, her bustled velvets do little to hide the broad hips and waist beneath, and her hair is peppered with grey scooped back into a low bun at the base of her neck, wisps escaping haphazardly. It is the broad symmetry of her face that people remember afterwards: that, and the animation with which she speaks on her beloved esoteric topics.

The outside bell rings somewhere below her in the hallway of the house and a slight quiver runs through her body as if she is waking from a long sleep, but in actuality she is returning from her evening meditation. A meditation and daily practice where she is in direct contact with her Master, who is living high in the mountains of Northern India but regularly instructs her through telepathic communication. It has taken her years of strenuous practice to reach this level of clarity, at first her extra sensory perception made her a target for every ghost and ghoul in the vicinity, her adolescence was strewn with the chaos of poltergeist activities. For some time she was seriously ill and her very life was feared for but nowadays she is in total control of her immense power.

She relaxes back into the chair and rings a small brass Tibetan hand bell that sits on the writing desk to one side of her. She has a visitor tonight, a girl from London; she remembers that much about her although she can't quite call to mind her appearance; yet she also remembers vividly the strange occurrence of their first meeting back in London at Halloween. Helena sighs and stretches, she very rarely indulges in "spiritualist" stuff anymore unless she needs money and that particular evening she remembers that she needed the money offered by the girl's rather flaky and semi hysteric mother to buy herself a boat ticket to New York. Indeed she had made enough money from that particular night to buy herself a wonderful first class ticket on a well-known liner only to forgo it and change it to third class in order to pay for a destitute Irish family to be able to make the journey. That's what comes of having a big heart but that uncomfortable journey is in the past now and she is almost ready for her next outing in the world.

That was then, she had met the people that she was supposed to meet and now she is preparing to return to India to set up the headquarters of the Theosophist Society. An admirer in Paris has lent her this house for a few weeks and very grateful she is to. A wind rustles the curtains the glass crystals shiver on the chandelier and she nonchalantly moves her hand to still the room, the spirits are fussing tonight, making their presence known and yet at her gesture the room breathes an audible sigh and settles into itself again. She learnt long ago the power over these unseen elementals, and they don't bother her now.

Footsteps clatter in the corridor and the door opens with a blast of colder air, the fire leaps and for a moment she sees only the shadow of a woman's figure in the doorway and something about it makes the hairs on the back of her neck stand on end. It seems as if the girl is carrying the shadow of someone else with her, someone tall and looming who towers over the diminutive presence. Helena passes her hand swiftly across her eyes as if to clear the view, then the illusion passes and she sees a very beautiful young woman staring quizzically at her. The girl walks forward and light billows around her dispersing the shadows, setting the crystal on the chandelier above their heads tinkling again but this time with a shiver of joy. The girl begins to speak and Helena sees laughter and love in her words, sees the images of a happy childhood and a rich tapestry of imagination and potential joy in the aura of possibilities of her life, unless.

'"Madame Blavatsky, thank you so much for agreeing to see me, I've been so looking forward to this: evening. Meeting you that night at my house has completely changed my life and I needed to come back to the source to ascertain exactly what it is that is going on. "

Blavatsky pats her hair and smiles gesturing to the chair opposite her.

" Sit down my dear, it's a pleasure to see you once more, I'm only sorry it couldn't be sooner for it seems that you have been trying to arrange a meeting for several months."

Without hesitating Nellie begins to tell her the strange story of her meeting in the woods with the mystery man and his two small sons the day after the séance.

"It was as if a split had occurred in the fabric of the sky and he had dropped right through it to be with me. "

Nellie explains wringing her hands.

"And then it seemed as if I had been waiting for him forever and yet he is someone both known and unknown to me., it feels like he is an intrinsic part of me and beloved by me but of course I had never seen him before. I'm not sure how to make you see this, but I feel quite definitely that I am not meant to be without him."

81

Helena picks up a piece of paper from her writing desk and crushes the lead of several pencils onto it. Then she simply brushes her hand over the paper in circular movements that hardly seem to touch the surface. Finished in a few minutes she hands the sheet of paper to Nellie who gasps in astonishment. In her hand is a perfect image of John as if drawn by a master portrait painter.

" This is the man in question I take it?"

Helena challenges her, a faint smile at the corner of her mouth.

" Yes, but how did you? Where did you, can I keep this please?"

Helena simply shrugs her shoulders and nods, words fail Nellie and she sits looking crumpled as if all the air has been sucked out of her and there are two small perfect tears pouring down her face.

"There, there my dear, don't cry, there is nothing to be upset about, all this is indeed particularly strange but , well the good news is that he doesn't seem to be a ghost, this man of yours. He is certainly alive and somewhere, but this seems to be a little beyond my understanding of the Universe and the machinations of time and space. I may have to consult with my Master to see if anything can be done about your predicament, for such it is. If you can give me this evening to ponder the problem tomorrow morning may gift us both with an answer.   At a guess the evening I spent in your home in Sydenham obviously rent the fabric of time as we know it; perhaps the house itself has something to do with it. I do remember feeling a particular sensation as I arrived there. There are certain places in the world which are power points, points where lay lines meet or geomorphic stress in the earth's crust can construct certain kinds of doorways or openings. I have found this to be true before and it obviously is in this case.

Now if you will excuse me there are things I have to get on with, but no I can see that you have something else that you wish to tell me?"

Nellie looks slightly embarrassed for a moment and then blushes.

"Well I was going to offer my services as a photographer if you would wish me to travel with you and document some of the marvels that seem to happen around you?"

Helena scrutinises her deeply for a moment but then smiles and continues the conversation in French, a language that she is much more at home with.

" I'm not certain that there will be anything very interesting to document my dear. Gone are the days of table rapping and my being plagued by spooks that really were of no use to me at all. You see child, most of the so called "ghosts" that continue to exist are only reflections of people that are stuck in one particular place because perhaps of something traumatic that happened to them. My training has led me in other directions, directions of the soul if you like. But if you wish to take a portrait of me that would be very fine and tomorrow morning would suit. Now the housekeeper will show you to your room where a light supper is waiting for you, I believe that your chaperone is already settled for the night. By the morning we might have some answers to your questions and some suggestions as to how to proceed in your matter of the heart."

With a gesture of the hand the door to the room silently opens and a smart looking woman in a maid's uniform appears hands crossed in front of her and head slightly bowed demurely waiting to escort Nellie. She follows her out of the room turning for one last curious backward glance at her hostess who seems to have reverted to the immobility of a statue in the flickering light of the chandelier. The woman is staring intently into the orange glow of the flames as if all the answers she is seeking are locked beneath the surface of the glowing coals. . As she leaves the sitting room it's cold,

83

extremely cold in the corridor and she can see the snow whirling in eddies outside the window, obscuring everything in a great blanket of white blindness, it makes her feel as if the walls are closing in on her. Immediately she senses a cold fear that flows through her and it seems to shift down into the very marrow of her bones filling her with a great tiredness that descends on her with the weight of the snow outside.

Solemnly and shivering now she follows the maid upstairs her travelling clothes feel wet and damp and she's delighted to see that there is a roaring fire in the grate of the pretty bedroom that the woman shows her into. From the adjoining room comes the sound of running water and a perky little teenage maid comes bobbing out of the room, scurrying to the door to follow the housekeeper. As the door shuts behind her Nellie suddenly realises that neither of the women had spoken a word and that thought makes her frown slightly. She goes quickly to the door on a sudden whim, just to make sure that it hasn't been locked behind her, but no, it swings open easily showing the shadows floating in the dark corridor beyond. Outside a dog howls and then there is a sound of a kick and a yelp and several unintelligible expletives in French, she shuts the door quickly and goes through into the cavernous bathroom that smells strongly of rose petals and is filled with steam.

Later lying in bed with her toes curling either side of the hot brick that nestles there she thinks back on the day's occurrences. The footprints in the snow this morning, John's prints she is sure of it and all the heart searching and sleepless nights that have led her here, and she closes her eyes to the silence of the snow and the pump of the blood in her veins.

The dream comes upon her suddenly in the early hours of the morning when she drifts up from the unconscious realms of exhaustion to the bright light of a summer's day in the garden, She's sitting in one of her favourite muslin dresses on the painted blue seat outside the summer house, the garden is full of roses and birdsong and she senses an infinite glow of warmth and contentment. She can feel the sun burning her skin slightly and smell the scent of lavender from the low bushes bordering the flower beds. Although she somewhere knows that this is a dream the smell is strong and pungent in her nostrils; while the hum of bees and the thought of honey are in her head. From a distance she hears the sound of children's laughter as it comes floating over the lawn from the orchard and she looks up to see the two small boys that she met in the woods the other day come running towards her. They're playing hide and seek she can tell that by their body language and the way they keep glancing behind them stifling the laughter that comes bubbling from them involuntarily, their small perfect faces full of the single minded joy that only children can experience.

They are almost upon her now and she opens up her arms to greet them but they don't seem to see her at all. Suddenly she feels cold and she has the weirdest feeling of being looked right through as they carry on past her to hide in the fuchsia bush on the left of the summer house. She can hear raised voices and looks up to see John coming around the corner of the house in earnest conversation with a thin dark haired woman. With a lurch somewhere in the region of her heart she understands that it must be his wife.

Instantly she wants to get away as quickly as possible but then she suddenly understands that there is little likelihood of her being visible to anyone but John. The couple appear to be arguing and the woman stops suddenly pointing and jabbing her finger at him and then turns brusquely away. She walks angrily around the side of the house and disappears from view. John falters for a moment staring after her, his shoulders slumped ,he looks rather sad and eminently hopeless, and then Nellie calls to him and he sees her sitting there glowing in the sunlight. He's there by her side in two beats of a thrush's breast, scooping her effortlessly up in his arms in the way that things can happen in dreams. She shuts her eyes as dizziness overtakes her and she can smell the muskiness of him, feel the solidity of his body enfolding hers. She begins to melt in a liquid haze of joy, his face is in her hair and he is whispering that he loves her in her ear. She feels her body

85

begin to deliciously dissolve into his as he kisses her and a flush of delicious heat runs through her from the space between her thighs up through her chest and explodes in light at the crown of her head. A vague thought comes to her that this must be the thing that is talked about in all the 2d novels that she has been reading. She is in total and undeniable bliss and has no idea where John begins and she ends, this is where she wants to stay for eternity, in his arms and melting.

Then the sound of the doorknob being turned starts to bring her back into the room, back into the here and now and she falls away from the dream down a long tunnel back to the present. Her face is cold from the drop in the room temperature overnight and she hears the maid bustling in to lay the fire and bring her early morning tea.

For a few moments she tries to recapture the texture of the dream but it's no good, so instead she simply lies there twiddling her toes basking in the afterglow. She feels wetness between her thighs and her cheeks are burning as if she has caught the sun from the dream. Sighing she sits up, the small blaze in the fireplace is beginning to warm the room, and she reaches for her tea which is highly perfumed and hot scalding on her tongue but it brings her back to her senses. She takes breakfast alone in the elegant morning room, the table laid for one with crusty croissants and swirling pats of butter and apricot jam to spread on them. She suddenly realises how hungry she is and concentrates wholly on the pleasure of eating letting the night's drama fall away from her. The tinkle of a bell sounds somewhere in the house and the maid comes to find her, the Madame is ready and waiting for her in the study.

The first thing that Nellie notices as she opens the door is the sunlight falling through the window onto the acres of floating dust in the air.

----"Dead skin, dead time aeons and aeons of it"-----

Is her thought as she waits takes a breath and takes in her surroundings. The room is lined with floor to ceiling bookshelves comfortably housed behind glass and in the morning sun she can see smears and finger-marks dotting the surface of the glass. It feels like she is alone, but then the sun goes behinds a cloud and from behind the bookshelf she feels the tug of a presence. The hairs on the back of her neck stand up and she holds her breath as she sees a luminous blue light radiating from under the small gap between oak floorboards and the bottom of the shelf. She listens intently, but can hear nothing; she clears her throat, still nothing, then as if an invisible hand has taken her by the elbow she feels herself propelled across the room around the bookshelf and there is the Madame sitting regally on what looks like an ancient Chinese throne.

Her eyes are shut, her hands rest quietly on her knees, the thumb and little finger held together like something from an ancient Hindu painting and she is breathing so quietly that for an astonishing moment Nellie wonders if she is dead. Nellie slips quietly into the seat facing the stillness of the woman and tries not to fidget. Her mind fills with stupid niggling thoughts that relentlessly taunt her and won't go away.

---Did she clean her teeth for long enough? How is Miss Tindley? The maid has said that she has gone down with a head cold and has stayed in bed this morning. Is her skirt ironed to perfection? Is she going to be able to photograph this enigmatic creature in front of her? ----

At that point her thoughts still of their own accord, as if they have slipped through a doorway in her mind and run away to play like naughty children. She begins to study the Madame with the intensity of a photographer scrutinising her subject. The face in front of her is serene and immobile the cheeks wide, the mouth gathered in a narrow line, the hair scraped back from the forehead and yet wisps of grey fall around her lace, giving her an untidy air. In repose like this she has few lines and Nellie thinks she looks rather like some of the Buddhist sculptures that Papa has acquired from the Orient. Her dress is drab and insignificant like the feathers of a grey pigeon; in fact she does remind Nellie more than a little of the pigeons in the park; the way her neck seems to escape from the confines of her dress and shoulders and jut forward slightly. She visualizes a pigeon walking across the floor towards her and at this thought an involuntary smile crosses her face. .As if she can read her mind the dark black eyes of Helena Blavatsky are suddenly fixedly beadily on her .and Nellie flinches as if she has been slapped.

'' Something amuses you my dear?" Blavatsky begins.

"I can assure you that the situation you find yourself in is not particularly funny, or indeed I would not find it so if I were you."

Blavatsky shakes herself and stands abruptly crossing to the window; the blue light that seemed to surround her coalesces and shrinks as it is instantly sucked back into her body so that Nellie wonders if she has imagined the whole scenario. Again her thoughts come crowding back this time like a class full of young children clambering for attention and she wipes a weary hand across her brow as if to shoo them away.

"No no I was just trying to see how I could create the best portrait of you, I didn't want to disturb you in your deep state of relaxation".

"That my dear is known as meditation in the Eastern world and I was telepathically communicating with my Master who is at this moment in Darjeeling high in the Himalayan mountain range to see what he had to say about your strange love affair. It seems my dear that if anyone in this situation is a ghost it is indeed you, the man in question who you profess to care for so deeply for will not be born this century."

Nellie feels a great faintness come upon her, she knew something was wrong about all this but the answer that Blavatsky is suggesting is ludicrous in the extreme. She licks her lips and opens her mouth to speak but her tongue seems to be stuck to the roof of her mouth and only a croak comes out.

"What do you mean?" She whispers.

"Exactly what I say, in the laws of the Universe which we as uninitiated mortals cannot hope to understand fully with our bestial type of logic, time is not linear but infinite and all at once and not at all, at the same time. You and your beloved have stepped out of time, through a cosmic glitch, you should never have been able to meet but perhaps because of my meddling that Halloween night it has happened. It seems you are karmically linked, but much more than that I cannot tell you. Tell me my dear is there anything about your house and its position that you have found unusual? My Master is suggesting that it may be a geomorphic problem, somewhat to do with lay lines and stress in the crust of the planet where an energy nucleus is created."

Nellie watches her mouth move, she looks above her head to the round clock on the wall, and she tries to breathe deeply to calm herself and splutters somewhat stupidly.

"Well the light has always been incredibly strong in the garden especially at the beginning and end of the tunnel that Papa had built for me. It always makes me very joyful to run through it and watch the light play on the mosaics of the ceiling and to find myself quite suddenly in the woods.

Blavatsky thinks for a second and then asks in a husky voice quite unlike her own.

" Is there any water nearby?"

"Yes the whole area is the top end of the artesian basin of which the city of London is made up, I read about it in the library and there are naturally occurring springs all over the hillside . Why Sydenham Wells Park has been renowned since the seventeenth century for the healing power of its waters. I know about all this because Papa showed me the tithe maps of the area that the architect used when designing the blueprints for the house and the tunnels beneath it. My tunnel goes into the woods but there is another one that is for Mama to attend the Saturday music concerts in Crystal Palace without having to get her feet wet or share her space with the ordinary kind of people that she so detests.

" Ah Mama and Papa, now is there anything that they have told you about the circumstances of your birth?"

"My birth? No not that I can think of ".

Nellie is beginning to feel very odd, as if her body is floating away from her and the voice that comes from Blavatsky is becoming fainter and fainter, she tries to form a sentence but all she can see are the colours in the sunlight, the bulk of the Madame and the shadow of a man who appears to be standing to one side of the woman. He is wearing long flowing robes and he holds his arms out diagonally above Helena Blavatsky as if he is protecting her Vaguely she tries to focus clearly on his image and her rational mind toys with the question of just when he appeared in the room and how. He reminds her of a Chinese Magician she once saw when she had sneaked out to the music hall in Crystal Palace with her old nanny. For a moment seven year old visions of the music hall come back and mingle with the ambience in the room. But then the confusion of the images all float away like the ending of a dream, the room becomes black and oppressive, it seems to be tightening around her as if it is a belt or a pair of stays that someone is lacing so tightly that they are taking her breath away. She is literally choking, the ground is falling away from her and she cannot stop it, she cannot stop herself.

"John, I don't understand how, it can be as you say, how he can belong to another time sequence from our own, he was there I touched him."

Is the last thing that she remembers saying as she falls to the floor and Blavatsky with a small sigh of exasperation reaches out to the table beside her and rings the Tibetan brass hand bell. From somewhere far away Nellie can hear the infinitely clear sound of the bell and tries to rouse herself but to no avail.

Later, and it must be a long time later, for she is on the bed in her room and the fire is lit, the curtains are drawn and it is obviously night time again. The day has somehow been stolen from her, she swims up from the deep water of unconsciousness, relaxed, pliable somehow empty and yet immediately she feels the old panic appear making her breathless and break out in a cold sweat She intuits the presence of someone sitting beside her and craning her neck she sees the young maid sitting on a chair with a heap of sewing in her lap that she is patiently stitching by the light of the oil lamp. The girl immediately drops the bundle of linen pillowcases and silk petticoats that swathe her lap and scrambles to her feet, muttering under her breath in a French dialect that Nellie simply doesn't understand. Nellie tries to raise her neck and the girl places her arm gently under her shoulders and lifts her to a sitting position.

" Drink this Mademoiselle, Madame has told me you are to drink all of it if you awake, you have had a big shock and you need to rest."

The girl lifts some sort of syrupy concoction that smells of laudanum to Nellies lips and obediently as if she is a child Nellie swallows the sticky mixture.

" Very good, very good, now you must rest some more and tomorrow will be another day, the snow is clearing and you can be on your way."

"But Madame, I am here to take Madame's portrait, I have to get up."

"Oh no Mademoiselle, you cannot do that, Madame left for the port this morning she is on her way to India on important business, I am afraid you are too late."

The laudanum is beginning to take effect ,Nellie feels totally relaxed and at ease now and the room with the girls voice is beginning to fade but the last thing that she hears is the girl saying as she leaves the room and closes the door behind her.

" There is a letter explaining it all, Madame has told me to advise you that she will be sending you a letter in the post."

With that Nellie is back in the dream, the ground of the orchard coming up to meet her, a song bird on the branch of the apple tree above her head and everywhere she looks are delicately floating petals of white blossom falling like snow, falling like confetti, covering her in their silken breath. Somehow they are telling her that it will be fine, all manner of things will be fine ,when she sees John again, when she kisses him for the longest of times, when they become one in body and soul, when she becomes his one true love.

Her head slumps back onto the pillow and her breathing becomes slow and shallow, the full moon lingers on outside the window, and somewhere on the road to Calais the fur bundled figure of Madame Blavatsky travels silently through the night. She notices nothing of the journey her thoughts are set on higher things, the purpose of the Master and at last her chance to travel back to the forbidden land of Tibet and learn the secrets of the Lords of Time in the wilderness of the remote mountains where men can become immortal and the dragon sleeps waiting for her to learn how to wake it once more.

*

Part Two

"If you are drinking wine or

sitting in the garden with roses instead

of seeking the Beloved

then you are wasting time"

Hafiz.

Chapter 8

John London 1994 November 2nd

When he wakes up this morning his first thought is of the girl, *his girl* he wants to call her now. The sunlight is filtering through the curtains and somewhere in his dreams he has the vague recollection of meeting her in a sunny garden. His sunny garden but not as it is now, as it must have been when it was first planted .The summer house was newly painted a beautiful cornflower blue and the apple trees in the orchard freshly planted and pruned, and the apple blossom falling around them as he bent to kiss her felt like wedding day confetti.. An involuntary smile flits over his face before he realises it and he feels like a teenager again, a warm sensation of pleasure washing over his body. He sighs and stretches the entire length of the bed, the thought of having those adolescent wet dreams make him blush slightly but it is true that the dream was so innocently erotic that he had woken with an orgasm and a wet spot on the sheets. He is alone in the large oak bateau lit that was a wedding present from Cecilia's parents, the sheets are finely threaded Egyptian cotton, the smell of beeswax lingers from the polished headboard and the other side of the bed is smooth and pristine where his wife is not.

That brings him to his second thought; and it stuns him with its startling simplicity. He doesn't love Cecilia any more: in fact he is unsure if he ever did really love her with the strength of the feelings that are now assaulting him. With Nellie not only does he feel this joyful sense of ultimate connection but he also wants to protect her and look after her a feeling that he certainly never entertained for his wife. What he felt for his wife was more in the realms of conquest and triumph at having

94

snared her when no one else could seem to. This over time has faded to bitterness, the shallow taste of triumph didn't last long after the boys were born, when he understood for the first time that the marriage had been somewhat "arranged" and not by him. No, he had been the sperm that cemented the continuation of the genetic DNA code of the De la Croix family, the name handed down from the ancestor who had found a peace of the "true cross " on his crusade to the Holy Land. Or some such popish nonsense he hadn't really taken much notice of the family history at the time. It was told to him over one of those endless French lunches at Cecilia's parents' house where there had been five courses and four different sorts of wine and all he had ended up with was a crashing headache. But he doesn't want to think about Cecilia now it will ruin his morning, he wants to just lie here and wallow in this new feeling of joy that he has just discovered.

He has certainly never felt like this before about anyone. It is almost as if his life has been catapulted into the realms of a B movie on a cinema screen through no volition of his own: *he is in love*, he has no doubt about that, but who is she and how does he find her again? He understands that he is in a state of enchantment, the very nub of this strange love connecting him to the source of all things. He's glad that he feels old enough and mature enough to deal with it, he can't imagine how intoxicating this would feel if he was a teenager. But he's not a teenager, he is a middle aged married man in love with a vision, and somehow he just knows that he has been waiting all of his life for this. He thinks of the slim form of his wife and the expression on her feline face as she turned to say goodbye to him, was it only yesterday? It feels like years since he last saw her, but of course that is ridiculous, except that time seems to be playing all kinds of tricks with him, what happened only last week feels like eternity and yet if his assumptions are correct he is in love with a mirage that walked the earth before he was even born. There, he has said it now and feels better for admitting it although for an instant a sense of impending panic begins to take him over again and he has to grip the sheets to remind himself that he is awake and not still dreaming.

A palpitation in his chest reminds him of his blackout yesterday, and he massages the tightness around the muscles of his ribcage; he has always suspected that death is linked to sex, but does it also go hand in hand with love? He listens for the boys but the house is breathing silently around him, he must have slept too long and they've already gone to school. Today he's going to concentrate on doing some research, try to find out who actually built this house of his and potter down to Dulwich Art Gallery and have a look see at the photographs that are on display. He doesn't really know all that much about the history of Sydenham, although there is a local historian who might provide him with some help if he needs it. He knows that the house is the other side of London on the curve of the artesian basin from Hampstead and he also remembers hearing that a series of spontaneous springs erupt now and again in the area. According to local Dulwich College gossip old lay lines cross from here down the Kent countryside to Canterbury and beyond, but history has never been much his 'thing" give him financial markets any day. He wonders if the original drawings for the house might be found in the Lewisham archives, he wonders how he is going to go about taking a week off work, and he almost becomes lost in a reverie of potentialities. Then the mobile that Cecilia insisted on giving him when she went back to work after her maternity leave begins to beep on the bedside table beside him.. He contemplates just ignoring it but he knows that she won't give up until she has spoken to him, it will be on her list of "to do" things and she will need to tick him off. Sighing he reaches out and grabs it fumbling with the answer button.

"John, it's me, how are the boys? Did you make sure that they did their homework last night?"

The clipped tones of his wife bark a series of orders down the phone at him, including instructions on Ollie's piano lessons and the parent teachers meeting that she is going to miss that he will have to attend tomorrow evening. He places the phone on the pillow beside him and waits for a lull in her voice before instigating a quick exit.

96

''Ah that's the front doorbell darling must go, take care have fun big hug.''

Before she can protest he hangs up on her and stuffs the phone under a pillow, he's never liked mobile phones much and he certainly doesn't intend to be at Cecilia's beck and call all day. He shakes himself and realises with a quick internal jump of joy that he is free of his wife , he doesn't give a dam what she thinks and the thought of her fury at being hung up on does nothing but fill him with a chuckle that bubbles out of him like spring rain, soft moist irresistible.

His morning passes peacefully enough in the study overlooking the garden: he finishes up a couple of articles for his editor but he keeps being drawn back to the delicate outline of the summer house there staring at him from the corner of his peripheral vision. All of a sudden he has had enough of trying to pretend that an internal spring isn't coiled in anticipation in his stomach. He gets up, puts on his down jacket that's hanging on the back of his chair and hurries across the scrunched fallen leaves to see if his hunch is true.

Pushing open the swollen door of the little building which squeaks and groans in resistance he quickly orientates himself into exactly the same position that he was yesterday when the girl appeared. He almost expects her soft breath and intriguing scent to materialise beside him, but the room is disappointingly empty, damp and cold, empty of the magic that he is so avidly seeking. For a moment he thinks that he imagined it all but then bending down to the fireplace he feels for the knob that the girl had shown him. His fingers know where to look although his mind has forgotten and within seconds he is pulling at a small black knob his other hand laid flat across his chest as if bracing himself for an attack. At first nothing happens and then he feels a slight movement in the handle.

Taking a deep breath he places all his weight on the lever half expecting it to come away in his hand, but no, with a creak and a groan the whole wall suddenly moves downwards almost making him lose his balance . The wall swings silently away from him and he is again staring down into the darkness.

This time however he is prepared and pulls a torch out of his pocket and shines it into the revealed space. A stench of rotting vegetation hits his nose making him wrinkle it in disgust and as he carefully manoeuvres his feet which seem suddenly to be too large, down the shallow steps he is not sure exactly what he is prepared to see. At first it just looks like any old tunnel, like a disused railway siding or the beginnings of a mine shaft; the floor covered in slimy mud the ceiling obscured but then as he reaches up and brushes his hand over the surface of the roof his hand dislodges some of the debris and a chink of light shines through onto the colours of the mosaics. The more he flails around with his hand the more the light pours in and the story in the mosaics that has been obscured for over a hundred years suddenly comes to light. Above his head he can see the face of a beautiful girl, an apple held delicately in her hand, she's looking away from him and down her barely clad back cascades handfuls of golden hair. She is nothing like his dream girl, but he recognises immediately the story line. Somewhere up ahead of him in the tunnel there is a rustle and a squeak, probably only rats but he carries on down the slippery path until he comes up against an iron grating and a wall. Although he shines the torch and taps and feels around the wall for a while he can't find a way out into the folly and after a sweaty twenty minutes of shoving against brick he gives up and returns to the garden.

Only when he is back in the garden with the passage closed behind him does he really draw breath again, he's been hoping upon hope that she will suddenly appear, but the air is the normal cold grey air of winter, the light is dull and smudge grey and there is no magic or metamorphosis in sight. He is alone in his garden on a winter's day feeling slightly stupid.

Brushing off the debris of sticky leaves and mud that seems to have attached itself to him he makes his way around the side of the house to the garage and grabbing the spare keys to Cecilia's small Alpha Romeo from the peg behind the door he slips into the driver's seat. As he turns on the heater her perfume begins to seep from the seats and he sighs irritably. He doesn't really want any tangible reminder of his marriage, not today; he just needs to be free of it, free of her, free to think as clearly as possible in his present heightened state of anticipation. But anticipation for what exactly he can't actually say and it's making his head ache. He drives down Sydenham Hill turning left to descend into Lordship Lane and a lull in the traffic gives him a moment to cast his eyes out over the cityscape beneath him.

It always makes him draw breath and hesitate when he sees this view, the newer buildings rising out of the indiscriminate morass of the city, Canary Wharf twinkles through the insipid grey light like a beacon of hope. Then he is swinging down into the traffic flow and passing Dulwich Park and the small cramped livery stables to his right where the pile of horse manure seems large and looming and the shabby shed where he supposes they ride the poor beasts backs onto the road with pieces of its wooden exterior splintered and unkept.. Dulwich College is on his left, solid and imposing with the immaculate cricket pitch and towering clock tower exactly as it must have been for the past hundred years and then he turns right at the traffic lights down past the multi million pound rows of houses that line the park.

At this time of the morning the Gallery is full of yummy mummy's and pairs of maiden aunts, it seems that he is the only man around and it makes him feel awkward. So this is what all these women do when their husbands are out drinking their way through their lunchtime meetings, and making the vast sums of money that are necessary to live in this part of London. They congregate with their buggies in corners of the village and drink lattes and eat carrot cake and then he supposes they spend the rest of the afternoon at the gym trying to remove the calories that they have eaten over coffee. All these thoughts drift in and out while he wanders through the looming crimson rooms of the gallery, past the landscapes and the token Rembrandt until he finally gets to the small side room that he is looking for.

The exhibition is entitled:

"Early Nineteenth Century Photography

1854 to 1894."

There is an unassuming middle aged woman selling tickets from a table top and he buys one readily, his heart beginning to bang a loud rhythm in his chest as he enters. The photos begin with early images of the Crystal Palace and misty views of Sydenham Hill in its heyday, he is hoping for a glimpse of Raven House but he can't quite make it out behind the trees which line the road. The High Street is looking resplendent with white awnings and aproned shopkeepers all standing in a row outside their shops in a carefully orchestrated shot. There are a few dreamy images by Julia Margaret Cameron, pictures that he has seen before in the Victoria and Albert museum, portraits of her niece, images of her interpretation of the three graces and other quasi classical poses. He stares at the women closely but they are remote and foreign to him .He moves on down the corridor disappointment seeping through his skin and then there around a corner are four portraits accredited to Nellie Weinberg, and his heart begins to pound again .

Two of the photos are of ladies walking in Sydenham Woods, mystical and serene their backs turned to the viewer, their skirts swirling into the early autumn leaves as if they are wood spirits or dryads of the trees. There is a photo of the stern rather puffy face of a young man and he screws up his eyes to read the small print beneath. Sir Arthur Sullivan of Gilbert and Sullivan fame stares back at him. The very last photo is of a girl standing on the seashore. She is walking away from the camera the sea spray flying up around her, her arms making a blurry arc in the long exposure of the photo. Her hair is loose and flies out behind her and she stands against a wooden building out on the sands as if she and the building had suddenly appeared on this vast expanse of shore from nowhere. Putting on his reading glasses he reads the small note beneath the photo.

" Self portrait of the artist on the shore in Whitstable kindly lent to the gallery by her Great Great niece Helena Weinberg."

He straightens up and stares again and then he sees something that makes him stop and clutch the wall for support. He hadn't really thought it could be possible but it is, this is the girl he saw in the woods, he's very sure of it now. Swinging out behind her in its own trajectory is the blur of the jewelled pendant that he saw a flash of the other day, and he can remember the feel of it intruding between them as he kissed her in his dream. Dropping nonchalantly from her shoulders and flying away into the shingle is the fur coat that she was wearing. This is the girl, this is his girl, his Nellie there is no doubt in his mind and he reaches out a hand to touch the glass of the portrait as if in some way it could connect him to her.

His thought processes slow to a slumped blur, this is ludicrous and his whole mind rebels against the idea, even though he toyed with it earlier in the day. The picture he is staring at has a date of 1875 a hundred or so years ago, it can't be possible can it? The woman he saw in the woods, the girl he can't get out of his brain, whose perfume he smelt and whose hand brushed his arm is right here in front of him in this mid Victorian photograph. If it is true then she lived on this earth more than a hundred years ago. The very idea of it is scary and inexplicable and makes him feel physically sick, he desperately looks around to make sure that no one is watching him as he sinks to his knees his face in his hands.

He has fallen in love with a ghost there is no other explanation and the idea of it fills him with horror and panic, the black band closes tightly around his chest again and he stares wildly around the room actively looking for a plausible solution. The blood is pounding in his head but somewhere deep down inside he begins to feel very calm. If he is completely honest with himself he knew that his meeting with Nellie was no ordinary meeting and the links that have been forged between them are precisely that. Links in a chain of time that will bring them together once more he is sure of it. .Luckily there is no one else in the small side room and within a few minutes he pulls himself together and has come up with some kind of a plan. The niece, of course that's the answer, he must go and see the niece, and she must be able to help him through this.

The next twenty minutes or so are invaluable while John uses his considerable, albeit slightly rusty and disused charm to wheedle an address from the curator of the exhibition. She is one of those rather flimsy blondes buttoned up and straightened by the cut of her very expensive suit. John has never had much truck for blondes in any shape or form but she seems to find him fascinating and goes out of her way to rummage through files and her address book to find him what he seeks. He flashes his journalistic credentials and every other dam connection he can think of and learns that Helena Weinberg inherited the Weinberg holiday house in Whitstable which apparently was beloved of Nellie who adored taking a different kind of photo down there. According to the blonde woman, an expert in her field although he can't really imagine her blue eyed mistiness as expert in anything, but he has to remind himself that he is being unkindly chauvinistic here. The Blonde woman named Sarah Smythe from the card she plunges into his unwilling grip tells him breathlessly with much batting of long black eyelashes that Nellie spent her time in Whitstable concentrating on capturing in almost documentary detail the working life of the fishermen and oyster catchers of the North Kent coast. Her niece Helena Weinberg has a fair number of the surviving pictures and the gallery is hoping for an exhibition of those works early in the New Year. He manages to inveigle an address and telephone number of the house in Whitstable from his unwanted conquest, and also to escape without agreeing to meet her for a drink or become. 'A friend" of the gallery. He makes a lucky escape out into the sunshine of the gardens the Henry Moore sculpture smiling down at him as if in cahoots. His head is pounding and his mobile buzzing with missed calls both from the office and from Cecilia in France. Wearily he walks through the park, his hands in his pockets, and a huge pit of blackness swirling just around the next corner of his mind.

The girl is real he's sure of it and when the boys come home from school today he's going to double check that they remember seeing her too. For the rest of it, it seems that a visit to the seaside is on the cards, it's the only place that he can think of to continue this quest. Some people wait a whole lifetime to fall in love and it never happens to them, if the past few days are to be his only experience of the emotion then they were worth it. But somewhere deep within him are stirring emotions that he never knew existed, the sort of stuff that he has always attributed to women's chick lit novels, and there has to be a way through to her, even if it is only for a moment to tell her how he feels, to see the same look in her eyes. He will move Heaven and Hell to find that path, but first he has to give himself space and time, find the right space and time, walk into the impossible unknown depths of the past, and search for the light that this love has shown him really can exist.

*

Chapter 9
Whitstable Spring 1875.

Nellie

All through the long winter months she has waited for this day, the first day of spring and the opening of the house by the sea. It sits in a row of pretty painted pastel houses just behind the beach staring out to sea with a long garden in front of it full of shingle and bulrushes and anything else that will flourish and grow in the salty earth which is occasionally flooded by the high spring tides. Her father built the house for them when they were children and Nellie and her brother spent hours on the beach collecting sea shells and seaweed and driving their Nanny mad with sand in all their clothes and hair smelling of seaweed, but they didn't care. There is still a corner of the garden dedicated to their precious treasures, pieces of cut glass oyster shells and the odd ancient looking bottle and driftwood twisted into shapes of smooth white wonder, nature's natural sculptures.

As they grew older they grew bolder and slipped out in the early morning to watch the fishermen mend their nets, even once stowing away on a small trawler and only being discovered by one of the crew way out to sea. She blushes now remembering how they had to explain that they were sailing away to become pirates and find their own desert island to live on. But it had been worth it, the Captain had let them watch the seal families dipping and diving from the sandbanks and their cheeks had chapped red and raw from the sting of the salt. He had made them hot sweet tea and fed them sardines and she hadn't regretted one moment of it all, that is until they had been hauled off the boat by the irate constable who had had to deal with the distraught Nanny searching for them. That was the first and last time poor Nanny ever slapped her with exasperation and relief at having her charges safe and back on dry land. At the time she remembers being bewildered by the seeming illogicality of their reception back on shore. Why slap her if she was so precious? She hadn't talked to Nanny for a whole month except in grunts and nods, and she had never really trusted her again.

She smiles when she thinks about the telling off they got for that little escapade, two days of being locked in the house like scowling baby seals tearing all that came within their reach with the frustration of not being allowed to roam free. Often they would be sent to the coast with just the housemaid the cook and the Nanny, Papa being too busy up in the City, and goodness knows what Mama did, but enough it seemed to keep her busy and away from her children. It was a childhood of watching the light play on the water and the nuance of every changing horizon that first drew Nellie to try and paint what she saw in front of her and then after that of course came the photos. She had discovered the unerring yearning to try and capture a little piece of the immensity that was this ever changing seascape, she smiles, and shrugs as the impossibility of the task beckons to her once again. She wants to grasp at the ineffable mystery of it all and catch it for others to see, but perhaps she might have made a better job of it if she had been a painter instead.

She is standing on the small balcony now hugging her arms around her in joy and anticipation of the months to come when she will be totally free to work here in peace without Mama constantly trying to make her suitable for the marriage market that she Nellie so obviously is not the slightest bit interested in. Until she had come upon John she had always thought that men were rather a waste of space, in her world at least. Yes they were necessary for the job of procreation, that much she knew, but what else could they do that women couldn't? She doesn't think that she has a maternal bone in her body so that part of the marriage equation is of no real interest to her. Other people's children are acceptable but the whole business of childbirth just seems too inextricably time consuming and messy to even consider. For this year at least she has been allowed to come here alone without the chaperone, thank goodness, Miss Tindley is definitely the most boring company she has had to bear, and she needs to be alone to recuperate from the bronchitis that had taken her winter away from her.

It was when she had returned from Paris her senses heightened by all that Blavatsky had revealed and not revealed that she had immediately been struck down with the fever and infection. There had been talk of her catching the bug from Miss Tindley who had travelled back from Paris with her of course: with a streaming cold and very red nose. It had been impossible not to catch it considering the shaky state she was in. There had been fears that she might not pull through, and January and February had passed in a semi-conscious haze of doctors and eucalyptus oil, and the sticky sweet laudanum which sent her reeling into vivid dream landscapes. Her bedroom had been dotted with humidifying burners and her diet consisted solely of steaming lashings of her mother's recipe for chicken soup. If she never tasted chicken soup again it could not be too soon. While she was in that nebulous nether state of neither being present in this world, nor truly out of it she had one quest uppermost in her mind, she had kept on trying yes had constantly tried in vain to reach out to John. But in the dreams that she could now remember being successful, and there were only a few; he always seemed to be walking away from her through the woods and vanishing just as she turned the corner to catch up with him. It was as if her lack of physical strength hindered her in some way from pulling the two of them together even in the subtle world of dreams.

She had waited and waited in vain for the letter that was promised from the Madame but it had never come, although she still holds out hope of it appearing, of being told how and where she can come to see him again. He has it is true recently appeared from time to time and more memorably each time in her dreams ,but that is all the contact that she has had with this man that she loves, this man that lives in another time from her. Madame's bland factual statement of the impossible still makes her heart beat too fast when she tries to wrap her mind around the ramifications of it all. She gives a small internal laugh, how ridiculous could it be that this has happened to her? It's the stuff of penny novels, impossible and completely ridiculous especially to one such as her who believes so strongly in the new advances of the research of science.

But for today she won't think about it, the whole concept is too exhausting and more than a little scary. It is enough to be here on her beloved shore again. The tide is incoming the "Old Neptune Inn" solid and reassuring before her gaze nestling in a pocket of shingle above the water line and the fishing boats setting out from the harbour for their evening trade. They look like so many swooping swallows as they bounce and bob on the current and the men set their lanterns a glowing in the bow. She shivers and pulls her shawl around her shoulders; she feels the chill more nowadays as she is still thin from the illness. Overhead she hears the cries of a flock of geese as they fly past in their habitual V formation low over the water at tide line, and the lights begin to twinkle more noticeably in Sea salter the other side of the bay.

There is just time for a walk before it gets too dark and she descends the outside staircase of the house which leads down from the balcony into the garden, and she then walks slowly and thoughtfully out of the peacock blue gate and onto the boardwalk which follows the curve of the bay. She heads east towards the small harbour where the oyster dredging fleet are anchored for the night, their rigging a forest of masts against the outlines and shadow of the small pitch and tarred fishing huts. The sands in front of their black tarred beach huts covered in drying nets that in this silver twilight look like so many giant cobwebs. She can smell the evening meals cooking in fishermen's kitchens and every now and then the brisk footsteps of one of the fishermen can be heard advancing distinctly on the cobbles before a figure appears from one of the narrow fisherman's alleyways. All these intricate maze of

107

pathways leading from the town to the beach have curious names like Squeeze Gut Alley or the Captains path and they weave between the houses connecting land to sea and house to workplace. The land is a series of reclaimed islands protected from the sea by sea walls and each separate area has its own feel about it.

Each time a shadowy figure appears from an alleyway she goes through the same prolonged chatty palaver of greeting and a small update on her health and her work, so her progress along towards the harbour is slow but joyful. She is known and loved here in the small town; it is totally unlike her daily life in London which can be so lonely and anonymous. The people of Whitstable watched her grow up as a child and now value her for her work and that thought warms her from the inside with a glow that for the moment keeps out the cold.

It's a small community, but a good solid community which is run by the Company of Oyster Dredgers, entry into which is passed down from father to son. The whole company works as a cooperative to farm the oyster beds and supply the London market at Billingsgate. Out in the bay the hoys that take the fish to market in London on Wednesdays Thursdays and Fridays are bobbing at anchor, their bow lights appearing and disappearing with the slight swell of the tide. She walks until the smell of fish becomes too much for her and then she turns back towards the house a quiet sense of peace settling over her, as her lungs fill with the sea air stinging slightly with the sharp salt of the air which opens them and soothes them for the first time in months. She yawns and stretches, something about this air always manages to relax her and this is the place that she sleeps properly in.

She likes walking through the streets at dusk like this and pretending that she is just part of one of the families that live here. Apart from the company of her brother, there have been many times when she has felt lonely, she supposes that it's because she's unlike normal girls of her age and since she was forced to leave school from ill health she hasn't really had anyone that she can call a close friend that she can confide in. Of course even down by the sea side there is the fashionable set that have taken up residence here and that she can visit if she feels the urge. When Papa and Mama come down from the city they take family outings to George Reynolds Gothic mansion in Herne Bay.

There the famous writer holds at homes with the like of Augustus Pugin and sometimes Rossetti pops down to Fostal, but Nellie prefers the simplicity of their own little house to the gawky and sumptuous décor of these mansions. Why Mr Pugin has his whole house covered in wallpaper emblazoned with his own crest, in gaudy orange and red. It quite makes her head ache when she goes there, The gothic interior is so full of escutcheons and emblazoning's, twirls and carving and all that colour can cover that it affronts her senses and leaves her feeling dizzy . Her thoughts have brought her full circle back to the small blue gate of her house and for a moment she turns and looks back across the shingle to the blank black canvas of the sea, the wind making her shiver and the fisherman's boats winking and bobbing in the distance like sea bound stars.

The house is far too ablaze with light as she approaches it, making her blink and as she opens the front door her heart skips a beat, for it is her house and it isn't. There is a smell in the hall of a perfume that she doesn't recognise and a bright glaze over everything as if she is looking at it through the lens of one of her cameras. She hears the light lilt of a woman's voice and an answering voice that she recognises immediately. Down the stairs comes a pale complexioned woman, slightly older than Nellie with a cascade of dark hair and slim hips tucked into what looks like a pair of men's trousers. She is laughing and turning her head up the stairway behind her from where descends a man in earnest conversation with her. The woman walks right by her as if she doesn't exist, the light playing over her aquiline face, a face that has some of the attributes that Nellie recognises as her own. But the man stops at the bottom of the steps and stares at her and it is him and he knows her. His face lights up and the space between them fizzles like electric soda pop for a second, she laughs and begins to run towards him holding out her arms like a child.

"Nellie" He whispers, " It is Nellie isn't it?'

She turns her face up to him bemused and opens her mouth to tell him

"Yes, I am Nellie and I am absolutely your Nellie where have you been I have been waiting for you? "

But then like a switch the vision fades, the night is again upon her and all she can hear is the sound of cook's voice calling her into the parlour for dinner.

*

Chapter 10
Place Vendome Paris Spring 1995

Cecilia

Cecilia wakes and for a moment forgets where she is, even who she is. Last night's dreams and echoes are still there on the tip of her consciousness almost alive and confusing. She tries to sift through them and discover what was real and what was dream but gives up with a sigh. She looks up at the heavy brocade ceiling in wonderment tracing the lines of the rich tapestry, and then she twists around to pass her hand over the fine cotton sheets that she is entangled in. The sheets feel hot and sticky to her fingers and she begins to unwrap her legs and fan them out to cool her sweating body She feels like a girl again ready to go out and discover the world but as she lowers her hand under the covers she touches her body and it is the body of a woman. All is softness, the soft of silken skin her breasts warm and heavy beneath her palm, her groin sweaty from the warmth of the bed. A slight noise issues from beside her and she turns her neck ever so slightly to see the beautiful lines of a young man lying next to her. He's spread out on his stomach his arms flung akimbo, dark curls covering the pillow and as she watches him one of his long fine arms reaches out and grabs her around the stomach and pulls her to him with a slight sigh of contentment. A slow lazy smile crosses his face his black eyes flicker open for a second take her in and she can't help feeling exposed and naked to him as he possessively places the palm of his hand over her stomach.

She smiles and shifts into the taut curve of him, adjusting her limbs to his, Louis, how could she ever for a moment forget Louis? Sunlight flows in through a chink in the heavy brocade curtains and she sinks back in contentment, and

© Victoria Mosley 2016

remembers everything. She's safe in her beautiful Paris flat, Bosnia and the agony of the orphanages that she has had to visit for her recent assignment are a long way away, she shivers and snuggles closer closing her eyes under her long heavy lashes. She remembers blissfully that she has time on her side, time to spend with this gift of a boy who is so much more a man than her husband ever was. The thought of John makes her heart palpitate slightly in irritation, but she stills it. She hasn't seen him for a few months, they talk on the phone sometimes about the children but that's it really. What with her work and Louis, her marriage seems to be drifting away from her like a leaf down a river, and she does a quick careful internal check to see if she really cares. The answer that drifts into her mind already floating on the edge of sleep is emphatically no.

The early morning continues on its way around them, the apartment is on the first floor of a large house in the square and rich in its original hangings, from the blue silk on the walls to the brocade of the ceiling. From each corniced ceiling hangs the lustre of the heavy teardrop chandeliers and the pretty fireplaces are clean and ready to have a fire lit in them, just as they have always been. The former occupants from other centuries drift through their daily tasks unnoticed by each other, layer upon layer of life and time passing and re passing but hardly ever colliding.

Somewhere in the house a bell rings, Cecilia moves in her sleep her eyelids twitching and Louis sits up on his elbow now watching her. At this precise moment he is perfectly content and if he could die now or stay here forever just holding her, watching her, it would be more than enough. For deep within him he knows that she is fiercely his and he wants no other man to touch her ever again.

The thought translates to his body and he feels his erection knocking against his stomach and it is no use he wants her again he has to have her, his need for her is all consuming, it consumes them both. Every time he makes love to her it seems to be more of an immense experience than the last. All of his feeling self combines with the urgency of his body into a crescendo of an orgasm, the kind of orgasm that leaves him shaky and disorientated. Yet as soon as he is finished and is lying spent beside her he is hard again and ready for her, it is a kind of drug, this sexual chemistry that they have between them, the more sex they have the more he needs. If he could keep them both locked up in this bedroom for ever that would be a life, but he can't. Outside of the confines of their intimacy where he is in control of her, outside of it their relationship slips from his grasp and she has the power. Sometimes she uses it against him and then quite simply he wants to kill her.

The thought slides through him as he begins to stroke her, caressing the soft lines of her stomach, delving between her legs where she is always wet and ready for him. She moans in her sleep and turns away from him slightly and that is enough to rouse him, he pushes her legs open and glides into her pushing hard, meeting resistance and the resistance excites him. He uses his fingers on her, softly where she likes it most, his mouth on her neck taking a grip of the soft skin under her hairline, holding hard , biting bruising marking her, making her his again. They tussle like dogs one getting the upper hand and then the other before she begins to move with his rhythm, giving in to the cadence of it all, giving in to his need.

Later driven out by hunger they lunch at the bistro on the corner of the square consuming great draughts of red wine with the meat of the plat du jour, as if they have never eaten before. She is flushed and beautiful from the love making, her face devoid of her usual make up she looks young again, and he has a two day growth of beard, hollows beneath his eyes still with that hungry look that she brings out in him. No one comments or notices the disparity of their years. For a while they eat in silence, again Cecilia drinks him in with her eyes until he laughs almost embarrassed.by her intensity.

"What is it Cherie, you're making me nervous?".

He reaches for her hand over the table their eyes are locked as if there is not another living soul on the planet, and she smiles a twisted smile and shrugs.

'' I like looking at you, it's been a long time since we've been together like this, too long, and I always think that I need to look at you because we're living in a fairy tale and each time I look may be the last time. The Universe might take its dues , take us away from each other, nothing is forever, we've only this moment , and in this moment you are mine.''

She pulls her hand away and blows her nose on a tissue and for a moment he looks angry, he turns away abruptly and orders an espresso.

"Where would you go? Where would I go? I won't ever let you go, I would rather you were dead than with anyone else"

She reaches over and touches his cheek almost sadly.

'' What fire and brimstone my darling, of course we are together but I am living in my own time too, I have a life, perhaps you need a life, a wife a child, something normal of your own. I can't do that again not even for you, no more children for me, I'm not the maternal type and then there is work, I just have a few days.''

He is furious now, and lifts his hand up abruptly as if to silence her and it works, she shuts her mouth and turns away slightly, her hand falling from his arm, her back stiffening, She knows that it would be easier between them if she could just keep her anxieties to herself, never share them with him, but they bubble up to the surface and out of her mouth when she is least expecting it, and then there is a row. His dark eyes flash, his brows are knit together and she realises that it's no good, she can't talk to him about the reality of it all, he can't cope with that, and he certainly doesn't want to. She will just have to exist in this nether world that they have created between them, where they fuck and talk like teenagers of a world that he conjures up in his head every time they are together. Or like now she will

114

have to deal with the consequences of his anger, which sometimes are not pretty. She shivers as she watches him pay the bill, understanding that he will make her pay later for the question mark she has placed next to their affair.

Her mobile vibrates in her handbag, the phone is a perk of her job and the newspaper company pays for it ,but when it rings it always makes her feel guilty as if it is keeping an eye on her and she jumps her heart tumbling into her mouth for a moment. She fumbles around in her capacious handbag and turns it off ignoring the "missed call" status bar. Louis sweeps his chair from under him and makes towards the door refusing to even look at her. She sits there and stirs her coffee and sighs, all of her muscles ache from the scrum of their mornings love making. For a brief moment she wishes that she was alone, maybe she's just too old for all this passion stuff. She watches as he stands on the corner of the street opposite the café window and lights a cigarette, his shoulders hunched in his navy blue Burberry coat, his jeans boot cut to his very French shoes. She smiles as she watches some of the young girls that hurry by who can't help but glance at him, he is so beautiful and he is all hers.

Then without a backward glance he flicks his cigarette butt from him scowls at her through the window of the café and heads back towards the apartment. She pays the bill and delves into her bag for the phone, a missed call from John and as she stares at it she feels someone looking at her and suddenly peering in through the window is the tall grey haired shape of her husband. Cecilia half rises to her feet and waves, he sees her and nods briefly before pulling his coat collar up around his shoulders and heading into the restaurant. She feels awkward her skin prickles she can still feel the dull ache between her legs from Louis and suddenly her old life has come to bang smack her in the face and the juxtaposition of it all is unnerving .

But why is he here? She hugs him smelling his familiar after shave; her body relaxes for a nanosecond in the old familiarity of him until she remembers all that is separating them. They haven't seen each other since they passed an awkward Christmas together at her parents and she is surprised that he has left the boys to come all this way to talk to her. It must be something urgent but for the first ten minutes they chat away about the children who are apparently being looked after by his frosty old mother and the au pair, but then the conversation turns to work and he surprises her with his opening sentence.

"I've taken some time out from work, something has happened in my life that effects both of us and I've come to ask you for a divorce. "

She pales and gives an intake of breath, obviously, he might guess that she is having an affair but she comes from an Old Catholic family, divorce is very rarely on the agenda, and marriage is forever. Does he know about Louis? His next words leave a heavy chill in her heart as he throws a letter onto the table and she recognises the hand writing.

" I received this last week from your boyfriend telling me how he longs to be with you, so I suppose you aren't going to contest the divorce , although this isn't the reason for it."

She gropes around for words that seem to have deserted her leaving her brain muddy and sluggish as if someone has pulled the plug from a bath of dirty water and she is the plughole that the debris is disappearing down.

" So what is the reason then John? And what do you expect to happen to the children? Of course they will come and live with me and my family."

"It doesn't matter what the reason is does it, you're in no position to question me with this little snippet of black and white evidence in my hands, although I would have thought you'd have more taste, some of his descriptions of your affair are quite disgusting would you like me to read you some."

He picks up the letter and begins,

"When I have the silky softness of your wife's tight labia around me I know that we are meant to be and nothing you will say can make me change my mind about this, she belongs to me and to me only you have no more claim on her than a piece of paper and a ceremony in the church of a God that doesn't exist."

Cecilia grabs for the letter but he lifts it clear from her reach and she only manages to spill her coffee across the white tablecloth, the brown stain slowly spreads and she mops at it ineffectually with her napkin unsure of how to proceed with this new forceful side of John that she has never glimpsed before.

"As for the children my dear I don't think you should even begin to think about using them as a bargaining tool, there is no court in the land that will give them into the custody of an adulterous mother who spends half her time fucking a boy half her age and the other half wandering about irresponsibly in a war zone."

" Bastard".

Slips from her lips, but then she slumps, he is right of course and anyway what would she do with the boys? They'll be much happier in that gloomy old house with him, who's she kidding and she will be free, free to be with Louis if she feels like it. This thought however doesn't appear as mesmerising as it would have done an hour ago, somewhere inside her the cement of her life which was John and her marriage, the anchor that gave her the upper hand in her affair is beginning to crumble away and she is immediately scared .

" John, this is silly, can't we sort this out? An affair is only an affair; a marriage is so much more isn't it?"

He leans back in his chair and looks at her and she doesn't like the way his eyes narrow, as if he is seeing her for the first time and not liking what he sees.

" I'm sorry Cecilia, I can't accommodate you anymore, we'll split everything down the middle, you can keep the flat here which is about on a financial par with the house in London. You see I'm just not that bothered about it all, I've found that I love someone else."

An icy chill weaves its way across her brow and she shakes her head in disbelief.

"Who is she?" She whispers. "I think I have a right to know."

He laughs and swigs his coffee back shrugging on his coat and for the first time ever she can see that he seems truly happy and it shocks her. She didn't really want him anymore that much is true, but she doesn't particularly want anyone else to have him either.

" You have absolutely no right to know anything at all about me anymore, my lawyer will be in touch to arrange access for the children, that's if you can tear yourself away from the young cock that you are so absorbed with. I hope he makes you happy Cecilia; I certainly never could although I have tried. Feel free to ring the children whenever you can be bothered, they miss you. Goodbye Ceci and very good luck, I think you will need it."

She is numb as she watches him stride off around the corner and out of sight, she needs to get out of here and walk for a while, the thought of going back to the flat and having to deal with Louis is just altogether too much. How can her life have narrowed itself to this in such a short and cataclysmic space of time? Why, just this morning when she woke everything was perfect and now what is going to happen to her?

She walks for half an hour without noticing where she is going and then suddenly she is alongside the river with the Ile de la Cite and Notre Dame in front of her. The soft pale stone of the building with its familiar sweeping lines feels comforting and without thinking she walks into the huge space of the cathedral

118

made suddenly thankful for the solidity of it. She is immensely grateful for the glowing rose window in front of her and the atmosphere of hundreds of years of prayer that comes rolling off the walls to greet her. She walks into a pew at the front of the nave and sinks to her knees burying her head in her hands and begins to intone the prayer of our lady firstly in English and then without thinking she slips into the Latin of her childhood.

'Our lady full of grace Our Lord is with thee Ave Maria, gratia plena, Dominus tecum, benedicta tu in mulieribus, et benedictus fructus ventris tui Iesus. Sancta Maria mater Dei, ora pro nobis peccatoribus, nunc, et in hora mortis nostrae. "

The familiar magic of what she always thought of as a secret language when she was little and a small child in her first year at the convent slips easily off her tongue and she feels almost as if she has taken a Valium, as the calm of the prayer creeps over her whole being. Later much later that night when she is lying beside Louis who sleeps at last, she listens carefully to the sounds of the house wrap themselves around her. She can hear the whisper of the *almost* laughter, the shuffling of the floorboards the moan of an icy cold winding itself like a cats tail around the square and her mind is an empty husk floating on the wind of where she has taken it, *pray for us sinners now and at the hour of our death.* Hums around her brain as sleep catches her and she loosens herself from her minds desperate churning grip and understands that she is with Louis now in a way that she never was before. The lure of this love of theirs is deadly and she may not get out of it alive, the strength of his obsession with her is just beginning to dawn on her, and she sees it float in with the patterns in the room as another miasma that can't be altered. After today she has realised that even the things she thought were unbreakable, like her marriage can be pulled down in an instant and for the first time she understands that sometimes love is a condition that you have to survive. Gently she moves a dark curl of hair from the sleeping lover's forehead, the hair soft as silk beneath her fingers, his breath as peaceful as a sleeping child. Who is this man beside her really? Now she is attached to him in a way that she never really wanted to be before, somehow solid, she needs him as she never did before. Somewhere she is scared of the hold that he has over her and also of the hold that his temper has over them both when he is angry she is never quite sure how far his rage will take him. She hadn't dared to mention the letter that he had written to her husband for fear of what he would do. But if she is honest with herself she knows that this letter disclosing her secrets is only the last crack in the edifice of her marriage, neglect is the thing that has dismantled it, years of both of them taking each other for granted.

She had never really wanted the love affair with Louis to be real, the magic of it lay in the way it could simply fly through her fingers and disappear like wood smoke from a summer BBQ. It was just an illicit affair that she was having that now had catapulted out of control in a way that she had never wanted it to. John was her safety valve and by leaving her he has set her floating in the sea of freedom which is a yawning chasm in front of her and she feels that she may never be able to anchor herself to solidity again.

*

Chapter 11
John

Whitstable Summer 1995.

He is driving south out of London through the dreary suburbs of Catford with its bleary eyed early morning joggers and dog walkers their footfalls spattering through the mud on the after rain pavement. He considers stopping at MacDonald's but then decides it would be too hideous to start this journey munching a Big Mac, his stomach rumbles but he ignores it, swigging instead at a cold cup of coffee housed in the cup holder by his elbow. He weaves through the traffic on the A205 and down into the filter road for the M2 motorway. Its early morning; very early it must be only slightly after six am, a full hour before the advent of any rush hour traffic. His mind is only peripherally on the traffic around him, he has switched into motorway driving auto pilot. The kind of driving where later in the day you wonder how you managed to get to your destination in one piece as you can't recall any single detail of its trajectory. His eyes search the horizon for his first glimpse of the sea, but as yet there are only rolling fields leading onto woods and the low scar of a morning mist hovering over the land. It's see through veil makes the landscape seem mysterious and he ponders on the history of the Kent countryside, the regular pillage and plunder of the coastal towns and the land around since Anglo Saxon times, didn't Alfred burn his cakes somewhere near here ?

He passes Oast houses and fields yellow with rape seed flowers; he looks blankly at vineyards and apple orchards, his internal dialogue preventing him from taking in the luxuriant beauty of the county. He's feeling excited and discombobulated as if he is going to a new job, but that's not it. On the seat beside him is the print out of an email from Helena Weinberg giving him directions to her house by the sea, the house she inherited from her Great great Aunt Nellie, his Nellie. He hardly dare say the words, in fact he doesn't. It's too ridiculous and he sweeps all thought of the notion from his mind. If he really lets himself relive the glimpses of the dark haired girl in the woods his mind threatens to snap, its neurons overstrung with disbelief its pathways burnt out and smoking from the impossibilities of the situation it might very well have conjured up.

He couldn't have made this journey before now although he had wanted to; there was stuff that he had to do first. He had wanted to come immediately after his original contact with Helena, his instinct was to get in the car and hotfoot it to the coast. But something had made him wait and as he'd waited the vision of the girl had faded somewhat, she'd become almost a beautiful memory of something extraordinary, but nothing more, and for the duration of the spring months he hadn't seen her. Everything had slotted back to normality but he had changed, his magic encounter had given him a slightly different perspective on his own world. He'd needed to try to sort out the mess that had become his marriage, or rather the beginnings of the ending of his marriage. He'd started to get suspicious of Cecilia's comings and goings after Christmas, drawn out of his own inner reverie by the noticeable absence of his wife. Then it had become apparent that something was going on with Cecilia that she didn't want to talk about.

He gives an abrupt laugh out loud to the humming of the radio and the swish of gigantic lorries going by. Thinking about it now indeed how could she talk about anything with him since she was never at home? Firstly she'd gone to Bosnia, much against his will, she was a mother for God's sake, and the boys needed a mother, even a shit one, although at the moment it seems to be the au pair who is taking on that role. But finally impatient with the lack of communication he'd rung the apartment in Paris when he knew that she should be there, and a man had answered. Suspicions aroused he'd got one of the investigative journalists who owed him a favour to pop over the channel, snoop around a bit and take a few photos, just in case he needed them in court.

There is no point in underestimating the De la Croix family, he'd done that before and it had got him pre nuptials and a huge bill for a wedding which he didn't want. He'd wanted something quiet and romantic on a beach somewhere but there had been no hope of his wishes once Cecilia's mother had got involved. The photos of this handsome young man and then the letter he had sent to John detailing in graphic detail the intimacies of their affair had led to his confrontation with her in the café and from there on in he'd decided he wanted out. If only to breathe the air again without feeling guilty or without having to worry about what he should be thinking and feeling as a family man. He needed to give himself back the right to be the master of his own destiny; he had wanted to give himself a chance. Life is short and he needs to give himself permission to discover whatever it has to offer. The boys deserve more than a pair of bickering unhappy parents; if Cecilia can't be bothered to be a proper mother to them maybe he can find them somebody who can.

Instantly his memory sends him the startling image of Nellie in the woods with the boys that first day he saw her and he smiles. She was wonderful with them and they still sometimes ask him about her when he is telling them a bed time story .He has spun a little tale for them all about the girl that used to live in the house a long long time ago, who sometimes comes back to visit and Ollie often snuggles down under his duvet and says contentedly,

"Tell me the Nellie girl story daddy."

He sighs and checks his mirror as a lorry pulls out in front of him, ok he can't completely blame Cecilia for the breakdown of their marriage, he is also in love with someone else but it's not exactly as if he could ever consummate this fantasy of his. The bold photos of his wife curled around some pretty skinny French boy were enough to hurt his pride big time. It hadn't helped when he'd pulled himself together and marched across the channel to play the indignant husband and found her entwined in a café with the man. He'd watched them both through their heated discussion and it was obvious even from the distance of the corner of the street that they had time for no one but each other. As he'd strode into the café to confront her he had very carefully checked his heart for hurt but had found nothing but a numb sense of weariness when he'd looked at his wife.

A loud honk of a lorry startles him as he swerves in front of it, and it brings him back to the present. The last few months have been busy, he'd been working to shore up his loneliness and his sense of impotence at the situation and then he'd decided to tackle the local historian and show him the tunnel down through the woods. Together they had found the original drawings for the house locked away in the archives in the Lewisham library and together they had spent several frosty days digging out some of the debris so that light and air again circulate around the beautiful mosaics. There had been more than a little mumbo jumbo about lay lines and galactic line ups or something but although it sounded scientific it clearly wasn't. At that point John had decided that he needed to know more, he needed to trust in this thing that has happened to him however weird it might be and investigate the impossible; so here he is trundling down the motorway on a high bright summer day with butterflies in his stomach and a sense of the inevitable hanging over his left shoulder.

It only takes him thirty minutes from Catford to the Whitstable exit on the A299, and suddenly he is on the crest of a hill looking out over the choppy waters of the North Sea with the Isle of Sheppey clearly visible. In the distance like the haze of giant children's mecano set are the wind powered electricity turbines on the headland. Following the directions of his print out he parks his car in Nelson Road next to the Windy corner café and locks it. As soon as he unfurls his leggy 6ft frame from the warm driver's seat the chill of the sea air hits him. Even at this time of year it carries with it a sharp bite and he shivers pulling his coat collar up to his chin. In a couple of strides he makes it down a tiny side lane labelled Marine Gap and is immediately on the walkway alongside the beach.

The beach is deserted; it spreads out in front of him simple and timeless in the early morning light; shingle and breakwaters, small arcs of sand, seaweed and oyster shells half buried dead crab legs and a wonderland of sea smells. The force of the wind almost rips his hair from his head and makes his eyes water. There are only a few wrapped up dog walkers plodding bravely down the beach their plastic poop scoop bags clutched at the ready. The air still carries the chill of the night and the fading tide. He gazes out at the Old Neptune Pub with its white weather board as it stands staunchly on the shingle looking as if it has grown upward from the sand itself. It's, romantic and desolate, through the windows he can see the brown stained walls and the wooden trestle tables a few locals hunched over the bar already with their pints of bitter. His eyes flick over the miles of mud flats exposed by the receding tide. In the distance he can see the barges of the Oyster Dredging Company and further out to sea the shallow water of the sand banks where he has read that the seals breed.

It all looks as it must have done a hundred years ago and he realises that he is looking at the same scene that Nellie looked at so many times as she was growing up here . He's heard a little of her story from the few telephone conversations he has had with Helena, who is writing a PhD thesis on her illustrious Great Aunt. Not knowing what to specialise in after her MA in media studies course she was inspired by the letters journals and photographs that Nellie had left which she discovered locked in a travelling trunk in the attic of the house. She has reached a dead end in her research for it seems to him that something is bothering the woman about her Great aunt's tale.

Nothing is known of Nellie after a certain age, she abruptly disappeared. Helena has found newspaper cuttings of a hue and cry over the missing girl. Apparently she simply walked out of the door of her house in London one evening and never returned. They traced her to Victoria Station and the train to Whitstable but after that she vanished. It all sounds a bit unlikely, there is probably some reasonable explanation for it all, an elopement or a trip somewhere where she had decided to stay but Helena reminded him the Victorian society was not really like that, it was unusual for a woman to vanish without trace. Even Jack the Rippers victims had been accounted for, if Nellie had gone abroad there would have been some record of her crossing to France and there is none.

He has booked himself into the bed and breakfast in a rather plush sounding hotel on the Island Wall which is the street behind the seafront and intends to spend the next few days engrossed in the details of the artefacts. First however he needs a drink before he faces the next step of his journey, his heart is beating too fast and the light is too bright it's hurting his eyes. He swings across the shingle and goes into the pub, a fisherman turns an impossibly weather-beaten face to greet him with a nod as he orders a malt whisky and a coffee and takes the glass to a table where he can sit and watch the front door of the house. His heart gives a leap as he thinks "Nellie's" house, but the dull bruise of disbelief settles over him again and soon enough the woman behind the bar brings the coffee and a plate of biscuits which he doesn't really want. He props up the morning paper in front of him and tries to read through the low hum of local gossip coming from the bar.

Half an hour later he finds himself in front of an aqua blue front door inlaid with stained glass his hand is poised on the knocker but it suddenly swings open in front of him. There in the doorway is a slender woman, curly dark hair swept up on her head, the light in her face, so for a moment he is looking into a pale mask. Then a cloud blocks the sun and Helena Weinberg is staring at him and she takes his breath away. She's wearing a pair of faded jeans and a man's checked shirt, he can smell perfume and the soft clean smell of soap but it is her face that shocks him. Her eyes are huge and brown under long dark lashes, he can see faint laughter lines in the delicate skin, but that's not it, she looks like Nellie. The similarity is striking but he can't quite put his finger on it, luckily she immediately breaks the spell by sticking out her hand and greeting him and her voice is nothing like Nellie's.

" John I presume? Gosh you gave me a shock I was just popping out to the shops to get us something for lunch, but it can wait do come in."

He feels like he is in one of his dreams as he follows her down the narrow hallway, on the walls are faded sepia photographs in dark wooden frames and of course they are Nellie's photos. He wants to stop and examine them immediately but politeness means he follows Helena's slim body up the staircase into the sitting room which is on the first floor with huge bay windows looking out to sea. She chatters away inconsequentially and he tries not to stare; at her, or at the authentic furnishings of the room which look like original period pieces and at a large photo of Nellie which is prominently hanging above the fireplace. Eventually noticing his silence she falters in her stream of chatter and looks closely at him.

" Are you quite well? You look like you've seen a ghost, can I get you a cup of tea?"

" Sorry, yes that would be lovely , no I'm just recovering from a bout of flu and the early drive this morning didn't help matters much. "

He has already decided that the less she knows about why he is here the better and he wants to be left alone in this precious house so that he can investigate the photo, really look at Nellie for the first time. As far as he is concerned it is Helena who is the ghost, Helena who shouldn't really be here, this thought comes to him strongly as she leaves him to his own devices while she clatters in the kitchen beneath them. Reverently as if he is in a church he crosses to the fireplace and examines the portrait, his fingers touching the glass in deference, she is even more beautiful than he remembers her eyes looking past him out the window, out to sea, her fingers entwined in her necklace the pearls curling around her slender fingers and the sapphire huge and catching the light.. As he studies her the light shimmers in the room and he gets the buzzing in his ears that he hasn't had these past few months.

127
© Victoria Mosley 2016

He hears the peel of a girl's laughter and the slamming of the door somewhere in the house behind him and his heart leaps. He turns away from the photo as the door to the kitchen clatters and the magic stills; Helena is there again bringing normality and a strong cup of sweet tea.

" You look better already ". She laughs " It must be that smidgeon of sea air that you got on your walk here this morning.

It's true that he feels better but he knows that it's nothing to do with sea air, it's because Nellie is here in the house with them and all he has to do is wait awhile and he is sure that she will find a way to him.

*

Chapter 12
Nellie summer 1875

Whitstable

Summer has come with the onslaught of the holiday crowd replete with their hats and muslins, their parasols, their chatter and of course their voluminous bathing suits. They are strewn across the beach in the afternoon sun and take tea on the balcony of their brightly coloured beach huts. Large veiled sunhats on heads and hands shading eyes that pretend to stare languidly out to see but in fact are busy scrutinising the fashions of the season. *Beach fashion* if it can be called that, she snorts inwardly at the absurdity of the woollens and collars leggings and pantaloons covering every possible inch of flesh, the men looking just as silly as the ladies but perhaps not quite in so much danger of drowning because of the weight of their clothes. They come to their cottages in streets named after London streets, Sydenham Street and Victoria Street being the seeming favourites this year, or they drive their carriages to the large imposing villas on Cromwell Road.

Everything is light and space both inside and outside her house, it seems to expand out into the ever changing vista of the sea that laps the shingle in front of it. She looks at the sea and wonders for a moment if love is like water, endless expanding relentless and painted with all the colours that God can imagine. This is her special house; she loves the simplicity and soft colours of Pebble cottage as brilliantly as she loves the imposing splendour of the house in London. Both residences appeal to different parts of her soul; here she feels a freedom that she never can in London where she is constantly buttoned up and on show. She loves to sit in the upstairs sitting room and watch the small sailing boats set out across the bay. She has settled into a calm rhythm of sorts; she gets up at first light and washes in the small bathroom which is situated off the back of the kitchen. Cook always leaves the stove lit for her so with much clanging of pipes she usually has a plentiful supply of hot water. Then she grabs a small slice from the freshly baked loaf set out on her breakfast tray and takes her early morning walk.

Sometimes it will be along West Beach usually deserted apart from the cockle pickers at low tide. If she is feeling like some company she will take her camera down to the harbour and set up a few shots on the harbour wall. The fishermen are so used to her that apart from doffing a cap or nodding a greeting they let her get on with her task. Then when she has completed enough shots for her work in the darkroom later in the day she makes her way back for breakfast which she takes in the upstairs sitting room.

Since that glimpse of John and the slim woman in trousers earlier in the year she has been happier settling into her home by the sea, before she felt anxious that she was abandoning him in some way in London but it is now apparent that he is here and indeed he is everywhere she is ever likely to be. They are linked by invisible threads that are gradually pulling them closer and closer together, and this morning she has an intuition that she is teetering on the edge of something huge and unexpected. Her early morning rise has made her sleepy so after the walk and the wolfing down of her breakfast, and on a whim she picks her skirts up and lies on the chaise longue in the bay window covering herself with the coloured quilt.

She watches the light play on the water out at Seasalter, and she can just glimpse the marshes with their panoply of wild flowers and the marsh birds wheeling in to their nests.

Soon she settles down into a light dose and reaches that interim place where she is neither asleep nor awake. To begin with all she can hear is the swish of the waves on the shingle and the low voices of walkers on the promenade at the end of the front garden. She sinks down deeper into the sofa, loving the warmth of the sun on her skin, her mind replaying an internal projection of all the photographic images she has taken this morning. She is the first of the new wave of photographers to be more interested in taking images of natural subjects under natural light than the studio organised shots which are so favoured. Apart from the documentation for the newspapers, this isn't a normal state of affairs. Julia Margaret Cameron prefers to use her studio for her studies, but Nellie wants to capture real life at the end of her camera lens, not some made up thing that floats through the zeitgeist of the cultural imagination.

She smiles thinking how horrified her contemporaries' would be at the smelly harbour where she spends most of her mornings taking photos of the gnarled countenances of the fishermen. She has a fascination with the way light lodges in the deep grooves of their skin illuminating their complex craggy faces which look as if they have been fishing the seven seas since time immemorial. She cannot understand how wind and water and salt have eroded their expressions as it would a piece of the landscape. To her the fishermen are living walking history, and on bright mornings when they are mending their nets she will sit awhile with them and listen to their tales promising herself to write them all down in her diary later. Of course she hardly ever does, she is such a visual person that the portraits will have to speak for themselves and the oral tradition will have to stay just the way that it's always been, handed down by tongue in public houses and around the mending of the nets never confined to pen and ink.

Above and beyond her dream state the murmur of voices in the sunlit room becomes stronger, and more insistent. She shifts position on the sofa and tries to find a place where her hip bone is not aching as it hits the wooden frame of the chaise longue. Instinctually she sighs, somewhere in her consciousness she is feeling slightly annoyed at the interruption to her dose, the voices are disturbing her snooze added to which the sun is really warm now almost making her sweat. She is beginning to get a crick in her neck and her pendant is lodged beneath her arm hurting her skin, she needs to change position. She fumbles to throw off the covers and turns her head towards the disturbance which seems to be coming from somewhere across the other side of the room and tries to open her eyes.

For a second she believes she is still dreaming; there behind her, sitting very close to each other and pouring over what she immediately recognises as one of her own portfolios of photos is the slim woman in the trousers, her head bent closely to a man, who is none other than John. The space between Nellie and these two seems to be thick with a fog like substance and immediately a stab of jealousy lodges itself quickly in her breast .She watches how the woman's hand inadvertently brushes against John's and notices the quick light smile he gives her. The woman is flirting with John and he isn't objecting.

Without thinking Nellie gets to her feet and walks towards them but as soon as she enters the fog it pulls her back towards the window. Like treacle, like a storm filled sea it has its own potent undercurrent and she has to use brute force to travel a few feet across the room to where the two of them are sitting. At first she feels herself to be totally invisible; she can tell that neither John nor the woman know that she is here, but then she concentrates on planting her feet to the floor and being alive in the spot she finds herself and immediately she feels a buzz of life flow back into her veins. This time it is Nellie who has stepped into his world, into his paradigm whatever that might be and for the first time since this began, she feels the prickle of a foreign wind in her hair.

Quickly and almost for reassurance she looks back to the window seat and she notices it to be bathed in a halo of calm light. It makes her feel stronger to know that her world is just over there and she somehow tries to draw the strength of that presence of place to her. To bring a bubble of her own world into this one so that she has substance. The light flows towards her as a narrow tunnel and as it touches her fingers she feels warmth and strength. It is at that precise moment that John looks up and looks straight at her and she knows that he has seen her. Inadvertently and instinctually she reaches out towards him and her hand touches the hand of the woman at his side, she looks down expecting to see two hands but there is only one, and her hand is tingling where it has merged into the body of the woman. Quickly and with a sick sense of horror she pulls it back and it appears again at the end of her arm, where it should be with a slight sound, a sound of tiny bells or a robin's cry, and the woman notices and looks up.

The woman is speaking excitedly to John and staring intently at Nellie and all of a sudden Nellie knows exactly what she must do. She sidesteps towards the body of the woman and as she meets it she simply carries on pushing. For a moment everything becomes dark and viscous and then she is staring at John, her hand next to his on the table. With a huge smile of victory and a gurgle of happy laughter she turns to him, and understands that there is only the two of them sitting here, the woman has disappeared completely or has she? But she doesn't stop to think about this, she's not interested in where her rival has disappeared to she is only interested in John.

Nellie's finds each breath hard to take as if she is wearing one of her mother's corsets that have been laced far too tight and there are other disturbing things too. Her eye lashes are annoyingly long and her hair is tied back on her head in some kind of a tight band that is pulling at her skin. She puts her hand up to tug at it and it is gratifyingly released to fall in soft curls around her shoulders, and then she gasps as she looks down. Her light muslin skirt has gone and instead she has some tight kind of blue material around her legs and she feels naked. That's when it hits her in the full force of what she has done.

The woman has disappeared because she has *become the woman* she has possessed her body. There is no other way to describe it, and yet already she feels the light in the far corner of the room pulling her back to where she really belongs but she resists it if only for a few fleeting moments so that she can truly talk to John.

He is leaning towards her his face chalky white and there is something wrong with her eyesight , he looks blurry and too near , he reaches out and pulls her to him and she is in his embrace, it is solid and real and he is talking into her hair as he does in her dreams, he is whispering to her.

'' Nellie, oh my dear what have you done? What have you done? But I'm so happy you've come to me.''

Before she can get the words out she can feel the woman fighting to regain control of her body, it's as if her very heart beat is trying to push Nellie away. She pulls his face away from her neck and looks at him and tries to tell him.

'' I can't stay, I really can't stay this body won't let me, but there must be a way, we will find a way.''

The last syllable slips away from her and like a cork popping from a champagne bottle she feels herself ejected with force, back across the room into her own space and time. For a moment she watches the woman slump onto the sofa beside John as if she has fainted and then the normal everyday noises from outside the window begin to take over, the strength of the light flickers and fades. When she looks back into the room there is only her own embroidery waiting on the coffee table and the clanging of pots and pans from the kitchen. For a moment she feels a huge sense of loss and desolation. He has gone from her again: but her despair only lasts a moment as she remembers what it was like to actually be human in his world and feel him touch her, it makes the hairs rise on the back of her neck.

The maid comes clattering into the room with a small glass of sherry on a silver platter, an aperitif before luncheon and leaves the tray on the table beside her. There nestling beside the glass is a letter replete with Indian stamps depicting the Viceroy of India and his wife. She reaches out to pick up the letter and understands that this might hold some sort of an answer, the answer that she has been waiting so long for. For here she is at last holding the letter that Madame Blavatsky

134

promised to write to her so many months ago. Her fingers shake as she slits the seal with the letter opener and she can hardly bear to read the eloquent and flowery handwriting as it begins.

The Kingdom of Bhutan May 1875.

My dearest Nellie,

In this country, the greeting is" Namaste" which means I am told

" The God in me, salutes the God in you.". And so, I salute you.

I'm so sorry to have taken all this time to write to you, but travel has been hard and the journey long and exciting. I hope this letter finds you well and not too perplexed at the situation that you find yourself in. One of the reasons it has taken me so long to write to you is that my Master insisted that I travel to this sacred Kingdom to find part of the answer to your conundrum. Bhutan is only accessible with an invitation from the King and as you can imagine it has taken some time and not a small amount of gold to secure this. I'm writing to you from the upper room in the Lamasery, I am not at liberty to give you any more information than this but suffice it to say that the view beneath my gaze is quite extraordinary. Peal upon peak of snow covered mountain top each one of them a God in the eyes of the local population. It is here that the dragon sleeps and in the thaw soon to arrive I will have the honour of travelling these secret passes into the mountains to meet with the most holy of men. You will be anxious for me to turn to your situation which is indeed a most strange and pertinent place to find oneself however I can only answer you in the same way as I have been answered and hope you might come to understand better than I do myself. These words were gleaned in a deep meditative state and I hope they might be some use to you.

"When the light follows you, strength is in the taking

There is only one life here though two are known.'

I can understand that you might find this answer to be too opaque to comprehend but it is given in good faith with every hope that it will point you in the right direction to find your heart's desire.

I would have liked to spend more time indulging myself of your talent as a photographic portrait artist but that was not to be.

With every good luck for the future

Yours Helena Blavatsky.

She reads the letter twice just to make sure that she has understood it and then very carefully puts it back in the envelope. She brings the envelope to her cheek to touch it, it's come from so far away and Helena Blavatsky's words have burnt a hole in her head where they keep drumming around and around.

----What can they mean? And do they mean what she thinks they do? ---

Suddenly she doesn't care anymore she just wants to be normal again and not bothered with all this stuff, suddenly she is young and alone and hungry. She impatiently pulls the blind down on the window to shut out the strong sunlight which is giving her a headache and gathering her embroidery in one hand she marches down the stairs to the dining room calling for her lunch. This afternoon she will develop her film in the garden shed that she has carefully blacked out for a darkroom and forget about love. Why should this happen to her when she is a young woman more of a scientific bent than most? She can think of plenty of the girls at school that would have been more at home in the situation she finds herself in than she is. If what has happened this morning is anything to go by the pursuit of her dream to be with John is going to cause dire consequences for someone and she just isn't sure that she is ready to go through with it yet.

*

Chapter 13
Helena Weinberg Whitstable Summer 1995

She closes the folder that contains all of Nellie's paperwork and printed photos and sighs deeply. She would so much like to have been a part of that era but she supposes that being a historian is the nearest that she will ever get to it. In fact being a historian is probably in a way better than actually living in Victorian England., She can imagine all the excitement and innovation of an era without having to be part of the daily nitty gritty problems, like cholera epidemics and tuberculosis: the incurable and the deadly stuff of everyday life in the nineteenth century that roamed the countryside and ravaged the unsuspecting. She thinks of all the graves in the small graveyard of the town, the deaths of children under the age of two being the most pernicious and upsetting, she thinks of the lack of effective contraception and the way that some poor women had eight of nine children or more with only a few survivors.

The medical establishment of the time were fairly gruesome in their treatment of even some of the most simple diseases and as for the mental health issue, the "asylums" it's best not to dwell too much on what went on in those hidden away Gothic mansions, where screams and cold water baths were the daily norm.. Why if she Helena had been born then she probably wouldn't have any teeth left by now, the craze for sugar from the Indies had been a very effective means to tooth decay. She shivers at the thought of laudanum and dentists chairs running her tongue carefully over her beautiful white teeth and healthy gums.

Of course it must have been fine and dandy to be the lovely Nellie born into a rich family with a fair amount of freedom at her disposal and the determination to be one of the "new women". But how truly awful it must have been to be living on the bread line, subsisting in the cold and hunger of the working classes. She pulls herself inwardly together and focuses on focusing her mind as it slip slaps away from her in all directions. She seems to be getting more and more absentminded and fanciful these days and it's not a good trait for an academic. All of this isn't really something that can concern her now; she has to keep focused on the matter in hand. It's lucky that she can turn her obsessive personality traits to her studies; goodness knows what kind of a person she might have become if she hadn't chosen academia.

She looks around the sun washed sitting room which she has restored as near as possible to how she thinks it might have been back then. She has kept it intentionally stark and pared down as she thinks Nellie might have wanted it to be, the walls are carefully painted in subtle shades of dove grey and faded green. It had been simple to do with the help of a little research and many pots of Farrow and Ball paint. On her carefully painted and then lime washed walls she has hung Nellie's stark portraits of the fishermen going about their business in the harbour. They are hung in the order that she believes Nellie took them, a row of incredible portraits taken with depth and precision and embodying the very epitome of the power of the times. The faces look as if they have been carved by a sculptress the lines and tones of the photos capturing a moment in time that was soon to disappear for ever. Helena never gets tired of staring at the images and wondering about their life stories, of running her fingers gently over the glass to trace the lines on the weathered faces. If she looks up above the fireplace, Nellie herself is staring languidly down at her in a carefully exposed self-portrait that shows the girl in all her intelligent beauty, her hair flowing over her left shoulder and her eyes reaching into the room in a questioning look as if she is trying to solve a riddle or find the key to a hidden treasure. For a second Helena feels a prickle of irritation at the beautiful and mysterious image of her distant relation. The woman was not only talented and a brave pioneer in her field she was alluringly lovely, any man that comes into Helena's life always seems to fall more in love with Nellie than Helena , but she supposes that is par for the course.

She gets up with the lithe flick of a sportswoman's body and walks to the window to gaze out at the choppy surface of the water, her movements are swift and intense and she is twisting her hands together one against the other. The woman is a coiled spring of nervous energy, relaxation is something totally alien to her she is constantly on the move if not physically then in her head her thoughts flying away from her in one direction and then the next . Yet this view of the sea never fails to calm her and today she is waiting rather impatiently it must be said, for this John person to turn up but as yet it's too early to expect him.

Helena has been single now for several years ever since her husband turned out to be gay, that was one for the books but she had tried not to take it personally. In a sense it felt easier to be abandoned for a man rather than another woman. She isn't at all homophobic but she couldn't help feeling slightly ill at ease when thinking about her first love turning out to be more attracted to the same sex rather than to her. She'd had no inkling of it, until it was too late; she was too tied up in her work she supposes. One day he'd simply brought a bottle of wine home and sat her down at the kitchen table and announced that he was leaving her and moving in with his boyfriend. End of. She'd drunk rather a lot of the bottle of wine mumbled at him incoherently for a bit and then locked herself in the bathroom to cry. The next morning when she'd woken up she'd carried on as usual, and tried not to think about it. He had already gone and the divorce was carried out by anonymous lawyers in an exchange of impersonal letters that were sent for her signature and that was that. Occasionally she receives a card from him from some exotic far eastern destination. But she hardly even glances at them just consigns them to the dustbin without a second thought. That was all a long time ago now and the lasting effect had been that she had found it impossible to trust a man or a relationship again and so had become even more engrossed in her work and by nature of that more obsessed with Nellie and her intriguingly mysterious story.

Helena had grown up coming to this house by the sea for her school holidays and vaguely remembers her great grandfather Ed with his whiskers and his pipe. A rather filthy old man at the end of his days, she remembers him as someone who smelt horrid and who refused to get out of his pyjamas. He was the only remaining child of Nellies brother Edmund and his namesake .He smoked a long curling pipe that gave him a rattling cough and made his visitors feel sick. The house had certainly needed a grass root refurbishment including demolishing the rather primitive sanitary arrangements and moving the bathroom upstairs and her father had willingly taken that on. Grand pop Ed had died quite suddenly in the upstairs bedroom relieving the family of the need to put him into one of the large rambling Nursing homes in the Tankerton area or the one overlooking the golf course which is where she Helena would like to be placed when she is old enough. In his will he had skipped a generation and left the house to her.

From the age of about seven she had been fascinated by the woman in the portrait above the fireplace and Nellie had in a sense become her life's work. With some success now it might be added, after the small exhibition in the Dulwich gallery the V& A had decided to put on a retrospective in the autumn, and then a book was promised in which Helena was to edit the journal and Nellies letters and spin some of the story of her life around the pictures in the photo album. It must be said that a great deal has been made of Nellie's intimate acquaintance with the intelligentsia of the times, the Arts and Crafts movement and the Pre Raphaelites of course, but Helena finds that connection intrinsically less interesting than the enigma of the woman herself. Something went on in her life that was very unusual and Helena needs with a burning passion to find out what that something was.

The house itself has always been a kind of haven for her, it seemed somehow to open its arms and surround her with its comforting areas of light and shadow. She often heard soft voices that moved from room to room in the house in the night when she had to use the loo and it was dark and spooky. At that time of night her parents were fast asleep, and sounds of gentle snoring could be heard issuing from their bedroom but the little girl heard whispers of voices that she didn't recognise and banging doors when no one else was there. She had stood immobile at the head of the stairway listening to the banging of pots and pans from the kitchen when she knew that the kitchen was empty. She could hear footsteps clacking over the floorboards, the slam of the back door and the sloshing of water as it was thrown out onto the back yard. None of these sounds were remotely similar to the usual everyday hubbub of her family but she was too little to worry about it and too afraid of being teased by her father to mention it to the grownups.

But none of this had ever been at all threatening to her in any way. She would occasionally see figures at the bottom of the garden, or a woman with long brown hair in tumbling ringlets down her back smiling at her from the end of her bed when she woke in the night. There was a maid in a starched white apron that drifted in and out hanging washing and emptying the pretty fireplaces of ash, all of this had seemed quite normal to her when she was little but from the age of puberty the world sharpened up and she no longer heard the voices or could see the shadows, until yesterday.

She pushes the thought of it away, trying to stifle the sharp remembrance of how in the night she had woken to the sound of laughter coming from the drawing room and the smell of oil lamps. She knows that's what the smell is because she spent a week or so last year living as a Victorian as part of an experiment for her PhD. The thought of the haunting of the house makes her slightly uneasy but in the strong sunlight glinting off the sea this morning she pushes the thought away.

Local cleaning ladies are loathe to be left alone in the house muttering of ''shadow people' 'and such like but Helena prefers to think of it as the former occupants still

141

© Victoria Mosley 2016

somehow in residence and taking care of her. She has certainly never been scared of the house and its murmurs, until now.

For today however she can feel a bubble of anticipation gathering in her stomach, she'd taken more than the usual care this morning with her clothes and had actually added a spot of perfume at her neckline and some mascara from an old dried up tube she'd found in the dressing table drawer.. Silly really, she sort of guesses that this John man must be married and all that is fine but here she is beginning to sound like a desperate old spinster at the age of thirty eight. Maybe she is desperate, her last proper boyfriend had been three years ago and that had petered out rapidly when he had demanded too much of her.

He'd been an alright sort of bloke, she's met him at a concert in South Bank, Southern Indian divorced with two small children that he was seeking help with .That had been the problem really, it isn't that she doesn't like children, she does, it's just that her work is her life and she's not prepared to compromise that for anyone. Anyway she is always too concerned about the woman's side of the story, she had been suspicious of him from the start, and it really seemed to Helena to be cruel that he had decided to leave his wife with two very small children to bring up, on her own. The affair had started to unravel when he had asked her to go flat hunting with him one weekend and she had a paper to write and so had told him that she was busy. He'd objected, called her totally self-obsessed and she had called him needy. A huge dramatic row had ensued which partly was her way out of the relationship. She could have easily diffused it if she had wanted to, but to be honest she'd felt trapped by his affection. Although the sex had been good, she feels a flashback coming on and blushes slightly, and she misses it at times that in itself was exhausting. All that sighing and thumping and body stuff, she screws up her face and smiles remembering.

As a species men are obsessed with sex even when they are too old to have it any more, whereas women can take it

142

or leave it. As for the "love myth" she kind of gets the picture of what that might be, she is sure that she must have been in love sometime but she can't quite recall how it feels.

In fact the human race as a whole is quite exhausting and she'd far rather deal with the dead than the living. At least the dead have an ambiguity about them which can never be fully solved, so she can mostly mould their stories for her own use. That brings her full circle back to Nellie and she opens the folder again, pulling out the strange letter in it addressed to Nellie from none other than the great Theosophist Madame Blavatsky. It had taken her a while to decipher the writing and then she had followed the travels of Blavatsky avidly by reading several of her biographies, but had found no mention of her actually visiting Bhutan although secret journeys into the forbidden kingdom of Tibet are hinted at. This letter and the fact that there is no record of Nellie's existence after the age of twenty one is one of the central mysteries of the story of her Great great Aunt. The only possible explanation that she has come up with is that somehow Nellie left England by boat from Whitstable or Dover to follow Blavatsky to India. It's a nice theory but there is simply no proof for it. Nor is there mention of Blavatsky having a young English photographer as a travelling company anywhere in the minutiae of the documentation of her life

The problem of her vanishing into thin air and the contents of the journal where names of the main characters are written in some kind of code make her job intriguing but difficult. It is obvious from some of the entries in the journal that Nellie was in love, but she refuses to name the man, possibly because he was already married. There is no reason to think that this couldn't have happened to a young girl in Victorian society, it would have been easier for her to mix socially with married men than those that were single. Or perhaps it was one of the sitters for her portraits, but there is no suggestion in any of the prints in Helena's possession that one of the portraits was the mystical lover of the journal. Except for the shadow of a figure in the photo of the summerhouse in Nellie's garden in her house in

143

Sydenham, there is definitely someone there and no mention of who he is but in the bottom right hand corner of the photo is Nellie's signature and two kisses. Just two faint "xx ', that is all but it has always made Helena wonder if this is the mystery love interest.

The tinkling of the front doorbell stops any further thought and instantly her curiosity gets the better of her as she momentarily lingers at the window to catch a first glimpse of the man who she has spoken at length to on the phone. The intensity of his fervour on the subject of her great aunt is slightly worrying but she will soon be able to judge for herself if he is a complete crack pot. His journalistic credentials are certainly impressive although when she talked to him she could discern an intrinsic sadness in the tone of his voice that hinted at some sort of a loss.

The doorbell clangs again, this time more insistently and as if he knows that he is being watched he looks up quizzically to the bay window. Immediately she jumps back and hurries down the stairs to let him in, but not before she has caught a glimpse of a tall grey haired man who must once have been handsome. Who is she kidding? He is still good looking and she feels her heart beat a little louder as she opens the door. She decides to be slightly startled at his presence as if she was just popping out and his presence has surprised her.

Their greetings are swift and formal and within a few minutes she leaves him perusing the photos in the sitting room while she makes him tea. He looks unusually pale and fragile, as if he is recovering from a hard nights drinking, as men sometimes do and she uncharacteristically feels a distinct need to try and take care of him, to make him feel better. This is not like her, why should she care about a stranger in this way even one who is stridently pushing his way into her life as this "John" seems to be doing? Now she thinks about it, it is so uncharacteristic of her usual mode of behaviour as to be decidedly weird.

By the time she has made the tea and returned with the tray stacked high with sugar and biscuits the sitting room is full of the morning's sunlight and he is beginning to look a better colour. They sit side by side on the sofa and she shows him the folder with the most important of Nellie's letters, her unframed photos and her journal that she has gathered together for him to study. But very quickly the intensity of his interest in Nellie, which he can't hide nor does he try to, has an obsessional quality that begins to make her feel more than a little afraid. What is it that he is looking for so intently in the musings of a girl who disappeared more than a hundred years ago? He folds back each of the pages in her journal with an almost reverential quality especially when he reaches the autumn of 1874. He falters and looks at her quickly asking with what he obviously wants to appear to be a nonchalant smile.

'' Helena would it be possible to borrow this for a few days? I'm quite interested in the day to day life of your Great Aunt and I can't really do this justice now. I'll take very great care of it all as I know it is precious archive material, even more so now that you are gaining a certain recognition for your work. I was very impressed with the small show in the Dulwich Art Gallery and I hear that you have just clinched a book deal, for a book on Nellie?''

To emphasise his question he places his hand on top of hers as if it is the most natural thing in the world to do. She feels the heat flowing through him to her, it's a long time since she has been touched in such an intimate manner and she blushes quickly removing her hand with a wary smile.

''Yes, a book is in the offing and I suppose that would be fine for you to borrow it for a short time. You can even take some photocopies if you want to, there is a print shop in the town that can help you with that, I'll point you in the right direction if you like''.

Then she continues with her train of thought while trying to gently glean some information while she tops up their mugs of tea. She has suddenly realised that he knows a lot more about her and her family than she does about him.

'' Tell me how did you first find out about Nellie and what magazine is publishing the article that you are working on?''

He has already mentioned that he owns the former London home of the Weinberg family and she is hoping for an invitation to visit. She has often driven past the house on Sydenham Hill and seen the two black ravens adorning the heavy wrought iron gates but has been loath to enter the long sweeping drive with its imposing cedar trees still intact and ask the occupants for a viewing. But he seems slightly embarrassed by her probing and his answer when it comes isn't particularly convincing.

'' Oh I saw an article by the local historian on the house suggesting that one of the original occupants had been a well thought of woman photographer and immediately became intrigued.. There is only one other noted Victorian photographer who was a woman and Nellie appears to have down some of her early work under the watchful eye of Julia Margaret Cameron but the two diverged quite a bit on what kind of subject was suitable for study. As for the article I work freelance so I will be tooting it around when it's finished. I'm quite happy to give you any mention that you feel appropriate.''

He looks up at her, all pale grey eyes and earnest expression and she is charmed by him. He carefully shuts the journal and puts it to one side turning to the letter with its Indian stamps beneath. There is a reverence in his voice as he tries to read the Blavatsky letter and she is just about to ask him what exactly his article is about when something begins to go very wrong. The sunlight in the room becomes blinding and although the room is warm she is sure of it, she feels deathly cold. She looks up at John but his face appears to be receding down a long tunnel away from her and although his lips are moving she can't hear his voice. The distance between them gets further and further and then suddenly she has the impression that she is sitting just below the ceiling looking down on him from a great height. This can't be so but it is definitely happening and yet there is still the figure of a woman beside him, but it can't be her can it for she is up here watching.

Helena looks down at her hands but can see nothing, and then she notices that the woman on the sofa talking to John has masses of dark hair tumbling around her shoulders. He says something and she laughs and in that moment she looks up and Helena can't help but cry out as she realises who it is. But then everything is coming rushing towards her again and she is falling, she is falling and tightness constricts her breath, Johns face regains its sharp outlines it is back in focus and she is there beside him on the sofa.

'' What is going on? She gasps, unable to help herself.

''I thought I saw someone here with you that wasn't me; I mean I think I have seen a ghost ''.

With that she bursts into tears and he gathers her in his arms handing her a carefully ironed handkerchief as he does so. She feels immediately better but then notices that he isn't contradicting her, he isn't telling her that she imagined it all and with huge eyes brimming with shock and disbelief she pulls herself away from him and asks.

'' I wasn't imagining it at all was I? Something strange is going on here and I think it's about time you came clean with me and told me what this is all about. ''

*

Chapter 14
John Whitstable Summer 1995

He sits in the pub staring out to sea a plate of barely touched scampi and chips in front of him which he randomly picks at without really noticing the automatic action of food to mouth. It's in the swallowing of the lumps that he has to concentrate otherwise he knows that he will choke on the food and suffocate. Something in his mind switches at the thought and he comes back to himself and looks around. The interior of the pub is brown, dank nondescript much as he'd noticed earlier in the day. There is a chalk board advertising an evening's live music with a band called "Nagasaki" and he somehow finds that appropriate.as a descriptive term for this morning's goings on.

The trouble is he is beginning to feel very guilty and more than slightly out of control. For the first time in his experience his life is spiralling away from him way out of his comfort zone and he is avalanching terrifyingly towards a destination where life and death have switched faces and yet both are grinning crazily at him. He had to get out of that house, suddenly the bright sunlight the crying woman the scent of Nellie in the warm sunlit sitting room had been too much to bear. There were questions he couldn't hope to answer and feelings that would take time to unravel. Added to which on swinging by the hotel there was a long garbled fax from Cecilia in Paris asking him to ring her, the words had a precise air of desperation in them that sent his heart plummeting down through his stomach to land somewhere underground and unbeknown to him. Quite simply the whole thing was becoming less delightful and scarier than he cared to admit.

Like a teenager with a new hobby he had been dazzled by the whole experience of loving someone or something unattainable but perhaps it isn't unobtainable after all; at least not in the way that he thought, but the price is so high that he is not sure that he wants to pay it. Even more disquieting is the thought that he doesn't have the choice and that the decision for all this "love " business has slipped out of his hands and is coming at him like an unstoppable freight train with terrifying power and velocity

He sighs and slugs back his pint crossing to the bar to order another, the beer is bitter and slightly sickly but it's all that he can think of doing to numb the encroaching terror that he feels. He's going to have to go back to the hotel and ring Cecilia in a moment there is no getting around that. His sense of duty forces him in that direction but first curiosity has its hands around his throat and he is itching to just take a look at Nellie's diary especially the short entry he had noticed on Halloween, the day that he'd first met her .

Sitting down again and pushing the plate away he runs a hand through his hair and grimaces as he recalls the garbled explanation he had given poor Helena about his former experience with Nellie. It had sounded like something straight out of a B movie, he'd mumbled about lights and noises and figures in the distance. Well he just couldn't tell her the truth; tell her that for a few moments there in the sitting room, her body had been possessed by a girl that seemed to be living both a hundred years ago and in the present. Anyway he really doesn't want to think about it, it's not as if he has conjured it all up like a black magician. It has arrived of its own volition and he is as much an observer as anyone else.

Carefully he opens Nellie's diary, it's mostly written in pencil and the marks are faint in places. She talks about her photos , the trips to Crystal Palace , some gossip about advances made to her , obviously unwanted by someone she describes as "Sir S". He holds the little book up to the light at the window to get a better view and finds the entry for Halloween 1874.

149

Last night Mama had the strangest "at home" yet. She invited the notorious Madame Blavatsky for the evening to hold one of her séances in the dining room. A few of our close neighbours attended, at first all was normal as one would expect apart from the glass between us whizzing across the table surprisingly fast. Everything was middling to nonsense until it was my turn to ask the questions. When asked who, I was to fall in love with the glass flew off the table and smashed. Then I did something quite unlike myself and fainted. My sleep was full of nightmares and this morning I have had quite a headache. After luncheon, I went for a walk in the woods to clear my head, through the tunnel that Papa built for me and came across two delightful little boys playing down by the old folly. Their handsome father was not far behind them. I decided to play a trick on him and took the boys up through the tunnel which of course leads back to my summerhouse, but then something went awry and I found myself alone, the boys quite vanished. Curious. I must find out in which part of the neighbourhood they live in as they did mention that their house was a big house on the hill. I cannot recall that any of our immediate neighbours has the handsome stance of this man.

His breath quickens as he recognises his first meeting with the girl in the woods and for a second his colour rises as he remembers just how she had managed to make him feel in that fleeting glimpse of her. He goes to turn the page and notices that his hand is shaking his brain almost in a state of flight as the phantasm that he has lived with becomes someone else's reality in plain black and white written a hundred years before his birth. There is no point even trying to work out how this has happened, but it has and for the first time he feels more than a little scared and a chill comes over him, he shivers as the door to the pub opens and then shuts behind a gaggle of tourists that clatter in.. He looks around the pub as if searching for unseen eyes that might be watching him, but no, no one is the slightest bit interested in the tall grey haired man with an anorak who is hunched in the corner. He stares up and out of the window, he can see Nellie's house quite clearly, the little pale blue gate the shingle path and the big bay window where an hour ago he had held her in his arms. But it wasn't quite that simple was it? Yes he had held her, but at the time she had possessed someone else's body. He shivers again and hugs his coat around him almost afraid to read the next entry written on November 1st of the same year. He is fairly sure what it is going to tell him but he reads it anyway.

November 1st 1874

Today the strangest of things happened and I am quite frightened by it although I might think myself a coward to say so. I was taking pictures by the summerhouse just experimenting with natural light when through my lens I noticed a shadow inside the little wooden house itself. On-going into the shed the man I saw in the woods yesterday was kneeling down by the fireplace. At first my heart beat faster and I was glad to see him although I did wonder what he was doing trespassing on our property but then there was an insubstantial air about him, too much light and space between us and he didn't seem to notice me at all until I bent over him and touched him. That in itself was astonishing he felt like paper, thin insufficient as if my fingers could snap him like a cracker and then he looked at me with very grey eyes and I knew his name was John and he knew me as Nellie. It only lasted a split second but I have no doubt that love has come to call in the strangest of ways. Immediately I felt dizzy and when I came to he was gone and all was back to its normal self. The only explanation that I can find is that it is something to do with Madame Blavatsky's séance, I will write to her directly tomorrow and ask to visit and see if she can furnish an answer to my questions of who is this man and where does he come from? She is the only person that I can trust to talk about this with, anyone else might think that I am insane and lock me up in the nearest lunatic asylum.

As he goes to shut the book his fingers feel a sharp edge on the inside of the back cover against the palm of his hand. Puzzled he looks down and notices that the back cover seems to be thicker and a different colour from the inside front cover. His fingers feel around the corner of the paper which seems to have come slightly unglued. Holding his breath he carefully peels back the thick sheet from its stiff binding and he finds a folded sheet of paper within between the binding and the paper. It is exactly the same size as the small leather book, with shaking hands he eases out the small square and unfolds it. He gasps and the room seems to fall away from him as adrenaline opens every pore. In his hand he holds a drawing, a detailed pencil sketch of a man. He stares at it mesmerised at the face that stares back at him, there is no question of a doubt in his mind that he is staring at a portrait of his own face. It is a pencil drawing and beautifully carried out, light and dark shading provide an accurate representation of him, and he strains his eyes to decipher two initials in the bottom left hand corner. A very faint outline of two capital letters, an *H* and a *B* carefully interlaces. He guesses that the letters stand for Helena Blavatsky, but how on earth? With that thought his mind snaps into a million shards of unconnected data and for a moment he grips onto the edge of the table to stop himself falling into a void that he feels reaching out for him, He takes a deep breath and simply understands that he can't possibly begin to understand any of this so why bother trying?

John shuts the little leather book with a snap and shoves it deep into his pocket, the drawing he folds carefully and places in the inner panel of his wallet. This Helena didn't know of its existence, so as far as he is concerned it obviously belongs to him. It is as if Nellie has sent him a present across the vast eclipse of time. His mind can't conceive of how the drawing originated or how they managed to capture such an accurate resemblance of him. Linear thinking has no place here and he is beginning to let go and let himself feel that he belongs in the drift of this; the newest of the Universe's miracles. He walks to the bar and pays and then without a further thought he walks back to his car.

He has to get out of here, he needs to clear his head and Cecilia's plaintive missive has made him feel guilty about giving up on his marriage so easily. The boys are fine his mother has moved into Raven House and is looking after them with the au pair but he owes Cecilia at least the courtesy of his presence. If she is asking him for help she really must be in trouble. His thoughts are a whorl with images of the three women, Cecilia the way he had seen her the last time in the café in Paris, Nellie in the woods that first day the sun a bright halo of angel dust in her hair and Helena this morning crushed and confused in his arms. He's not an emotional man but all of a sudden he has emotions running through him like water in a water wheel, and he feels his mind tilting towards the rapids.

As he is so near the channel he doesn't think twice and simply heads the car in the direction of Dover, he'll ring the B&B later and explain that an emergency has arisen. As for Nellie he wants to put some space between them, she looks so beautiful and harmless yet what happened this morning has scared him. He is being stalked by a ghost who is in love with him. The whole idea is ridiculous except that it is extremely real and a large part of it is of his own making. As he reaches the ticket office and navigates the car onto the ferry he feels a sense of relief come over him, as if he is escaping a danger that is imminent and threatening. The little leather journal is still in his pocket and as he places his fingers on it the scent of summer and light and that soft subtle perfume that he has come to know as Nellie wafts around him and comforts him.

He's alright, it's all going to be alright, maybe there will be some possible solution; maybe his imagination is just playing tricks on him, perhaps he'll confide in Cecilia and see what she has to say. The motion of the boat lulls him into a light sleep, he is huddled in a comfortable corner seat in one of the quieter rooms and the engine hums a background noise in his dreams. He dreams of being on a train, a train rather like the Orient Express, he is wearing a dinner jacket and a liveried waiter is pouring the wine. A beautiful woman is leaning across the table at him, her arm swathed in a cream kid glove with buttons, he looks up expecting to see Nellie, but the woman sitting across from him with her jet necklace and diamonds at her wrist turns to him and he starts back in fear. Where he was expecting to see a pair of huge brown eyes and a lavish smile, there is nothing. The thing that is leaning towards him from across the table has no face and he wakes to the churning motion of the cross channel ferry with a start, his mouth dry , his hands in a cold sweat . What he had thought of as a love affair is turning into a bad dream with a trail of broken promises stretching out behind him and the future grinning at him with the only certainty being that he is uncertain of everything. Where once was the concrete certitude of his life , his marriage, his job all has fallen away to a diaphanous sea built on an infatuation which has no substance , unless he allows it to, and he is beginning to realize just what the repercussions of that might be.

*

Part Three

"You think the shadow is the substance."

Rumi

Chapter 15
Place de Vendôme Paris

Summer 1995

Cecilia sits in the café looking out over the square and stares fixedly up towards the windows of her apartment. She stifles a nervous yawn and shivers hoping above hope that the windows will stare back at her as empty as they are supposed to be; as blank and impersonal as all the other rows of windows in the building. She feels a nervous tick twitch at the corner of her mouth and puts up a finger to try and calm it but in vain, she has to admit that she is feeling seriously rattled. Louis is away thank goodness, he has been gone for a week now. His internship at the newspaper office is over which has meant more freedom from him so his father has sent him off to look at a new coffee plantation in Ethiopia; and the communication links between Paris and Addis Ababa are tenuous to say the least. It's been more than a little strained between them recently, his young man's sense of ambition and terminal navel gazing have driven her crazy, every other conversation punctuated with existential angst centring on his role in the world, his role in her life and of course whether or not he needs to change his hair dresser . She hates to admit it even to herself but she has missed the calm nonchalance of her husband, that independent aloofness that used to drive her crazy when they lived together. The English reserve and emotional tautness of John which is outwardly reflected in his stern good looks and the way he carries himself, so upright and unassuming, she bites her lip remembering just what she is throwing away by divorcing him,. Never mind about all that now she hasn't really got the time or energy to be sentimental about her past, today she just needs John here with her now more than she ever did before.

Louis is a lovely boy he still gives her all the passion that was missing in her marriage and of course she stills loves him, or "lusts" him. Which is it? Does it really matter? The sex is fantastic and he continually thinks up new things to please her, the sort of things that her catholic upbringing hasn't prepared her to imagine, erotica of a kind that makes her tingle just to think about it .But his obsessive jealousy of her work, her friends and even the rare phone calls and visits she has with her boys have started to take a toll. There is going to be no way of easily escaping him though even if she ever wants to, she knows that now.

--- That's if she ever really needed to ---

Louis is very clear about some things and one of them is that they are in this relationship together for the duration; he can't wait for the divorce to be final so that he can marry her. That will be the next sticking point because she is equally sure that she never ever wants to get married again. Today she is beginning to think she has given up rather a lot for this love affair of hers. He has taken over her apartment in exactly the same way that he has taken over her life, completely and dramatically, marking his territory like a terrier.

Then last week when he was called away for work the apartment itself had started to play up. It's the only way she can think of describing the things she has been seeing, and she's beginning to be worried that she is losing her mind or perhaps is in the grip of a "possession" in the Catholic sense of the word. Her early childhood years where she went to school in the local convent has left images of the devil and fire licking hell lodged deep in her subconscious and after last night's little episode she just can't rid herself of the notion that this is some kind of divine retribution for her sins.

---The sin of adultery. ---

She knows logically that it is ridiculous to think this way, in this day and age but her parents haven't really made things easy for her; it is fairly obvious that they regard her divorce from John as a failure on her part. The De la Croix family just don't get divorced, yes have a love affair if you must,

157

French upper class society allows for that, but marriage is sacrosanct.

She has tried in vain to explain to them that it is John who is so adamant that he wants a "clean break" as he calls it, but they have no time for this sort of solution. There have been rows, there have been tears and at the moment there is eerie silence between the daughter and her parents. The battle ranks of her parents' marriage are drawn together and they are determined to exclude her in the vague hope that she will come into line and stop all this nonsense. They are obviously hoping that she will go back to her children and forget about her career and her love affair with the "pretty little pimp" as her mother refers to Louis. For the first time she can see why their marriage is so successful, they are simply emotionally brutal in their attitude to " failure" of any sort.

Another good reason why she has asked John to come and see her today is his no nonsense Anglican atheism when it comes to anything vaguely "New Age", he will be able to convince her how silly she is being. She's desperate for a drink even though it is only midday, her heart is racing with unwanted adrenaline and she needs to still it.

She orders a carafe of the house red, maybe if she gets slightly drunk she will be able to handle this better. John called her from the port earlier in the day and she has assured him that he can spend the night in the spare room at Place Vendome. After all until recently it had been as much his apartment as it was hers, but first they'll eat and swap stories, for when he called her he also sounded fraught and as if he had something to confide to her. Perhaps this wonderful lover that he is so besotted with that he has refused to disclose the identity of to her isn't all that she is cracked up to be.

The café fills up and all around her are the normal early evening noises of couple greeting couple, she watches them idly noticing the nuances between each, but soon a voice at her elbow brings her back to the present with a jolt, it's

John. He's looking pale and strained and for the first time she notices the signs of age are creeping up on him. His hairline has receded more than the last time she saw him and the wisps of grey above his ears are more pronounced, the rest of his hair is no longer dark brown but now definitely salt and pepper. His skin looks tired and his jawline has a saggy edge to it where before it was sharply defined. He bends to kiss her cheek.

" Ceci, hello, what's up?"

She smiles and gestures to the chair beside her, and they sit side by side and elbow to elbow and for a moment sip wine and say nothing. The rancour that was so evident between them in the spring is not there anymore, like an old married couple they are relaxed about letting silence settle between them without finding it uncomfortable. They look at each other occasionally and smile and then eventually when the waiter has been to the table twice with his notebook in hand and they have ordered the set menu John turns to her.

" So really how are you? You look tired, lovely of course but tired none the less".

She gives a laugh and a shrug and then runs her slim fingers through her hair and looks at him.

"Well I'm not really sure where to start, but I think that I'm being possessed or something."

He tries not to look panic stricken at her words but he involuntarily he grips his wine glass even more tightly and says nothing waiting for her to continue, which she does after another glug of wine. She's surprised that he is so obviously perturbed by her statement. She half expected him to look bored and poo hoo the whole idea of nefarious presences in the flat immediately and his state of anxiety only succeeds in making her heart beat even faster and her palms feel sweaty. She reaches for her wine glass and lets the wine sink into her system which it does quickly as she can't remember having eaten today. She wills it to blur the edges of her fear, round out

159

the panic and then she takes a deep breath and continues slowly.

" I've always heard noises in the flat and thought nothing of it , I just thought that it was old plumbing and the floorboards stretching or warping or whatever floor boards do, but last night something else happened."

She stops to light a cigarette and he moves away from the smoke but says nothing. Cecilia has always been an occasional smoker except when she was pregnant with the boys; she takes a deep lungful and continues.

" I woke up in the middle of the night and went to switch on the bedside light but it didn't work, I tried the wall light but again nothing, so I thought"

----- Oh bugger the trip switch has gone----

I opened the door to go to the kitchen and sort it all out. It was then that I saw light flickering under the sitting room door and I could hear voices. I was still half asleep so didn't really think about it just went and stood outside the door to listen and there were two women talking in French, both of them with accents that told me that they weren't born French. One had a strong burr to her voice she sounded Russian or Eastern European and the other was obviously English. The light under the door was flickering as if from a fire, but how could it be a fire its summer and anyway no one has lit a fire in the fireplace for years?".

She stifles a sob and blows her nose noisily, John says nothing but she notices that he won't actually meet her eyes, and she continues talking while twisting her white linen napkin in her hands.

" It gets weirder, anyway I opened the door and looked in and at first I could only see the fire in the grate, but then I noticed that the room had one wall that was full of books, I wasn't looking at our sitting room I was looking into a study and

160
© Victoria Mosley 2016

in a large Victorian chair facing me was a corpulent woman with grey hair talking to someone that I couldn't see. ''

She takes a good slug of wine and the waiter brings their starter, goat's cheese salad with beetroot and red onion chutney. For a few minutes they eat in silence, John breaks bread and still he says nothing except to nod for her to continue her story when she is ready. She pushes the plate away and stares off into the middle distance trying to capture the essential essence of the scene she is trying to convey to him, she wipes her mouth lights another cigarette and continues.

'' The thing is, it was very cold inside the room, as if it was winter , there were thick drapes across the window and the woman I could see was wearing a heavy shawl across her shoulders as if she was cold. The other woman, I had the impression that she was younger , was in a high backed chair with her back to me so I couldn't see her at all, but she had a young girl's voice and she was the one with the English accent. So I tried to walk into the room to ask them what the hell they were doing in my apartment in the middle of the night, ludicrous I know but somewhere my brain was trying to make sense of it. I couldn't enter the room, it was as if a force was holding me back, or I was watching a play that I had no part of and no access to. After a few minutes I began to shiver violently, the door knob flew out of my hands and the door slammed violently propelling me back into the hallway and that was it. I don't remember getting back into bed but when I woke this morning it was all still crystal clear in my mind''.

He pours her more wine and the waiter clears the plates then brings them steak frites, Cecilia is expecting John to laugh or tell her she is being ridiculous or something,, anything but the silence that is looming over the table like a vacuum. It sucks them into an unreachable place where the white table cloth feels like the huge expanse of the frozen wastes of Antarctica. Still he says nothing although several times he looks like he might be about to. He briefly leans across the table and grips her hand sympathetically but then seems to concentrate

© Victoria Mosley 2016

solely on the plate in front of him. He watches her from beneath his lashes spearing one chip after another with single minded dedication, yes he watches her glumly as she twists her napkin into knots between her fingers.

She has lost weight there is no doubt of that , and she looks wild eyed almost hysterical, he is going to have to say something to calm her down but how much of the truth should he tell her? How much has she a right to know? He might think that all this could be some kind of kinetic coincidence the fact that Cecilia is suddenly having a nineteenth century visitation in the night: but he knows that it can't be. He had stopped for a coffee in Calais and because he was itching to know what else was in the little leather journal that was burning a hole in his pocket he'd flicked through it briefly. One thing that had stood out in the early entries was Nellie's description of her visit to Paris just before Christmas 1874. She booked an appointment with the Madame to try and glean some help from the famous Madame Blavatsky. She had needed to make sense of their meeting as much as he does now and Blavatsky was the only person that could throw light on it for her.

The Victorian's were much less phased by the possibility of a ''spirit'' world than the present agnostic culture of the twentieth century. That was mainly because they had to deal with death on a daily basis and it hadn't yet been blocked out of the collective psyche. Nellie had briefly mentioned the location of the house that she visited and stayed in several nights after the meeting. It was all very brief, she had been ill of course, some sort of flu that had later become serious, but he can vividly remember his heart give a skip and a beat when she mentioned that her destination in Paris was the beautiful Place Vendome.

Is he supposed to believe that it's another twist of fate that the apartment they were given as wedding present by Cecilia's parents is part of the house that the Madame lived in when she was in Paris? It can't be a coincidence, somehow the past and the present are so fused together that it is inevitable

162

that this should happen. He is beginning to see that now, even though he is loath to admit it; but that doesn't help with the very real problem that his wife is being haunted by the life of his lover. He can't say that it's the "former" life of Nellie because he isn't sure how these things work, can she really be dead if he has touched her and smelt her and just the other day watched her inhabit the body of someone else?

Recently he has come across various semi scientific theories in the press by a man called Rupert Sheldrake that could provide a framework of sorts. Following on from Jung's archetypes which we all have individually and also experience in the collective unconscious Sheldrake supposes a theory that there are such things as "fields of memory", that exist outside the confines of the brain. Could different time periods co-exist simultaneously in just such a framework with some sort of catalyst like the Blavatsky séance aligning them so that they overlap?

He sighs and pushes his plate away, these questions have no answers so there isn't much point asking them, he just needs to deal with the dangerously volatile state that Cecilia is in now. Sort her out; perhaps take her back to London with him, always depending of course on the situation with her lover. He can't tell her about Nellie that's obvious she looks pretty shaky and the telling of his story might just push her over the edge.

---- Whatever edge she might be near, how can he tell anymore, nothing is as it seems and everything is falling from his grasp into a non-specific void that is orchestrated by obsession-----?

He leans over and removes the napkin from her fingers which are sticky with sweat, he touches her gently as he would touch a child and tells her.

"Come let's go for a walk, it's beautiful out there and the worst of the crowds have gone, Paris is so lovely after the fifteenth of July when everyone goes "en vacances' let;s walk a bit it'll make you feel better, we'll take a coffee in St Germain and watch the tourists."

A wave of heat hits them as soon as they open the restaurant door and Cecilia coughs and then smiles up at him apologetically.

"Sorry ,I always tell myself not to be in Paris in the summer , it's so dusty and polluted nowadays but I just can't help staying here , the city is magic in its own way when everyone leaves it to go to the seaside., let's just meander and see where it takes us. I just want to get as far away from the apartment as possible. "

She glances nervously behind her at the long elegant windows that face down into the Place, as if they will somehow dislodge and follow her, but the windows look back at her empty as they should be and she relaxes her shoulders in relief. She links her arm through John's and they walk along like this for a full fifteen minutes or so saying nothing. They're happy to be part of the anonymous crowd of tourists swaying gently through the city in the intense heat wafting off the pavement after the day's sun. Eventually as the sliver of a moon rises above the water they reach the river and stop to listen to music floating over the water. All along the bank groups of people have stopped to watch dancers who are swirling and dipping in time to tango music blaring from ghetto blasters at their feet. The women have exactly the right kind of heels on their shoes, black skirts and red flowers in their hair. The men wear high waist trousers and have slicked back hair. For a moment it is as if they've stepped into another world and again the idea buzzes through John's mind of interconnecting synapse of time requiring literal attention in the here and now. But this is not a mirage, this is happening in front of them and in time the music stops, the crowds drift away and he is left with the dregs of a failed marriage languishing tiredly on his shoulder and a problem as to what to do next. Cecilia solves it for him, she points to a nearby hotel with a liveried footman outside.

'' Let's just book into a hotel, we can afford it and I don't want to go back to the flat tonight, I need to sleep and so do you by the looks of you. We can have a twin bedroom and unless you've started to snore you won't disturb me.''

Tugging at his arm she leads him through the revolving doors and before he knows it they've ordered a bottle of whisky and some tea from room service and are lying on their allotted beds watching an old Brigit Bardot film on TV. In the flickering light he glances over at his wife and smiles, she's still his wife, the final divorce the decree absolute hasn't come through yet and he is glad that it hasn't. Somewhere in this mess of things they seem to have found a common theme this evening and he sees her again as he must have done when he first met her. Her eyes alight by something that interests her and a languid stretch in her body that he once found so fascinating. He settles down beside her and refuses to think about anything but the film that is passing in front of their eyes on the flickering screen. He reaches into his jacket pocket and feels for his wallet, removing it and placing it under his pillow. Partly for safekeeping, and partly because he wants to be near his drawing, his present from another world. Tomorrow he will start thinking about what to do but for now let it all pass through him, for now he is glad to be alive and simply human with all that that really means.

*

Chapter 16
Nellie September 1875

The summer has slipped gently into a cooler autumn, the holiday crowd and day trippers have departed for another year the railway platform is no longer crowded with Londoners clutching parasols and packed lunches, and Nellie knows that it's time for her to depart too. She has a list of pressing commissions to fulfil back in Sydenham and the promise of a show before Christmas at the elegant Beauberry House overlooking Dulwich Park if she can get enough of her photos framed in time. She has had letters from Rossetti urging her to return to town he has promised several sitters for her, but every morning she wakes up in her little French bed in her pale grey bedroom listening to the sound of the sea and she knows that she doesn't want to leave yet.

This summer she has created some of her best work, a new form of camera has enabled her to take her pictures with quicker exposures and therefore her long suffering subjects in her morning sojourns to the harbour have been relieved of their duty of standing still for minutes at a time. She has captured the calm weathered features of her favourite fishermen and the squalls of youngsters roped in to mend the nets. She's been made welcome in blackened kitchens by their wives and has helped to tend the children when fever strikes. All the inhabitants of the town know and like her and she feels more at home here than she does anywhere else, or if she is honest *nearly* anywhere else.

She has walked by the bathing huts each morning and at times she has sneaked out at first light to bathe without anyone seeing her. She undresses carefully in her beach hut, a grey one that belongs to the house, number 33 to be exact, and then she dares to venture forth in her slip. It just so happened that as a child the cook's daughter, a sun kissed girl two or three years older than the siblings had volunteered to teach them how to swim one summer. It was thought prudent after their stowaway escapade on the oyster boat just in case the next time they ran away to sea they weren't so lucky .As it was everyone knew that the Captain who had found them as red cheeked red handed stowaways had threatened to throw them to the seagulls the next time he caught them on his boat without permission, though she did think that he was joking. Nellie was very glad indeed to learn the art of floating on her back or striking out towards the deep swell where the seals play. Mama hadn't objected although it was highly irregular for Victorian ladies to know how to swim. Their huge ballooning bathing suits always threatened to pull them down at any moment if they ventured out more than knee high in the water, but Nellie has never bothered with one of those, she simply wears her cotton camisole and hopes nobody sees her and although she is now the age of twenty one she still can't think of herself as older than a teenager.

Once she has got used to the chill of the water she lets herself float in the incoming tide, her limbs languid and weightless her mind emptied of its questions. Her hair streams out behind her and if anyone had been watching they would have thought her very beautiful, but no one sees her except the pale sliver of a setting moon and the red streaks of the rising sun placing its stamp on the high, soon to be blue cerulean sky.

The house is waiting for her when she returns damp and tingling, her toes slightly blue with cold, and yet she never knows *which* house it will be. Mostly it is the house she has known since childhood but lately it seems that more and more often on returning from her morning swims she finds herself in Helena's world and yet John is nowhere to be seen. She lets herself in listens carefully to the silence and registers the faint humming in her ears that tells her that she is on the edge of that other world, Helena's world but more importantly John's world. She has decided that she needs to know as much about it as

167

possible about the other woman but the only way to do this is to "become" Helena. Swiftly she pours herself a glass of milk from the pitcher cooling in the outside pantry and pads up the stairs barefoot leaving wet footprints on the stair runner. Vigorously she rubs her hair with a towel, its length reaching down to her hips and impossible to dry in any kind of a hurry. The light is bouncing around her, ebbing and flowing prickling with anticipation and below the sitting room she can hear the sound of footsteps and the faint echo of music.

The pull of the music answers a pull in her blood and with a mounting air of fear and excitement she finishes dressing and slips silently down the stairs into the cosy snug. Opening the door she is flooded with light and sound and the potent image of Helena sitting in front of a machine by the window typing. A stirring in the atmosphere as if fields of resonance are opening between them and the light between her and the woman in the window pulsates with expectancy. Helena turns with a quizzical expression on her face, holding a hand to her head as if she has a headache coming on, but Nellie doesn't hesitate, the magnetic pull of the other woman is too much to resist.

She is beginning to crave the confining pleasure of this morphing sequence, this blending totally into another in an almost God like bliss, that really is the only way she can describe it. What was at first strange and terrifying has become addictive in the way that she has seen her mother crave laudanum or her father a strong whisky on his return from work. But that belittles the experience, as when two become one over time and space it is more like a love affair than anything she has ever experienced and she is beginning to wonder if she can do without it. The feeling it gives her is akin to some of the dreams she has just before waking when she is walking in the sunlit garden with John and then his hands are around her waist and he is kissing her and she is melting into his kiss, and then she wakes up still tingling , her body flooded with warmth .

She shakes the distracting thought of him from her mind and glides across the interim space between them. For a second it seems as if Helena looks her straight in the eyes, but it must be a trick of the light for she doesn't think that the woman actually sees her. No, this is all under Nellie's control and she justifies it to herself by telling herself that she is conducting research in the knowledge of John's world so that she can eventually be closer to him, but she knows in her heart of hearts that this isn't true. There is another reason which she can't admit to herself, not yet anyway.

Taking her last breath and holding it she slips into Helena as she would slip into an evening dress, the feeling is now soft, silky, sumptuous caressing. Nellie has never had a lover but this feeling that she gets as she slides into the muscle bone and flesh of the other woman is how she imagines it would feel to be touched by a lover. Her vision blurs for a second and then she is looking out at a different world through a new pair of eyes and it is all terrifyingly new and uncharted and yet she knows exactly what to do. For she has gained in an instant all the knowledge that is an intrinsic part of Helena, all the memories that the other woman cherishes and all the feelings that she has ever felt. It comes to Nellie like the heady rush of a waterfall filling her to bursting with a new kind of life, a life where she feels true freedom for the first time. For no one can tell her what to do or where to go. She finds her fingers on the keyboard of what her brain now tells her is a computer keyboard and she sees that Helena is engaged in writing a letter or email as she calls it to John. Her eyes scan the print and a burst of what can only be described as jealousy runs through her, and then she sees that Helena is simply inviting him to come down at Halloween and watch the fireworks out on one of the Oyster barges moored outside the harbour. She smiles when she sees this as it is one of the delights that she remembers as a child and it makes her feel safer to know that one hundred years later the same traditions are still being upheld. She examines herself carefully then gets up and walks to the window.

At first she could only manage to maintain "the merger" as she likes to think of it for seconds at a time but gradually those seconds turned to minutes and today she feels confident in thinking that she can take a look at her surroundings without worrying about the giddy feeling that she always gets before she finds herself back with herself. Outside the beach is very similar to how it always was except that the people walking along it look very different and there are no visible signs of the fishing fleet that she is so used to seeing out her own window. She wonders what has become of them all, and looks over to the pub which is exactly where it should be, yet there are wooden tables outside and a group of people milling around in the most outrageous of clothes, she can hardly bear to look at the ridiculous things the women are wearing. Yet if she looks down at her own legs it makes her gasp to see her legs clothed in the trousers that Helena wears. Along the edge of the beach are pounding figures of the occasional runner and she wonders where they are running to and why.

. A loud ringing coming from the corner of the room startles her, but she ignores it and turns instead to look at her own portrait another Nellie portrait, above the fireplace. She steps closer to stare at it and catches sight of her own face in the mirror that hangs just to the side of the fire. She peers closely, it looks like her but doesn't it's almost as if her features won't stay still as if Helena is pushing her way back in. That's when she begins to feel fuzzy about things;

--- The unsettling knowledge that she is herself looking at herself and yet she isn't, --

Causes a huge knot of fear to lodge in her stomach, and then she is losing grip on it all again, Helena's body seems to shrug her off as she would discard a winter overcoat and she is stuck in the interim blackness of it all, and then she is falling falling falling.

She wakes up with a thumping headache on the rug in front of the fireplace in her own sitting room, and for a moment she lies there stunned looking out the window where she can see a line of geese flying in a V across the smooth calm silvery veil of the sea. She takes a deep breath and tries to move but can't, her limbs feel leaden and she's deathly cold. The cook finds her like this when bringing in the morning coffee, her eyes are wide open but she seems unable to speak. Fearing some sort of seizure the doctor is called and she is piled back into bed with blankets and hot bricks to warm her. Gradually after half an hour she comes to herself, her eyes focus on the room around her and she begins to shiver violently, she has a fever and the rest of the day and the next night she hovers between consciousness and delirium.

The visions come thick and fast and there is nothing she can do to stop them, sometimes they hover at the end of the bed playing games with the light and she knows that she is only seeing things which aren't really there. But as the morning fades to afternoon her strength fades and more and more she tumbles helter skelter into the gap she has created in time which looms like a windy corridor pulling her down its whispering expanses.

The fever drips into the sheets soaking them, her hair is stuck to her forehead which is shiny with sweat and Nellie tosses and turns in the grips of her uncharted journey of the soul. The fever acts as a centrifugal force spinning her out into the realms of delirium where she has nothing but her love of John to hold onto. The cook and the parlour maid like efficient crew members run up and down the stairs with cooling tisanes and herb packed sponges to wash her body down with, Cook mutters under her breath about the ills of Nellie's bathing regime and how she always knew this was going to happen.

-----Just a matter of timer, silly girl , worrying us all like this, I've told her before that these mornings are too cold, to be out there swimming in that freezing sea. She should have stopped the sea bathing at the end of August like all the decent people do and now look at her------

Her voice drones on and on as she wrings out the sponges and replaces the crumpled pillow case with a fresh laundered one smelling of lavender straight from the airing cupboard. She pushes back the streaks of hair from Nellie's brow and can't help shedding a few silent tears as she watches the girl heave and shake in her delirium.

The young parlour maid is wide eyed and frightened. She likes the uniqueness and vigour of Nellie, who is loved in the small seaside town by all the fishermen and their wives for her kindness and beauty. She is only young and has never seen anyone this sick before and the things that Nellie she is saying with her cracked lips and the look in those wide black empty staring eyes of hers. The young girl crosses herself and tries not to think of her bible stories, those stories of possession and the devil.

----Why the Madame is a good girl, everyone knows that she is, she certainly doesn't deserve this kind of sickness. -----

As the afternoon wallows on towards twilight, a gigantic red sunset spreads out over the mud flats beyond the window. A portentous sun the locals call it fearing that it foretells of some disaster to come. Down here folk often let superstition take over their hazy reasoning when something untoward takes over and this sun is hovering for far longer than usual before it sinks to the flat horizon of the sea. It leaves pink pearly streaks of light to slowly disappear in the encroaching opaqueness of the night and the twilight is full of the call of the starlings as they flock to settle for the night. Small posies of wild flowers are left at the little grey gate leading in to the garden to wish the girl well. Her lips are bleeding now, harsh gashes in the lamp light and her hair sticks like glue to her brow, and still she mutters her eyes moving rapidly under their glued shut lids.

She is in a place now where none can reach her , it looks like the inside of a disused fisherman's hut and she is shut in the dark with the pungent smell of fish, she bangs and bangs on the door yet no one comes. She calls for John but her voice fades out into the darkness until she can call no more for her voice is gone. Then the scene switches and she is back in the library of the Place Vendome with Madame Blavatsky who is telling her something really important, she knows it's vital but she can't hear it. She leans forward to catch the voice and then there is a draught behind her as if someone has opened the door. She turns and in the doorway she sees the woman who was walking in the garden with John, his thin cross looking wife, and the thing is she knows that the woman can see her too; she knows this by the look of sheer horror on her face. . She tries to rise and go to her but her legs don't work, the woman and the vision fades and at last sometime in the early hours of the morning her fever lessens and she falls into a deep dreamless sleep.

The cook wakes once from her vigil by the bed noting the change in breathing and the cool pallor of Nellie's skin and sighs in relief. Her Nellie will be fine again in the morning, nothing to fear, and she douses the lamp and settles back down under her blanket to rest.

*

Chapter 17
John September 1995

It wouldn't do, it simply wasn't right he has been a total wanker he understands that now and he has decided that he definitely needs some help to try and get a grip on the situation. This past year has been like a sabbatical from his real life and he's not sure that he likes what's happening any more. He certainly isn't in control of any of it in the way that he would like to be. The revelation of meeting Nellie in the woods and everything that has followed from it has been a bit like a peak religious experience; except that he is beginning to think that there are shades of the devil or madness lurking in there somewhere He has read about these things in books by people like Stanislaw Grof, it seems the fortieth year of one's life is prone to strange occurrences. Is it the brain playing tricks or something trying to get through from the intelligent mind of the Universe or something worse? He has all the questions lined up, they go around and around in his head in ever increasing circles, until he feels that his head might simply explode with it all: but he has no answers.

She is an obsession in his every waking thought and he can't seem to get her out of his system. He should have been appalled at the scene in the house in Whitstable, he should have stayed to help poor Helena and at least explain to her some of what he thinks is happening but instead he had run back to the familiar, he ran back to Cecilia and that has just complicated matters further.

He walks along by the river to his twice weekly meeting with the Jungian analyst that he has been seeing this past year his feet dragging as he nears the front door of the basement flat in Pimlico. Somehow he always feels that he has to tell her as near a semblance to the truth as possible and this is becoming increasingly difficult. He'd found her through a friends recommendation, she'd done wonders in helping him through his divorce but she doesn't appear to be enabling John to make much headway in the present situation.

His hand falters over the brass nameplate and bell to the right of the door. Dr Abigail Simmons, and then a whole load of unintelligible letters after her name of which he has no idea of the meaning of. She could have made them up for all he knows. The door when it opens lets out a smell of stale cigarettes and cabbage and the fleeting thought crosses his mind that she must be some kind of miser , the money that he and all her other patients pay her ought to go a long way towards helping her live more luxuriously than this. The door has opened of its own accord; she has an electric switch system for her patients so that they never in fact need to meet each other. He trundles down the long gloomy corridor into a waiting room lined from floor to ceiling with books, and there is a desultory fish tank sitting in the corner where several goldfish are making mouths at each other in the murky green water. He has just sat down when he hears the click of the front door that means that her previous patient has let themselves out and it's now his turn to enter the inner sanctum. He uncurls himself from the creaky leather chair and opens the door into the adjoining room.

Abigail sits there surrounded by even more books and a side table containing a dusty looking jug of water, various bottles of homeopathic remedies including rescue remedy and of course the proverbial box of tissues strategically placed between them. She looks up and smiles at him gesturing to the seat opposite her. He can never remember what she looks like once he has left the confines of the poky flat but looking at her now he tries to think about what she might have looked like in her younger years. This is practically impossible. Looking at her salt and pepper hair, her crinkled face and stumbling figure wrapped in its bandages of charity shop clothes she is the epitome of the invisible post-menopausal female that crowds buses and book shops of the city, without anyone ever noticing them. Her wire rimmed glasses are perched on her nose and she peers at him from behind them like a startled bird. He can't ever imagine her having sex or kissing anyone, but that is just him being chauvinistic and horrible. Of course she must have been younger and in love sometime mustn't she? He wonders what makes people become analysts, happy to sit in virtual darkness for hours every day listening to other people's problems. But then he stretches back into his chair and sighs, he's not here to worry about her is he? He's paying £50 an hour to try and get a grip of exactly what is happening to his own life.

She rearranges herself as if she is a pigeon ruffling her nondescript plumage and settling down onto her nest and folds her hands in her lap nodding at him to begin. That's the difficulty, while he is here in his allotted hour he can say as much or as little as he likes and she will listen and occasionally make comments. When he doesn't want to talk about the matter at hand he has taken to occasionally making things up, but it crosses his mind that he couldn't actually have had a vivid enough imagination to make up Nellie, could he? Here in this sepulchre of a room it is as if he has entered the subterranean regions of his own mind, a shadow world where he is never quite sure what he will come up with or what will come at him. He finds it easier if he doesn't make eye contact and so fixes his gaze on a spider's web in the corner of the room, watching transfixed as the creature delicately embalms its prey in its sticky web.

He tells her of his visit to Paris and his night in the hotel room with Cecilia, which hadn't led to sex although he must admit he would have liked it too. He hasn't had sex for so long now that he is beginning to climb the wall and have vivid wet dreams where he wakes in the morning with a throbbing erection and dreams of Nellie naked in odalisque swathes of see through muslin, dancing along the banks of a river. But he can't tell her of the erection part, although the dreams of Nellie are a constant topic running through this analytical conversation that he and "the bird woman" have between them.

When he had first come to her it had been in the flush of what he thought of as his first ever love affair, with Nellie of course. As he realised just what had begun to happen he and Abigail have begun to talk in code about the situation. To her the appearance of Nellie at this time of his life is a resurrection of his inner archetypal ideal of "womanhood". They didn't talk about her as a living human being, until the "possession scenario", when even Abigail had begun to look concerned and suggest that perhaps some kind of medication might be the answer. He had been switched from "mid-life crisis" to "delusional" in the sub text of her mind, so now he has gone back to talking less about Nellie and more about himself. He talks solidly for five minutes about Cecilia and then there is a lull and a silence where Abigail strategically sips from her glass of dusty water and pops a little white pill from the one of the bottles into her mouth. She sucks glumly and he can tell that she is about to say something by the tick that appears in the corner of her right eyelid. She clears her throat and leans forward slightly, fixing him in an intense stare.

" What is it that you feel you should do about this situation with Cecilia? It seems that a barrier of sorts has been dropped between you both; Instead of being locked in a "husband and wife " battle you are beginning to see each other as people again. This is a very common occurrence at the end of the beginning of marriage breakups, you have both taken back the projections you imposed on the other and again can see the person that you actually liked to begin with."

He sighs and leans' forward staring into his hands, what she says is very true but he had opened Pandora's Box in his own heart the day he fell for Nellie and although he can now see again what he saw in his wife when he married her, his life has moved on since then. He gets an internal image of bat like harpies flying across the space between them and rubs a hand across his eyes in disconcertion He looks at Abigail and suddenly feels a surge of anger. He's paying this woman to come up with some sort of a solution and so far all she has done is churn out remarkably useless platitudes, plus she

177

doesn't believe in Nellie. He twists a strand of loose thread from the cushion he has placed on his knee in what he knows is a childlike attempt to place a barrier between himself and this 'all knowing all seeing bird like woman''. A fleeting image of leaping across the space between them and placing the cushion over her head to block out her annoying face crosses his mind but then he shakes it off. Traditional transference, he's read about it in psychology books, he's transferring all his anger onto harmless Abigail and he's at the stage in his analysis where he is obviously a menace to himself and others. Folding his arms firmly across the cushion to stop it jumping from his lap and doing something obviously stupid he tells her.

" Yes I see your point and to a degree you are absolutely right, but really the emotions I feel towards my wife are mainly pity and guilt, which is hardly something to hinge the beginnings of a new relationship on. Cecilia has gone to stay with friends in Paris now and we've decided to put the apartment up for sale, better that way. She did suggest getting in the Catholic priest to exorcise it, sprinkle holy water or whatever they do , but I pointed out that neighbours talk and it would affect the value price of the sale if it got out that the building is in some way haunted. I thought I might as well place a logical bent on the situation where at all possible."

She gently intercedes with the most obvious question which they have both avoided talking about

" What about the boys, how are they taking all this?"

"Oh they seem fine, my mother is being absolutely marvellous and there is of course the au pair, Cecilia was never a very hands on mother, it's not all that different for them. Except of course they don't have to put up with listening to our rows anymore. They seem to be doing very well at school which is the main thing; no it's more a question of where I should go from here. Cecilia has her own problems with her boyfriend who it seems is more than slightly a control freak, but she says that she is used to that because I was , in a different way but still she found me incredibly controlling."

Abigail pauses and lets the light and the dust settle between them, they listen to the hum of the traffic from the Embankment and the tick of the clock on the wall above his head. Then she reaches for the bottle of rescue remedy and pops a pipette full into the cavern of her mouth .He stiffens in the chair, he knows that something stressful is coming, it always is when she does this, and she clears her throat and looks at him with her watery grey eyes.

'' The dreams? Are you still having such vivid dreams of the young girl?''

John blushes as the thought flies into his mind that perhaps somehow she has found a way of flying into his head and spying on his sexual dreams of Nellie, but then he realises that she's using the word ''dream'' in a general sense in order to not tread on the shaky ground of what Abigail refers to as the ''manifestation of his inner anima in the outer world''. He decides to throw the ball back in her court, all this analysis business is becoming a tiresome game, the thing is he doesn't want to talk about the important things to this dusty old woman, and Nellie is of the utmost importance, so he replies vaguely hoping upon hope that the hour is nearly up.

'' Oh yes lots of dreams thank you, now I was just going to explain Abigail that I won't be coming to our little chats for at least a few months , work and travel you know , of course if I get stuck I can always ring you ?''

At that moment the doorbell rings and he breathes a sigh of relief, the next patient lets themselves into the waiting room with a click of the door and he knows that he's got to the end of another excruciating hour without actually saying anything useful, anything he wants to say. He shuffles around in his pocket for his cheque book and writes her a cheque big enough to get him out of the situation without any monetary embarrassment. Later when he remembers he'll get his P.A. to

179

send her an email telling her that his sessions are at an end. Whatever happens next will be under his own volition, he doesn't need a nutty woman in a basement to tell him whether he is crazy or not. He might very well be, but as Jung so eloquently pointed out psyche isn't bound by the confines of the mind, and it seems that neither are he or Nellie

*

Part four

A love affair

"Pretty as an antelope with Oriental eyes"

(Lord Byron)

Chapter 18
Whitstable autumn 1995

John and Helena

He sits across the table top from her, candlelight sending shadows scudding around behind them. The restaurant is close to the shoreline in one of the converted warehouses of the Oyster Dredging Company and if you listen carefully to the silence between the murmurs of the other diners you can hear the sea. Soporific languid unrelenting, pummelling and perfecting the shoreline with its endlessly gentle whisper "here I am, here I am". He hears voices in the silence and silence in the voices, he hears the call of sirens calling him to his doom and yet he is more than ready for love. Helena is looking beautiful tonight; the soft lighting erases the fine lines around her nose and mouth. Her mouth, which is open wide in laughter now as she reaches a slim hand over the white cloth to touch him his arm.

He's been in the little seaside town a few weeks now after his escape from London, his escape from trying to pretend that everything is normal, *that he is normal* when he so obviously isn't. He'd packed a small bag, some books and an empty notebook and returned to the bed and breakfast on the Island Wall that he'd fled from earlier in the year, again he had booked the best room with a sea view. If he lies in bed and cranes his neck a little he can watch the equinoctial tides rising and falling, rising and falling only a tennis court away from him. The thought makes him shiver as he remembers stories of the high tides and flooding in the fifties, so each night when he falls asleep he fully expects to awake submerged in icy water.

His dreams are full of murky scenarios, always far out at sea, where powerlessness seems to be the overriding theme. He's relieved that he doesn't have to explain them to his analyst, *no more analysis* a worryingly expensive waste of time that only managed to open wounds that he had thought cauterised or healed. All the endless talking had revealed is that they are still slowly seeping their poison into his psyche, but he doesn't have to pick the scab to uncover the festering. He spends nights tossing and sweating as he finds himself on ships that burst into flames and disintegrate around him forcing him to jump overboard. Then comes the drowning, him drowning: being pulled under the water by the freezing grey might of a riptide. His lungs fill with the cold dark salt of the sea, until he wakes up alone in the night his heart thudding his breath coming in splutters; and listens to the wind on the chimney pots and the rain slashing at the window panes. His morning dreams are full of women with long dark hair that call to him and then walk away from him into the waves, women that turn and look at him with antelope eyes. Nellies eyes, always the girl in the woods calling for him out there in the vast expanse of an unforgiving ocean and the overriding problem is that he follows her without question, deeper and deeper into the cold dark profundity of being.

At least it has been like that until tonight, tonight he intends to stay for the first time with Helena, and that thought makes his heart beat so hard he can hardly breathe but this time with trepidation. He might have picked up a tinge of French Catholicism from his ex-wife; he hasn't slept with another woman for so long he is afraid that he has forgotten how it is done. Some small part of him ticks away in a guilty fashion as if he is committing adultery as if he is about to cheat on Cecilia when in reality it is long over and the two have become edgy friends with a history in common and nothing much more sentimental than that. They will always have the boys as a testimony to something good and strong coming out of their marriage but that is about the sum total of their years together and nothing about him regrets any part of it now. No this guilt isn't about Cecilia it's the thought that he being unfaithful to

Nellie that worries him, but then there is so much of his lovely girl in this woman that is facing him across the table isn't it more like an earthly homage to a heavenly obsession ?

He lifts his wine glass to take a sip and looks at Helena again, at some angles and especially in this light she looks remarkably like Nellie, an older softer Nellie, but he has come to care more about this woman and less about the one he met in the woods that day last year. Or has he? Does he just need to do something about the physical frustration that he is feeling , what is sure is that he is thinking too much, for once in his life he just needs to surrender to the moment, *be here now*, and see where it takes him.

It had happened gradually over the last few weeks; this softening towards Helena, when he'd first arrived from London he'd felt taut and agitated. Tightly strung, like an instrument that someone had made out of tune: rasping angry at something or someone without knowing who or what, just angry at the situation. It had occurred to him that he was being selfish, that he should just go back to his life in the city: settle down to normality; nine to five in the city and playing with his children every evening after work. He could manage to be a single father; there were myriads of them in London. He knew a few, and they went to "single father groups" and usually could be recognised from a great distance by the level of exhaustion that followed them around like an odour. He should do that and maybe he would have done if he hadn't had somewhere to go and a riddle to work out.

Nellie had been appearing less and less in his dreams and then not at all at the corner of the room or a fleeting image of her lit by sunshine next to the summerhouse, as she used to. He couldn't smell her perfume any more that scent of ambergris that smelt of another time, another century, and some part of him had started to forget her. To be honest with himself it had been something of a relief, like the lid of a pressure cooker being released, he relaxed a little not expecting the unexpected at the corner of every street, forgetting to look for phantoms and mirages forgetting the girl in the woods, just a little. The numinous nature of their meeting had begun to pale and it felt alright to just let it be.

So he had begun to talk to Helena, he looks at her now chatting to him across the table her hands flying expressively to prove a point , high colour at the edges of her cheekbones and her eyes shining like the exploding core of a distant nebula. Looking at her now he has a sudden revelation as to her state of mind. She is in love with him of course she is, and the thought makes him happy that he is the object of her desire, he is the reason she has suddenly become so beautiful.

Helena pauses for breath and can't quite remember what it is she is talking about, the wine and the evening, the presence and attention that John is giving her have all gone to her head and for the first time in a long time she feels happy. The day he had turned up again on her doorstep had been a good day, she hadn't had one of those awful black outs for a while and was feeling more herself, her old self. She isn't sure what's been happening to her since the spring, it had started that day John had come to visit and then continued on and off. She would be engrossed in a normal task of research on her computer and then suddenly the whole day had slipped away and she would find herself alone walking on the mudflats at low tide with no recollection at all of how she got there. She'd gone to her GP who had ummed and aaahhed and diagnosed some kind of inner ear infection that could disturb balance, but she knew that wasn't it. For part of her could remember what had happened during the periods of amnesia, like a body memory that's the best way she can think of to describe it. But she doesn't want to linger on that now, think what it really might be. John had appeared out of the blue and he looked like he needed to talk and so she had opened the door of her house and it seems also the door of her heart to him.

Slowly over the following weeks they had walked in the wooded areas of Dunkirk and along the shore for miles in silence, and then he would tell her a little of the story. The

185

"Nellie" part of it she hadn't wanted to believe at all at first, but either he was delusional or something odd was happening to them both. When he had divulged what he'd seen that day in the house the first time he had visited Whitstable, the thing that had made him run from her, it felt like the truth and in a way it made her relieved to have an explanation: albeit an unbelievable one. After all if the reason for her blackouts was that Nellie was trying to get a grip on the present by somehow snaking her way into Helena's body, surely that might be an easier thing to sort out than if she had a psychosis that would require heavy chemical drugs? Surely a "possession" could be cured with garlic, or a priest, something solid and down to earth done about it, and since John had come back it hasn't been happening at all, so why worry?

So the mystery made them closer, and then of course they were both lonely , that helped move things along slightly, and what had started as a friendship was now about to turn into a love affair, she could feel it. She cared for him, and she knew that he felt the same. Yes he had fallen for a mirage but what he really yearned for was a flesh and blood woman, wasn't it? Wasn't that what all men thrived on, physical connection and sex? Maybe the sex will be a disappointment, but she doesn't really care, for tonight it will be enough for her to just hold him in her arms, to just have a body that she cares about next to her in her bed. It's been too long that she's gone to bed at night alone and woken up alone. Tonight she will stay awake and watch him sleep, tonight she will make every single second count, for time is her enemy she has begun to understand this, and not only the future but more savagely the past that is stalking her, Nellie and the past .

She toys with her steak pushing the pieces across her plate and pretending to eat a stem of broccoli or a sprig of green bean all the while feasting on the way his mouth moves, how his eyes crinkle at the edges when he smiles and how her body hums when he gently touches a hand or her bare arm. They move on to desert, a chocolate mousse with fresh raspberry coulis that they share between them with tiny teaspoons and large glass mugs of mint tea, the mint unfolding in the glass as they watch like something from a Moroccan Riad. He tells her of the boys and how he would like to bring them down to the shore to play on the sands and pick shells, maybe get them a dog to play with. She's not sure how she will feel about another woman's children but she puts that thought on the back burner for the moment, there are other things to worry about first.

There is a distinct chill in the air when they leave the restaurant, she buttons up her coat and leans into him for extra warmth, the sea is an unknown blackness to their left, and there is no moon, its dark and she stumbles a little on the cobbles in her high heeled shoes. Shoes that she hasn't worn for years and he gently holds her elbow to steady her. She thinks about the difference between this and love affairs when she was younger, how easy they were, how confident she was and now she isn't sure of anything, not even who she is. She's worried about silly things like what her body will look like to him when she takes off her clothes, will it be too slack, will he really desire her, what if it is a disaster, and she will lose a dearly loved friend.

'' Are you ok''?

He stops and turns her gently to face him, her expression is unknown to him, he leans towards her and feels for her mouth, its soft and yielding and his tongue moves between her lips as his body starts to flame. It's the first physical sense of being alive that he's had for a long time and in the moonlight he could be kissing anyone, *all women*. It's simply a fusion of hormones and needs and its carrying him on a rising tide of body feeling that he'd forgotten could exist. They kiss and then she pulls gently away from him her breath coming quickly her heart beating hard under his hand, his hand that has somehow been placed on her breast her nipple erect and straining underneath her thin silk bra. They don't talk but continue quickly down the narrow walkway till they reach the house, she fumbles with the key and then they are in the

187

hallway and their clothes are falling from them in soft billowing heaps.

Later they lay side by side hands entwined staring at the ceiling, again he asks her.

" Are you ok?". He asks again worried by her silence.

In reply she presses a finger to his lips, it smells of him and it smells of the salty liquids of their bodies. She doesn't want to talk, for once there is nothing to say and she moves to lie against him, skin on skin, marvelling about how soft he feels and yet the muscles under the flesh are hard like those of a boy. She runs a hand over the fine down of his stomach and feels his hardness come to meet her. Almost wearily they begin again the steps of the dance that they have just found access to, slower this time he pushes and probes pleasure from her in a way that he never knew he could. In reply she utters the gasps of a girl and stretches up to meet him, the night continues around their dips and troughs and with each incoming wave of pleasure she loses a little more of herself to him. By dawn when at last they pull apart to sleep the sheets tangled and wet;, sweat drying in rivers on their skin, she is amazed at how transparent she feels, as if she would be blown apart by another kiss, as if another thrust of his hips would send her under, and with this thought lying like a beach of pebbles between them they turn away from each other and sleep.

*

Chapter 19
Nellie Sydenham

October 1875

She wanders through the high ceilinged rooms of Raven House, running her fingers over favourite objects and looking out through the sparkling windows at the garden beyond. Every room contains a memory of childhood, a happy childhood where she and her brother were allowed a remarkable amount of freedom for children of their class. Her mother simply wasn't bothered that much with them as long as they turned up polished and bathed before dinner to spend the allotted fifteen minutes with their parents. Papa spent more time with them of course; he would seek them out in the nursery and take them for pony rides in the park and as she grew up her mother had become more and more aloof. Now she was away travelling in Europe and Papa was up north in his factories, he has promised to return for the day of her birthday lunch, and she is looking forward to that. Her brother Edmund is of course up at Oxford, at St John's College and making a nuisance of himself at the Oxford Union so she is alone and unfettered apart from the servants.

It had been hard to leave her little house by the sea, but she will be back there soon for the Halloween fireworks out on the barge moored outside the harbour .The Indian summer is over and after her illness and recovery the house had been unusually silent. No sign of Helena and the light and delicious feelings that went with her, and nothing to say that John had ever existed, she sighs glancing out to the garden missing the signs of his presence that she sometimes gets. Leaves rustling with invisible footsteps, a tall figure of a man just heading off down the garden to the stables, the front door banging and the sound of his voice. All of these she has experienced sometime over the past year and now she is lonely without him. Yet in her dreams at night she is often lying entangled in his arms and he is murmuring in her ear, sweetly softly telling her that he loves her as he moves his body against her with a sense of urgency. She should wake up blushing with the memory of it all, it is so vivid as if she has travelled from her bed here to be in his arms on a nightly basis, but she isn't shy. Instead she wakes with her cheeks flushed and a sense of loss that she cannot see his head on the pillow beside her. It is only a dream, but somehow her dreams have more substance that reality now and it is as if she is on top of a cliff just waiting to launch herself off the edge into the force of this love and begin to fly. In the meantime there are her affairs to put in order here in London and her newly shot sequence of photos from the coast to label and archive and of course her journal to bring up to date.

She isn't sure how much of the truth she should disclose in her writings but that's something to worry about later. For now she has a whole week of freedom before her birthday when of course Papa will expect them to take their habitual luncheon complete with French Champagne and a cake especially baked for her. This year it will be just the two of them as she hasn't thought to invite any of her friends although she would have liked to get to know the French painter Millais who is staying nearby. Too much to do and not enough time to do it in, she is pleased that unlike other young women of her age she has her own life and no girly acquaintances to keep up. Why, most of her school friends are married by now with a rosy baby or two in tow. Even the heiresses have given over all their fortunes to their husbands as the law still insists; she shivers at the thought of it. What use is education and girls being allowed to take the exams to get into Cambridge if marriage makes virtual slaves of them? In fact slavery is probably considerably better as there is always the chance of freedom, for a woman who is married there is none. Divorce if it comes at all always make a ruined woman of the wife while the husband gets away scot free in most cases. The woman will be pursued with the whiff of scandal for the most of her life, and probably be unable to see much of her children, the children belong to the husband which seems ridiculous to Nellie. Those rare women in the suffragette movement who are campaigning to change all of this

190

are mostly spinsters, most husbands wouldn't stand for their wives to be politically dilly dallying.

She sighs, pressing her nose against the window and staring down onto the frosty ground around the summer house which looks mournfully back at her its windows darkened by the early evening light. Twilight, that time when certainties become fogy and the things of the everyday takes on an energy of their own, slightly dark and malevolent, she shivers. Can it only be a year ago she took that fateful walk into the woods and came across the two little boys and of course John? She smiles to herself smoothing down her soft blue silk dress; she wonders how they all are with a wistful air, some part of her shut off from believing that she will ever see him again. But at least this kind of love affair brings freedom with it, even if the freedom has so much danger attached that she can't really formulate her thoughts clearly. No, best not to think too deeply about what has been going on she would rather just follow her instincts, move from one action to the next without questioning.

As for the promised commissions that had drawn her back from the seaside with a sense of work to be done, why these have simply vanished. Rossetti has left town for a lodge he has rented in Sussex and Jane Morris appears to be visiting him so the commission she was to undertake of Jane has been postponed and she worries that it will not get done now. She has spent most of the day overseeing the hanging of her portraits in Beauberry House down in Dulwich Village. They had sent a carriage for her and with the gardeners help she had carefully stacked the twenty pieces wrapped in tissue and cushioned with wool on the opposite seat from her.

The gallery owners had been very helpful sweeping her into an elegant sitting room to discuss the opening party while the photos themselves were taken from the carriage and hung as they should be. All the usual culprits would be invited from the "Hill "although she won't be here to see whether it is a success or not. She rather likes the idea of a party going on

191

without her, everyone waiting impatiently for her to arrive, but she will never arrive.

She walks over to her desk and takes out her journal, skipping the pages over until she reaches the next blank page, then sits and dips her pen in the inkpot and begins to write. She writes intently for twenty minutes, describing the events of the past few days and then carefully blots her page and shuts it. The light is fading over the park as she dons her fur coat for her evening walk. Tonight she is to go to the theatre with Mr Morris on her arm. She always wonders why his wife prefers the slightly mad and dangerous Rossetti to her husband; Nellie has always thought William very handsome for an older man. Not as handsome as John of course but she thinks a man over forty has a lot of gravure, unlike the odious young Arthur Sullivan who has still been leaving his card monotonously in the hall downstairs.

The garden is very silent as if holding its breath before nightfall and her small kid boots crunch the leaves underfoot making her almost wince at the noise. She walks down to the stables near the old apple orchard and stops to pick a few of the small round russets left on the tree to feed to the carriage horses and her old pony. She loves the smell of the hay and the evening feed and the comforting sound of munching from the animal stalls. The old pony wickers recognising her footsteps and she feels a flash of guilt for neglecting him and then immediately his soft nose is in her hand and gently nudging her pocket for more. She strokes his silky neck and tears gather in the corner of her eye. It is the first time that she can remember relaxing for a long time and she sits on a bale of hay to immerse herself in the evening routine of the animals. She sits there until it is completely dark and she can see pools of light on the flagstones from the gas lamp in the courtyard outside. She knows it is time to go back into the house and take her bath and get dressed for her evening but she is loath to leave this place where as a child she spent hours grooming her pony and oiling his bridle which now hangs cracked and disused on a hook by his stable door.

At last she can't put off the moment any longer and gets up to give him one last stroke before shutting the stable door gently behind her. For a moment she thinks how wonderful it must be to be a well-loved animal with no inkling of the past or future and no decisions to make. But the feeling fades as she walks towards the lighted house and a sense of the unfolding of her destiny dances through the last of the leaves that rustle in tune to the wind of time. An old moon rises from behind the apple trees and she knows that whatever happens she has been truly happy in this house, she could never have wished for a better place to be born and grow up Why if she had been born anywhere else she might never have met John and then what would her life have been like?

*

Chapter 20
John and Helena

October 1995

Helena is in love for the first time in her life and it feels extraordinary. All the little everyday things in life are lit with an incandescence that carries with it the gossamer threads of a childhood fairy-tale. Not only does she feel different, she looks completely different, she no longer sweeps her hair back in a ponytail or up on top of her head in the morning. She lets it lay softly around her shoulders, her cheeks aglow with the nights they spend making love, her chin slightly red with a rash from the scratch of his stubble. That's the other thing that's so new and so astounding in her life; every morning when she wakes up she props herself up on an elbow and watches John sleeping. He wakes slowly some part of him gently realising that he isn't alone and his eyes are out of focus, for a second he looks like the young man he must once have been and then he looks at her sleepily before smiling at her and pulling her to him so that they both entwine again in that musky place where their bodies meet and reality falls away.

The room vibrates around them as if the murmurs of their love making are a kind of music that make up an important ingredient in the symphony of living that blends with the cry of the gulls and the swell of the autumn tides outside the window. The mornings are chill now and they take it in turns to run barefoot downstairs to turn the heating on and make the tea. Then they sit up in the big brass bed that has always been here in the room that is still the soft dove grey colour that Nellie liked so much and stare unseeing out at the expanse of the horizon. Both of them completely satiated and speechless from the intensity of their intimacy. She could sit there next to him all day in their special place, but time begins to push at them, in the way time does, and morning turns to afternoon where she runs around the small streets of the town buying food to cook for their evening meal. She buys fresh sea bass from the fish shop, corn fed chicken from the butcher and herbs from the grocers, along with big juicy potatoes and tender purple shoots of broccoli.

Helena has never been a cook before, she's always been too wrapped up in research on her favourite topic her great aunt Nellie, but Nellie has faded into the background now, her thesis can wait. Meanwhile for the first time ever she is turning her house into a home for the pair of them. She doesn't know if he will stay, she doesn't dare ask when he has to return to the city, she simply lives minute by minute, hanging onto the magic as long as she is able. It frightens her, this great outpouring of feeling that sometimes overwhelms her so much that she can hardly speak, and when he isn't there where she left him when she returns, her heart beats with gulping palpitations until she realises that he hasn't left her; he has simply gone for a walk or is out on the mudflats watching the wild birds as he so likes to do.

John has thrown away his moral turpitude, his doubts about his divorce and his dreams of a phantom girl in a flowing summer dress. At least he tells Helena that he has, but Nellie does still creep into his dreams and beneath the sheets of the lover's bed, he knows she does. He has seen her when he is making love to Helena, feeling only Helena and then a softness of the skin and a taint of ambergris hints at the phantom girl. Sometimes he forbids himself but if he lazily narrows his eyes he can see the palest of female skins beneath his hands, the softest of curls and the large brown eyes of Nellie smiling erotically down at him as she pretends to be coy. At first he felt guilty when this happened as if he were betraying one of them though he couldn't say which one but now he has surrendered to it all knowing that nothing he can do will change the magic, nothing he can say will make it go away and in a way it heightens the sex, never knowing quite who he will be entering, the older or the younger woman, the lover or the beloved.

This evening there is a storm breaking outside the window and in time to the crash of the waves and the flicker of the fire he has lit in the grate, he rises and falls above Nellie, for it is her. Her body younger, softer, rounder smoother paler, than Helena's her hair falling all over her face. She is a shimmering hologram of being superimposed within the confines of Helena, and something in him bursts open as he whispers, the words he never uses, the love words.

'' Oh my darling, oh my darling, yes my love, yes I love you, never leave me.''

Then it is Helena's voice in his ear whispering that she too loves him and his mind explodes with the perfection of it all. Afterwards he lays there and sips at a large malt whisky that he has poured himself , the sweat dries on his shoulders and he is completely content and doesn't want to look at the woman snuggled against his stomach her hand stroking his chest hair for he knows that the beloved has left him again and the lover is back.

Days like this have turned into weeks, time plays with them a little more and they try to snatch their moments as if soon something will wake them up and laugh at the pretty illusion they are creating. Soon it is the last week in October and the whole town is gearing up for the huge firework event out on the Barge in the bay which has been turned of late into a floating Heritage Museum. Even at this time of year the boats ply like child's toys out of the harbour taking the visitors out to the Oyster beds and the seal sand banks with a meander around the exhibits on the barge for the return journey. John tries to work with little success, his laptop is full of chatty emails from Cecilia which he can rarely be bothered to reply to .She sends him images of her journeys, her pale face barely visible under large sunglasses and hat to keep out the desert sun. She is travelling in Egypt and the Sudan, she is at a conference in Washington, and she wants to know when they can talk, when she can spend some time with the boys.

He sighs as he feels a stab of guilt about his sons; they've been down to the coast to stay with them on several occasions his own mother staying in the other spare room as she refuses to be parted from them. It hadn't really gone to plan, Helena has absolutely no experience with small children and is rather hopeless at it all, getting easily irritated and flustered when presented with the many questions that small enquiring minds need to ask. He couldn't help feeling that Nellie was so wonderful with them that afternoon in the woods, they still occasionally ask where the "beautiful lady" has gone and there is no adequate reply that he can give them.

This evening as he lingers in the bay of the window and looks out, the sea is calm. The Old Neptune Pub sits there its white weatherboard staunch ballast on the foreshore and the odd dog walker meanders by beneath the window, head tucked in towards their neck to protect themselves from the rain. On a whim he goes over to Helena's desk where he has stowed Nellie's diary. It's been an unspoken thing between them that they have let their affair take them over and not delved further into the woman whose ghost dominates the house, but on a hunch there is something he needs to know. It's a whole year since this drama first erupted and if he remembers correctly Nellie disappeared about this time of year in 1875 when she was only twenty one years old, though why or how or more importantly where the girl had gone to, he doesn't know.

His heart always starts beating violently when he picks up the journal, stroking the smooth leather of the little book, bringing to his nose to see if he can get a hint of the perfume that he associates with Nellie. But all he can smell is the mustiness of years between the girl who wrote the journal and himself and without thinking it brings a lump to his throat and a tear to his eye. He mustn't cry, he really mustn't cry it's ridiculous, but more and more in these weeks with Helena when the present of their love affair is making the world so vibrantly "here and now" yes more and more he thinks of what has happened to him, that keeps on happening to him as a kind of possession by the ghost of a girl long dead.

197

Blowing his nose volubly with a large hanky he keeps in his jeans pocket he settles down on the window seat and opens the book, flicking gently through the pages with the tiny copperplate writing until he gets to the last entry. He perches his reading glasses on the bridge of his nose and trying to stop his heart battering he begins, not really knowing what to expect.

*

Sydenham Halloween 1875

Today I have put my affairs in order and packed my small leather satchel with the best of my photos and later I will add the journal I'm writing in now to take with me to my house by the sea in Whitstable. My pendant I have placed in its pouch along with some of my most precious negatives in a hiding place that only I can find. A last lunch with Papa today although he didn't of course realise as he presented me with my birthday present. A magnificent Canadian mink coat this year and my usual lemon drizzle birthday cake. I must be quick now in writing this, the light is failing and the woods are calling to me once more. I hope I don't come upon the Dulwich College gamekeeper as I have quite regularly these last few days. He knows that Papa has right of way through the woods but it would be too too funny to be shot as a poacher in the half light of twilight. That would indeed set all my plans awry. Or he could perhaps think that I am a ghost come to haunt the woods as very few people know of the exit of the tunnel into the folly.

So what must I say here? Little of the journey to come just that I wish no harm by my actions, but it is my love for John that is impelling me to do this, either that or live my entire existence wishing that I had tried. Perhaps "Nellie" will vanish completely this night who knows but someone said that to be brave for love is the main thing and I am ready to give my all.

This is her last entry, slightly smudged by something that could be a tear, he can't tell and his eyes ache from trying to decipher the small intricate script. Not that the entry tells him much, it only intimates that her last known journey was to this house. The door swings open and a whiff of roast chicken rises up the stairwell from the kitchen. He relaxes back into the cushions staring out at the sea, the night and the flickering lights of the small fishing boats on the horizon. He's loathe to go out tonight; something is prickling the skin at the back of his neck as though in warning but the sight of Helena beaming and bringing him a whisky before dinner soothes him.

---What's he afraid of? It's only a firework display---

Truth is that he's more than slightly spooked by the obsessive nature of Nellie's feelings for him, which have just been reinforced in his mind by the small entry in the diary. Whatever he imagined that he felt for her in their brief meetings was obviously magnified tenfold in her young and impressionable mind. She believed in miracles, he doesn't really if he is honest with himself. He's suddenly very tired, the past year has been so dramatic, so many turns and twists that haven't actually led anywhere, except perhaps to Helena. He looks around the soft furnishings and Nellie's portrait staring down at him from above the fireplace and smiles, she is so beautiful and however he tries to kid himself when he looks at her his heart still does a skip and a jump.

Helena is full of the heat of the kitchen and the delicious aroma of cooking food as she bends to kiss him she doesn't register the way that he pulls away from her slightly.

" Supper's ready, do you want it up here or shall we eat in the kitchen? It's cosier down there."

" Yes that will be fine how lovely, you are clever, I'll be with you in a moment thank you."

She starts at his unusually formal tone and then she notices the little leather book on the seat beside him and a fiery blush covers her cheeks, her heart plummeting to somewhere near the floor. Nellie's diary, he's been reading it again. They have talked around the subject of the other person in their relationship ever since that day, that terrible day that she doesn't really want to think about now. Her mouth twists itself in a sharp straight line but she pulls herself together quickly saying

199

nothing. As soon as the door is closed behind her she leans against the wall breathing deeply for a second she feels dizzy , the floor rising up to meet her and all her joy vanishes.

'' Breathe breathe.''

She mutters under her breath and from somewhere in the house she hears the banging of a door, laughter and the soft sound of a girl's footsteps and she knows from some instinctual place deep inside that it is all about to happen again, her life is floating away from her and there is absolutely nothing that she can do about it.

*

Chapter21
Halloween 1995

It's chilly on the quay, the couple stand in line with all the others, wrapped up in anoraks and Burberrys, fur coats and gloves as they wait for the little launch to ferry them out to the barge. Some of the children are playing tag their parents jumpy and chafing keeping their eyes fixed on the small leaping bodies, worried about little legs tripping up and ending up in the black depths of the harbour. Helena watches the black water slurp and slap against the side of the quay and shivers. John has his arm firmly around her and yet he is looking out to sea, impatient to be out there in the darkness of the bay with the black sky and the stars above.

The launch eventually arrives its smell of diesel and dead fish wafting before it, and they are all crammed in, far too many she thinks for health and safety. She clutches the side of the boat her hands slipping on the wetness of it, salt water splashing through her gloves and making her fingers wet. She wishes that they'd stayed indoors and watched the fireworks display from the balcony of the house but it's too late now and soon enough they are climbing the ladder which hangs perpendicular to the side of the barge, John's face upturned beneath her a blank canvas in the light from above as she swivels to look at him. She climbs, the muscles of her arms pulling against the metal her body hanging heavy away from the side of the boat and once again she feels that buzzing dizziness in her body, that sense of watching herself from afar and yes again she has to reel herself in to stop her thoughts disintegrating into terror.

" You alright honey?"

He's there beside her at last and the unusual endearment goes some way to stop her stomach turning. He's looking at her with consternation; at least she thinks he is. He may in fact be looking straight through her, or he may be looking at Nellie. She feels the other woman very near to her tonight shimmering on the edges of the moonlit deck, her laughter ringing in time to the children's excitement.

'' Damm you Nellie.''

She mutters under her breath, batting her hands around her head as if trying to dislodge a swarm of bees or a plague of locusts that have come to feed on her. Slowly she brings her attention back to the present as the first of the fireworks begin to whoosh and whirl around the night sky, set on fire from the small platform just in front of the barge. She looks back out towards the shore trying to pick out the lights of her house but she can't tell from this far away which one it is. Something in the reflection of the light makes it look as if the whole of the foreshore is on fire for a moment, but that is ridiculous it can't be happening, and she blinks rapidly as the vision fades back into black night. The fireworks continue around them in time to the ooo's and aaahhsa of the crowd, she watches the pink and green sparks, the orange fireballs, and the indigo Catherine wheels until her head aches.

There is a dull thud somewhere at the other end of the barge and the crowd cranes its collective neck in unison to see what is happening but there doesn't seem to be any reason for the noise and so everyone quickly turns back to the crescendo of the firework display. The sky is a dark velvet backdrop to the vigorously exploding gunpowder breaking into chunks and fireballs lighting up the night like so many tiny super nova above their cricked necks. Someone is at her elbow with a tray of piping hot mulled wine; she greedily sniffs in the comforting aroma of the cinnamon and herbs and takes a sip of the sugary substance. She can feel it descending like a globule of warmth down her throat and as the alcohol hits her stomach and she immediately feels more than a little drunk.

The evening begins to wind down, the first of the spectators embark on their journey back to the harbour, the children waving sparklers as they go the adults looking weary with the strain of keeping their chattering over excited brood safe. She is beginning to feel pleasantly sleepy the wine warming her and she lifts her face to John's for a kiss. His lips brush hers gently and she smells the soft scent of his aftershave, the whiff of fresh sea air on him and she thinks again how lucky she is to love this man. That's when it happens, a siren begins to whine and get louder and louder so that she covers her ears with her hands, from below deck smoke is billowing from a hatch up into the night air and she suddenly realises that the barge is on fire.

Everything happens very quickly after this, several of the crew begin to hand out life vests, the Captain makes an announcement telling them not to panic help is on the way. There are only about twenty or so of the spectators left on board apart from her and John and she can almost smell the inherent panic in the air along with the smell of smoke and burning oil. It occurs to her that the water surrounding them is very cold and deep and she is suddenly gaspingly afraid. Then a huge explosion rips the night air and the blast knocks her off her feet, dragging her away from John and catapulting her over the side of the barge and into the freezing depths of the water .She hits it with a resounding smack that knocks her out, yet just before she hits the water she gets the same impression that she had earlier this evening a glow in the sky above the shore as of the town burning in front of her.

It's all instantaneous and yet happening in slow motion, her plunge over the side of the heavily listing barge, smoke and chaos behind her, and Nellie, all at once Nellie is there. She can see a laughing pair of girl's eyes watching her and then pain as she hits the black concrete of the sea and she is unconscious, a sharp cry that seems to come from someone else and then blackness everywhere.

Where a few minutes previously all had been light and joy, excited children and fireworks, now the choppy North Sea is covered in a burning sheen of fuel, bodies and debris. John is blown clear and although the shock of the cold water is seeping through his skin he is alert and aware of everything around him. He swims strongly through the waves searching for Helena and at last finds her, but the way she looks frightens him so much that he forgets to breathe and a wave sloshes over him making him choke with the gritty taste of the ocean. Her head is slumped forward bobbing in and out of the waves, she is unconscious and for one horrible moment he thinks that she is dead. But no, picking up her icy wrist he can feel a faint pulse like the whirring of a butterfly deep within her body. He sweeps the long hair back from her face turns her over and gently calls her name , but then there are strong arms lifting them both out of the water and up into the coast guard launch he is wrapped in blankets and she is whisked away from him.

The night continues to unravel in ambulance sirens, police cars and flashing lights. The injured are carried away and he is looked over by a waiting emergency crew of Doctors and pronounced unhurt and then left with a hot mug of tea in the covered fish market which has been opened up as a rescue centre. Out in the bay pieces of the barge still burn and it's a miracle that no one has died, or at least it seems that way but the blast has done something to his hearing and he can see people mouthing words at him but can't hear their voices.

Ten minutes later he has had enough of being a victim and has no intention of hanging around and talking to the police, he needs to get himself to the hospital and find out what has happened to Helena. A helpful Detective Inspector tells him that she has probably been taken to Canterbury, that's where the seriously injured have been airlifted to and he hitches a ride in a squad car determined to be by her side whatever the cost to himself. He is shivering his head pounds and he is still coughing up sea water but within half an hour he is sitting outside intensive care watching through a small glass window the figure of his lover in a bed with tubes protruding from every part of her.

A doctor is carefully explaining stuff that he doesn't understand something about damage to her spinal cord and breathing difficulties and MRI scans. All he knows is that in that bed is the woman that he thinks that he loves and the woman who also holds the key to the mystery of his relationship with Nellie and whatever happens he is not going to lose her now.

*

Chapter 22
Nellie Halloween 1875

Whitstable.

She can feel them both in the house with her, as soon as she opens the front door with her little brass key the light begins to shimmer and hum around her and she knows that the walls between their world and hers are gossamer thin. She can hear them moving in the room above her head, the bed creaks and she knows that she has done the right thing by coming here tonight. Madame Blavatsky had intimated that something was possible on this night of all nights where the dead and the living pass so close to each other they can hear each other breathe. Although if you asked her she couldn't tell you who was alive and who wasn't and she doesn't really intend to get metaphysical about it all. John and Helena are here with her and a voiceless joy creeps over her as she begins to understand that her instincts are completely right and destiny has led her to this pivotal point in time for a specific reason.

She's not sure what's going to happen next or how it's all going to unfold, but whatever it is she has to do, she won't flinch from the task .She has watched them many times make love in the big brass bed, her bed of course who else's would it be, it seems that the bed has been in this house all the years that she hasn't. But can she really talk about the gap in time like this or is it all a continuum of some sorts, their lives paralleling hers? Only God can answer these sorts of questions and she doesn't think that now is the time to try and solidify a connection with the Almighty. She has never been that interested in religion and tonight definitely isn't the moment to start.

She amuses herself drifting in and out of Helena's body while John is naked and thrusting above her, if she concentrates really hard she can stay there long enough to feel a modicum of the pleasure that the lovers are indulging in and she knows that John can see her Nellie, and not Helena. Yet Helena's will is always strong enough to push her out and at last she gives in and sits by the bay window in the sitting room looking out into the bay and the preparation for the firework display.

She might have dozed off for a while it seems that way and when she wakes the house is silent around her. Hurriedly she gets up to make ready to go out to the harbour and watch the display, she washes her face with warm water from the boiler in the kitchen and places a dab of eau de toilette behind each ear. Walking briskly towards the quay there is an unusual silence in the air, she can hear the sea, but that's all; no Halloween revellers or children knocking on doors demanding tit bits, where has everyone gone? There is a mist creeping in from the Oyster beds and she hopes it won't spoil the vantage point for watching the show.

Then she hears it: a dull thud as if of an explosion coming from the fishing huts behind her and suddenly a wall of flame engulfs the pitch and tar filled wood and the sirens are out screeching. All around her now are people running and the smoke is overwhelming, soon she's choking on the smoke and decides to head down Squeeze Gut Alley towards the comparative calm of the harbour. Soon she is catching her breath and wiping the smut from her face while she watches the mayhem behind her as the fishermen seem to run past her and through her forming a human chain with the buckets of water and she notices that they behave as if she didn't exist.

With a supreme effort she focuses her foggy mind and immediately she finds herself out on the barge with Helena and

John watching the fireworks, she smiles with relief immediately creeping to John's side, pushing Helena out of the way and he looks at her his eyes full of love and consternation.

Another thud shakes her and this time it comes from the barge itself more smoke billows out on deck and suddenly people are flying through the air and out into the blackness of the water their bodies limp like so many puppets. The barge is listing heavily to port and the screaming fills the air, yes she can hear screaming but she keeps her eyes focused on John and that's all that matters. He's in the water with Helena and she is beside him, this time when she slips effortlessly into her bitter rival there is no objection from the woman, and she settles her mind peacefully in a hidden corner of the woman's broken body. She is supremely calm and at home in the knowledge that all will be well now, she just has to wait a little bit longer and everything that she has ever dreamed about in the past year will be hers for the asking, hers for the taking. Nothing and no one can stop her now.

*

Chapter 23
Sydenham summer 2000

It's hot, the afternoon sun beats down on the leaves of the park, and she sits on the steps of the summerhouse watching John and the boys high up in the branches of the large oak tree at the edge of the lawn. They're just putting the finishing touches to the tree house that they've spent the holidays building. They could have all gone to the South of France to the small cottage that they've bought high up in the hills above Nice but no they wanted a tree house here in their magic garden in Sydenham so that's what they've done. The cottage in France was bought with the proceeds from selling the house in Whitstable, sad though it was to sell it after the accident that dark autumn night neither of them really wanted to spend any more time looking out at the sea which nearly cost them their lives. And there was always the thought that Helena might be lingering somewhere nearby, at least that thought was uppermost in Nellie's mind. So they had packed up all her precious belongings and brought them back to where they should be at Raven House.

The sun glints on the pendant which again swings around her neck above her open necked silk blouse. She absent mindedly twists the pearls on the chain and smiles thinking how silly she was to have been so worried that anything bad was going to happen and pushes vaguely at her hair that is sticking in curly damp tendrils to her neck now in the heat of the day. She nudges it back up under her large brimmed straw hat and gets up to go to the kitchen to get that jug of ice cold lemonade that she had made for them earlier. It's strange having a ready-made family, but strange in a good way, it means that she never has to consider the rigours of pregnancy and childbirth as generations of women have done before her.

Many things are certainly strange these days but she's had to get used to that, she runs her hand over the smooth painted walls of the kitchen, pauses to look at the bright shiny appliances and listen to the hum of the huge gleaming Bosch fridge that belts out ice at the push of a button. A mobile phone vibrates its way across the granite work top but she ignores it, filling up the carved Chinese tray with large coloured plastic glasses for the two boys, crystal for her and John and a plate of lemon drizzle cake which she has become an adept at baking. She swings her long plait back over her shoulder and wobbles her way outside clicking across the flagstone floor unused to the heels of the straw wedge sandals that she is wearing, and she calls them to her as she goes.

The summer house is cool and shady, painted just that tone of cornflower blue that she's always loved so much and there is a through breeze blowing in from the top of the hill. She sighs with pleasure and picks up her embroidery only to lay it aside as a chattering tells her the boys have arrived. Oliie scrabbles up onto the seat beside her, at nine he is too big to get onto her knee any more although he would very much like to. He looks up adoringly at her and unhooks his fingers to show a long furry caterpillar he is delicately holding there.

"Look Nellie isn't he lovely, he tickles though, what do you think he eats?"

She bends over the little creature and runs her finger tip over it lightly and they both laugh as it curls itself up into a furry ball.

" Well I expect it eats the leaves from the tree that you found it on , so you'll just have to go and pick some later , but for now settle down and have a drink, you look very hot and thirsty."

She swishes to her feet and pours the lemonade onto the ice in the glasses and John watches her hungrily. She has a grace that never fails to amaze him and his heart floods with the sense of wellbeing that his life has become this rich and this contented. He watches the children as they chatter with her, both of them itching to get as close as possible to her, and the

210

way she affectionately strokes a cheek or pinches an ear to emphasis what she is saying. Toby is, eleven now and soon on his way to Dulwich College from his prep school he has lost all the awkwardness that used to hamper him. His teachers are full of praise for his aptitude at school and after school, and at weekends the big old house rings with the sound of children's footsteps banging doors and laughter. It's the laughter that is so infectious, it brims out of Nellie and fills them all, she brings an ''other'' worldly charm and significance to their lives that he never would have thought possible before. Ollie still has touches of his baby blonde curls but Toby's hair is dark and short and he's a serious little boy always asking questions and delving into the life of things.

He catches sight of his own face reflected in the glass and hardly recognises the sun swept features and new bundles of crinkly laughter lines as his own. The old dour public school stick up his arse John has .disappeared leaving this gentle slightly rounded man with an effortless smile and a swing in his stride. He drains the cool sticky liquid and sighs contentedly settling back on the cushions and idly listens to the conversation bubbling around the room. It's Toby his mouth full of lemon drizzle cake that begins to quiz her.

''Nellie, why are you called Nellie? It's not a usual name is it? I've never heard anyone called that. ''

''Don't push so much cake into your mouth, Tobias you will choke. ''

She admonishes him gently using his full name to emphasis her displeasure.

'' You'll choke badly and then what will we do? Turn you upside down and hope it all comes out?''.

The children chortle and dance about but Toby wants to know the answer to his question he's not going to give up that easily. John wonders whether to rescue her but decides to let her get on with it herself. The children are flourishing under the

211

firm yet loving care that she gives them, and he is nothing but grateful for her way with them. She sighs and picks up her embroidery glancing at him and raising an eyebrow before answering slowly.

'' Well I've always been called Nellie, my Papa liked to call me that when I was little and it stuck ,although of course it is a shortened version of Helena , quite a few ladies called 'Helena' have Nellie as a nickname .''

Toby is quiet for a moment thinking about something and then he turns to John and says.

'' But Dad, wasn't that the name of the lady you sometimes used to go and see by the seaside in that nice house with all the shells in it? Although she wasn't at all like this Nellie was she? Not as nice, at least not to us, not as pretty, a bit stick like really and definitely not as much fun.''

John squirms and decides that the best course of action is to divert the conversation and says sharply.

'' Come on you two only a few more nails to bang into the floor of the tree house before its finished and we can invite Nellie up there for a state visit. We'd better hurry up, your mother is coming for dinner tonight and that means a jolly good bath and brush up for both of you. ''

Nellie looks at him gratefully and gathers up the empty glasses to take them back to the kitchen. She pauses before entering the back door to look up at the house, her house, the Raven as proud above the front door as it was when it was first carved there all those years ago. Raven House smiles back at her, it seems to shift and sigh and sink further into the soil on which it is built, floating away the sudden sadness that she feels for all the things that are past, all the things that can never return. She doesn't dwell on all the things that she might miss, there is too much to do here and now, too much life to live and love to discover with this big brave man of hers who is now to be seen hanging upside down from a branch

212

of the tree, a hammer and nails in his hands. She can't bear to think of how much she misses her Papa or how worried he must have been when she didn't return to him.

No everything in life demands some sort of sacrifice it seems and for the love and happiness she has now she is quite happy to have given up everything known to her. Why it all seems like a distant island in a sea of nowhere her past life, each day it recedes further away from her and soon it will be as if it has never been. She laughs a little ruefully at her own ruthlessness, for that is what it is, and she believes that it comes from her staunchly Victorian upbringing. People nowadays just don't have an inkling of what you sometimes have to give up to achieve your heart's desire and that is why she has succeeded where Helena obviously couldn't.

She carries on her trajectory to the kitchen where the au pair is just putting away the food for the evening that the caterers have delivered. Nellie has discovered the joys of picking up the telephone and ordering things, especially when the imperious Cecilia is due for a visit. Cecilia who makes her feel like an ingénue, all fingers and thumbs and puppy fat, beside the slender elegance that is John's ex-wife.

'' Radna can you make sure that the strawberries are soaked in the almond brandy please; everything else is easy to heat up just twenty minutes before hand. I'm going to check the table and then have a shower before the boys come in.''

With that she drifts into the dining room where the table is covered in a beautifully ironed white linen cloth. It has taken her several years to search out the kind of linen that she was used to. She had looked from car boot sales to antique markets and local auctions in order to regroup the sort of bed linen and tableware that she liked. John couldn't quite understand her fervour and suggested that she simply go to John Lewis instead, but if it amused her and helped her to find her way around the city by bus and train then that was fine with him. As long as she was safe, as long as she didn't get lost; as long as every evening he could come home and find her sitting there waiting for him.

She smiles thinking about how much he loves her each and every night, five years later it still sends shivers down her spine to remember the first time it ever happened, the sheer physicality of it all. She had never realised before that her body had this life of its own, this root of pleasure that could be tapped into. A shadow on the stairwell startles her and she shivers; only a shift of the light, she thought that she was over all the nightmares but apparently not.

The water in the shower is blissfully cool and she lathers her hair trying not to get soap in her eyes, from outside the window she can hear the laughter filtering in from the garden and it makes her feel warm to know that it's her little family making all that raucous noise. She is the centre of their universe and more than that she has started to have notice taken of her photographs, John had bought her a Nikon camera as a home coming present and showed her how to use it the first week that they came back to Raven House. Together with the negatives that she had retrieved from their hiding place in the cellar she had produced works that were so unusual that the arty world has begun to remark on it.

Out in the garden the tree house is finally finished and John leaves the boys with Radna to put the tools away and get ready for their bath while he sneaks off to the drinks cabinet and pours himself a large gin and tonic. From upstairs he can hear the sound of Nellie singing, albeit in a rather tuneless monotone, he can't quite catch the words it's probably some kind of obscure nineteenth century psalm that she learnt as a child. That's the side of her that he loves so much the stories that she can tell him from an age that in some ways was gentler yet in others far more brutal than anything he has ever known. A shadow passes over the window and he looks up quickly but can see nothing, he's still jumpy anything can send him back to that awful night and the agony of the weeks that followed.

He throws back the drink swallowing hard; the gin bites the back of his throat and quickly pours himself another. It's not like he's become an alcoholic or anything but sometimes he just has the need to numb down all this joy that he's feeling, sometimes it just feels like he and Nellie have stolen something from the Gods and any minute now a reckoning will be happening. He's not sure if he is expecting thunder and lightning or the devil appearing or if it will be an accident to the boys, the taking away of someone that he loves. How does the Universe restore balance and how have they interfered and changed it with their love?

All these thoughts crowd in on him whenever he is alone and a little bit tired, he remembers back to the hospital and Helena broken and unconscious in the bed. The days he spent visiting her and the mutterings of the doctors about how the brain scans showed that there was no appreciable activity going on, how she was brain dead. Even now it doesn't bear thinking about. Then there had been that morning when he was sitting there holding her hand and the fingers had squeezed him and she'd opened her eyes and looked at him. Such a look, such beautiful oriental eyes as pretty as an antelope, he remembered from somewhere in his memory the words of Byron. Except of course it was Nellie looking at him, Helena had gone somewhere else, and there he was with his beautiful girl alive and in front of him and his forever dream had started to happen right about then.

He smiles as she walks into the room bringing the freshness of the shower and that unmistakeable scent of Ambergris with her. It's not as if she even uses perfume it's just the odour of Nellie that he remembers so well that always seems to pervade the air. He looks up at her and his heart gives that hop skip and a jump he has become so used to, her hair is damp and she's wearing a long white muslin dress and no makeup, she looks younger than her twenty six years, how does she love an old bloke like him?

'' Hello darling come and see the tree house the boys are really proud of it and I must say that I am too.''

He gets to his feet and grabs her by the hand and pulls her laughing outside protesting as she goes.

'' I can't climb a tree in this dress for goodness sake, and our guests will be here in a moment John , and you really need a shower my love much as I think you are delectable you smell rather like one of my old cooks overripe cheeses.''

He swings her around and clasps her in a strong hug pressing his lips down on hers.

'' Are you saying that I smell like an old man?' Is this you politely trying to tell me that you don't love me anymore because you know darling I was just about to ask you to marry me ?''

Her eyes turn almost violet when she is aroused and the light catches them now, the intensity of them takes him aback and he holds her away from him at arm's length just drinking in her beauty. She gasps and nods and then she has pulled his face down to hers and she is kissing him. The minute she is close to him she melts she just can't help it, white lights go off in her brain and the future spreads out in fields of sunny summer's days to tempt her on. She has made this body her own and it has become so, she doesn't quite know how it worked out that way but who cares. That night is so long ago now it feels like another lifetime which indeed it was; that night when she ran away to Whitstable not quite knowing what she was going to do but somehow guessing that there was a way into this life with John if she could be brave about it.

As he kisses her now she remembers back to that day in the hospital when she had opened her eyes and he had looked at her and she knew that she had won, that Helena was gone somewhere where she could never come back and that she Nellie had done it. The kiss lingers too long and the heat starts to drown them both until the sound of a car on the drive brings them back to the present. The slam of a door and the running footsteps of the boys greeting Cecilia.

'' Mummy mummy we built a tree house come and see what we've done. ''

John draws Nellie further back into the shade of the tree and they both stand there and watch as Cecilia bends stiffly to greet her sons, Louis stands awkwardly behind her his eyes hidden behind a pair of designer sun glasses. Cecilia looks sleeker, younger than she did when she was married to him as if someone has taped her face tightly to the bones in her skull as if she is made from brittle glass ready to shatter into a million pieces at any second. John thinks this as he savours the warm voluptuous body of Nellie beside him, and thinks how strange it is that the woman who used to be his wife is now completely in the thrall of a trumped up slip of a boy man who controls her totally. Cecilia sweeps her eyes across the lawn as if searching for something and then she finds John and Nellie close together in the shade as if they are spying on her and something resembling her idea of a smile instantly fixes itself to her face.

'' John hello and Nellie, lovely to see you both. How pretty you look in that dress, Nellie almost like something out of Victorian novel.''

Her words manage to sound patronising and Nellie feels a cold band press itself around her heart and twist, how ridiculous that she can feel this way just by looking at the woman. There is something bitter and slightly desperate about Cecilia nowadays that was never there before. John feels Nellie stiffen and he gives her a quick hug, whispering.

''It's alright darling just ignore her, please ply them with drinks while I go and have a quick shower.''

''Don't leave me with them for long she gives me the jitters John you know she does, and as for him I can't understand a word he says''.

Nellie looks up at him pleadingly loathe to let go of his hand.

'' I think you give her the jitters too darling and the house certainly doesn't like her, just watch out that she doesn't get locked in the downstairs cloakroom like she did last time she was here.''

Nellie giggles remembering the fiasco at Easter when Cecilia had come to pick up the boys to take them on holiday. She'd disappeared for half an hour and when they had eventually gone looking for her she had managed to jam herself in the downstairs cloakroom. It's true the house really doesn't like her; if she listens carefully she can hear it almost groaning when the woman steps over the threshold. Doors slam for no reason or get stuck, or door handles fall off leaving Cecilia disgruntled and Nellie's eyes dancing with mirth. She watches John step out of the shade of the tree and into the glare of sunlight on the lawn, he executes the proverbial three kisses which are expected of him on Cecilia's sallow cheek and shakes Louis hand abruptly, then cracking a joke he leaves them there with the children while he continues on into the arbour of the house.

Walking up the wide staircase to the bathroom he passes two portraits hanging side by side on the stairs and pauses to smile and touch them briefly. There is the very beautiful self portrait of Nellie that they brought with them from the house in Whitstable and next to it is framed the drawing of John by Helena Blavatsky. The two seem to be looking at each other their eyes each turned towards the other portrait. Nellie insisted that they hang them like this as a testimony of their love for each other, this "other" worldly love. She had also told him of the wonder of that night when Blavatsky had swirled his likeness into being and Nellie had known for sure that they were always meant to be together.

He glances out at the figures below the window in the garden and frowns slightly; Louis is smoking a cigarette pacing up and down the lawn and obviously bored, while Nellie is still hovering under the tree looking uneasy. It annoys him that Cecilia can just saunter in and make them feel uncomfortable like this but she is the mother of his kids so there's nothing he can really do about it. Cecilia is sitting on the lawn her head bowed while she listens to the boys explaining excitedly the ins and outs of their constructive genius that has been harnessed into the branches of the oak tree. She looks thinner but younger and he wonders what kind of surgery she has put herself through in order to keep her boyfriend. It's funny how being with this younger man has made her less sure of herself, how the power has shifted, how now it is Louis who is so obviously in control. He sighs, he's not looking forward to the evening, but he'd rather have them all here on his territory than send the boys to Paris.

Cecilia had eventually pulled herself together after the semi psychotic breakdown that had her hearing voices and hallucinating pieces of the past. At least that's what she thought was happening, but he and Nellie knew the real truth of the situation although they couldn't help anything by trying to explain and the doctors certainly weren't going to believe them. So she'd taken a long "rest" in Switzerland and while she'd been gone he'd sold the flat in Place Vendome for her, handing over the chimera of Madame Blavatsky to the next owners and put the money in a bank account for her to use later . She and Louis live somewhere near the Jardin des Plantes now, which is useful for the boys to go roller skating in, but he's never wished to visit them and knows that he never will.

Nellie busies herself in the kitchen, Radna has the evening off and as she plates up the smoked salmon and blinis she feels a sudden sense of exasperation. In her world there would be servants to do this kind of thing and she would be free to sit in the drawing room and laugh and look pretty and make polite conversation. But actually she is itching to get this evening over with and get back to her work in the darkroom where she want to develop the photos that she took yesterday.

When she and John had returned to Raven House she had retrieved some of her own negatives from a locked iron box at the back of the cellar and of course her beautiful pendant from its smooth velvet pouch. The things that she had hidden so long ago in a place where she knew she would be the only one to find them suddenly came into the world again, her new world. Using the old negatives together with her new work she has created a photographic collage that is unique and unrepeatable. She thinks it will create an immense stir in photographic circles and launch her into the kind of career that she needs.

She wants John to be proud of her although they have almost argued over all this. He thinks it's too risky to bring too much of her past into the present, how will she explain it if questions are asked? But she's simply sure that it's impossible to guess what has happened, why even the lovers can't really explain it so how would anyone else? It had been fairly easy to fade Helena out of the equation, John had sent an email to her department at the University saying that she was taking a sabbatical, in a little known part of the Indonesian archipelago and no one had really questioned the fact that she had sort of disappeared. After two years she had been reported as a missing person and probate on the house in Whitstable had been served. It transpired that during the time she was with him Helena had made a will leaving all of her belongings to John. So they had simply packed up the Whitstable house and sold it as quickly as they could and Nellie had come to London as herself. As yet they haven't had much trouble with new documentation they simply changed the dates on her existing birth certificate, scanned it into the computer and built her a life in the twenty first century.

Even now it makes her smile to think how Nellie Weinberg born in 1854 has become Nellie Weinberg born 1974. Nellie's heart gives a little leap as she thinks about her new work and her hands move automatically over the kitchen surface chopping and garnishing the hors d'oevres.

From the oven comes the aroma of Thai curry heating itself up nicely and she realises that in fact everything is perfect. In this world there is so much time to discover the things that she wants to do and here she is in her own house with all the freedom she could possibly ask for. Upstairs she can hear the water running for her dream man, who loves her, but more than anything she has all the freedom she needs, much more than she ever had before. The kitchen door slams and suddenly there are the boys chattering and climbing up on the bar stools to pilfer some of the smaller pieces of salmon and her thoughts whirl away from her as she is sucked into the life of her new family , the one she chose all those years ago one autumn day in Dulwich Woods. Was it accident or fate? Was it meant to be or just hazard that brought them all together? The questions rise like dust on a sunbeam and then fade just as quickly back into the envelope of time where all things are potential letters just waiting to be opened and read.

*

Epilogue
The House in Whitstable Autumn 2000

Helena

It's a sea fog rolling in again, slowly like a smoking fire that can't be put out, she can't see a lot through it, and it's getting thicker by the minute. The beach unrolls at low tide and she is watching the cockle pickers out near Sea Salter, she can almost feel the thick slurp of the mud under their feet and the raw wind picking up and whipping their faces. Yes she can almost feel it but not quite, she can't really feel anything anymore, just vague impressions of what it all used to be like. The fishing boats out on the horizon disappear from view one by one, like light bulbs popping and even the pub is fading away, the fog swirling across the narrow pathway in front of the house and locking her in its damp obscure shell.

For a second panic hits her, she can't breathe and she feels herself start to disintegrate back into the shadows of the room. Maybe it's the blackness coming back sooner than usual, maybe she is going to disappear again. Helena prowls along the window pane itching to get out but she can't. She remembers stories from somewhere way back then, that ghosts are supposed to be able to slip through walls but it doesn't seem to be true in her case. Now she is just an echo of someone, a *has been*, a hologram of a place and a time that doesn't exist anymore, and a casualty of a violent accident that she isn't allowed to forget.

The house is empty now for the winter, all locked up and battened down: the dust sheets covering the furniture and the fridge empty of food. It was bought by a rich London family from Notting hill when John decided to sell it, back then that autumn five years ago now when life as she knew it ended. It seems a long time but to Helena it is yesterday, yesterday and tomorrow really the only tomorrow she will ever know. Anyway John wouldn't recognise the house now; it has been stripped down and completely redone in pared back white and black monotone. The floorboards painted black and all the feature fireplaces removed so none of the original house remains except the shape, the bricks and mortar that Nellie's father had built for her holiday house all that time ago. Though when she is actually here, and that isn't always, she can see all her old possessions shimmering along the edge of the wall where the fireplace stood, covering the old sofas cluttering the bookshelves.

It's tricky explaining these things, even to herself: how she comes to be here, but she thinks that when she is here; it is nothing but a respite from all that will happen next. For every seven days as regular as the sun rising and setting she has to relive her death. There is no other way to put it, she understands all too clearly now that the Buddhist sages had some kind of insight into the life after death scenario that is now hers, and she wishes that she had paid more attention to it all when she could . She vaguely remembers reading that the Dalai Llama's daily meditation consists on meditating on death and now she can understand why. She feels angry when she thinks about it but anger only has the effect of disintegrating pieces of her mind so that she floats disunited across the room never being able to catch her thoughts and gel them together. So anger is something that has had to go. The pathways in the brain seem to hang onto memories even when there is no physical brain to hold them in, and there is certainly nothing physical about her nowadays.

She laughs and the laughter echoes eerily around the house cascading up and down the stairs and back to her. She watches as the mist comes in tapping on the window again with its clammy fingers and whispering her name and knows it has come to get her.

It is time to relive it all again, each seven day sequence brings more of the memory back and yet she is impotent to change it, impotent to stop it.

Sucked back through the tunnel into the blankness of oblivion, back to that Halloween night when she hit the water so hard and the last thing that she remembers before the smack of cold steel that was the North Sea rising up to engulf her is the sight of Nellie sitting on the crest of the waves waiting for her. Yes she remembers thinking that it must be the shock that was making her see the girl there for it wasn't possible. Why she never even believed the stories about Jesus walking on water so how the hell could Nellie be sitting there? The next thing that happens with droning regularity every week now is the moment she regains some kind of consciousness in the hospital bed, the tubes in her mouth choking her yet giving her breath, John sitting slumped in sleep by her side snoring gently. It must be the middle of the night she knows that now and the only other sound that she hears above the faint puffing snore of John is the bleep of all the machines that are monitoring her.

And then the figure of Nellie is there by the bed, as if she is patiently waiting to slide inside her again in the way that Nellie always does and usually she wouldn't mind that much after all it feels like a delicious moment of respite from the reality of life but this time Helena isn't strong enough to force her out, to make her go away as she had always managed to do in the past. This time there is a glint of determination and malice in those perfect eyes as if she Nellie knows that Helena doesn't stand a chance against her. Yes the impossibility of trying to stop Nellie from getting inside her, from capturing her makes her heart beat pathetically faster and faster as if it is going to explode, why doesn't someone come to help her, where is the nurse when she is needed?

Nellie's eyes, those pretty innocent oriental eyes that look at her so gently and with such sympathy, and yet Helena knows what she wants what she is demanding with no mercy. She wants this broken body which Helena herself has no strength to mend. All she can do is let the machines breathe for her and wait for it to happen again, her skin sweats in terror and she knows that these eyes are the last thing that she will see.

The light is there above her, that big bright light that everyone talks about, but there doesn't seem to be a tunnel, and yet she's not sure if it's the hospital light or God that is blinding her with his omnipresence:, but suddenly her body is vomiting her out, evicting her like a squatter and the machines are crazily bleeping and she is floating free above it watching as Nellie slides in. So sweetly so comfortingly so perfectly, leaving Helena perfectly free of her body and knowing that no one is going to notice except John .

There is absolutely blank nothing for a while after this, blackness nothing at all, like the deepest of night time sleeps but then gradually she becomes aware of the house again. Pulling her back moulding her together locking her in a time warp over which she has no control, if she believed in any kind of religion this would be what they call limbo or purgatory wouldn't it? At first she is conscious only fitfully and in moments. The first time that she found herself back in the house she thought that the Halloween show and consequent fire had just been some terrible kind of nightmare, that John would walk in any moment and her life would be back to where it should be again. She didn't have to wait long, although she has no idea of the formation of time any more, it's just.

Wake up or

Replay or

Blank out.

Three modes of being which she has no control over. Yet it's taken the replay over and over again for her to come to any kind of catharsis in the Greek sense of the word.

She wasn't sure quite what had gone on until that first time when John walked back into the bedroom of the house closely followed by Nellie.: A Nellie wearing Helena's body, although already it was moulding itself into Nellie's body or Nellie was moulding herself to make it become her body .Oh she could go on thinking like this forever and there is no answer, the questions just make a splintering sound in the empty chambers of her non-existent field of reference. Why she felt herself split and scatter, split and scatter and she didn't come back for quite a while. Not till after the house had been sold and all the old bits of her life were thrown away, just like she was. She thinks that the Buddhist scriptures have a name for her state, they would call her a "Hungry ghost" but she isn't, when she can manage the effort of solidifying into anything at all it is a very *angry* ghost that she has become.

The mist grinds in and the high tide slaps the wall at the bottom of the small shingle garden. The locals make a detour now to prevent passing in front of the house, for the whole town knows that it is haunted. Children dare each other to pick a pebble from the front garden and lovers pass hand in hand at sunset and wonder about the woman that used to live there. Some say that she recovered and went to live in London but others who know better talk of possession and a forbidden love affair. On stormy nights the fishermen swear that they can hear her calling to them and the odd drunk has stood and watched her by the lighted window, only to take a second glance and know that their eyes are cheating them. For the windows are shuttered and there is no one there.

*

After you read this book enjoy from Victoria Mosley

Free download

The Red Dragon Bed

& news of new releases.

Join me on my website

www.victoriamosley.com

Hurry to get it while you still can, the intelligent reader's

50 Shades of Grey!

[Please leave a review, thank you]

About the Author

Victoria Mosley is a poet novelist and spoken word artist. She has published five poetry collections

She has run events and club nights in London and beyond, from the Groucho Club to the ICA, Austin Texas to Indonesia, from Jazz nights and Charity Events to new bands. She has worked for the British Council in Surabaya and in Canada, has produced and presented her own radio shows... She has worked as Artist in Residence in the Film and Media Studies Department at the School of Oriental and African Studies London University, and the Astro -Physics department of Imperial College where she taught her own courses on Creative Writing and Performance and wrote an MA option. She is presently concentrating on writing novels. She has written eleven novels all soon to be available on Kindle on Amazon. Check out her other books on her Author Profile. https://www.amazon.com/author/victoriamosley

Join her blog on www.victoriamosley.com

Follow on twitter @victoriamosley

Printed in Great Britain
by Amazon

15135260R00133